The Sea in Birmingham
Short Stories

30 Years of the Tindal Street Fiction Group

Edited by Gaynor Arnold and Julia Bell

First published in October 2013
by Tindal Street Fiction Group
www.tindalstreetfictiongroup.com

A CIP catalogue record for this book is available from the British Library.

Paperback ISBN: 978 0 9528246 8 8
Ebook ISBN: 978 0 9528246 9 5

The Sea in Birmingham is typeset in Book Antiqua.

Cover design and typesetting by Raffaele Teo at Arteo Graphik.
Printed and bound by Berforts Limited, 17 Burgess Road, Hastings TN35 4NR

Visit www.tindalstreetfictiongroup.com for more information about this title or to order further copies of this title.

Contents

Foreword

To most of us landlocked here in Birmingham the distance from the sea doesn't seem to be much of a problem. It isn't such a long drive to Barmouth, west Wales nor to Weston (-super-Mare). Brummies can manage without the ozone, and don't feel sentimentally attached to the seagulls that pummel the parkland grass or scavenge the chapatti and roti breads kindly left out for the pigeons. They can smell the country air beyond the city limits, only a short hop and it's Salop, Staffs, Warks and Worcs: Long Mynd, Cannock Chase, the old Forest of Arden, Malvern; and the rivers that flow: the Severn, the Stour, the Avon, the kind of country streams Brummie anglers a generation ago used to head for in their thousands at weekends, rods strapped to roof racks. Incomers like me might occasionally miss the orientation that a coastline provides, but Birmingham is central, everything outward and arterial from its pulsing centre.

Outsiders might think a city has to have a big river to be a proper city, to be able to boast of a Tyne or a Mersey. But as this city's greatest poet Roy Fisher – author of *Birmingham River* – has reminded us, it has two: the Rea and the Cole. Not big rivers, admittedly: unobtrusive; walled up, culverted-in places; hidden, unshowy, hardly noticed; Brummies don't boast. You might need a birder's eye to see the kingfishers on the Cole, which is the stream that goes through Tolkien's Sarehole Mill. The same Roy Fisher fashioned the line 'Birmingham is what I think with'; and Midlands writers today have been inspired by that unusual thought.

Two and three-quarter million souls live hereabouts across the urban West Midlands. Red, silver and blue West Midlands Travel buses reach as far as Coventry (Cov with its auto-industry connection; its two-tone; its rebirth as a new city); stylish Leamington, next door to Tudor Warwick; and all the glorious old-fashioned yam-yam hill towns of Dudley, Stourbridge, Walsall, Brierley Hill, Wolverhampton, all abutted in a modge next to each other. This is a world in miniature, a place in its own right, like Frankfurt or Chicago, Birmingham's twins overseas, not just somewhere to move on from. And as this anthology of twenty-two urban pieces demonstrates, this heart of England has stories to be told.

So what is it with Birmingham and its image problem beyond the Midlands? Why should it be the butt of cheap jibes from stand-ups, tin-eared approximations of an accent no more dumb-sounding than Cockney? Nationally, the city can still seem beyond the pale of possible interest. It could be Birmingham suffers, like most regional cities, from not being London. And yet its very difference must define its curious downbeat charm, so well hidden from outsiders. In any case, writers want to tell stories about complex people in complex places, not write tourist copy for city breaks. And short story specialists must take heart from the example of Man Booker International winner Alice Munro, and her beloved North Western Ontario, whose 'provincial' work is quite capable of representing the world.

I know from book launches for regional writers published up and down the country that 'not-London' has been a burden that writers in other English cities labour under. A chuckle of recognition always greeted the regional city appeal I was keen to champion when speaking of Tindal Street Press authors such as Anthony Cartwright or Catherine O'Flynn. Incurious *Granta* often seems to think the only writing worth reading is American or metropolitan, whereas regional writers applaud Milan Kundera's claim that 'Life is Elsewhere'. The likes of Liverpool and Newcastle are openly proud, couldn't care that London can only condescend, but Brummies tend to keep their heads down, understanding implicitly how their city works, taking for granted its tolerance and pragmatism, its unpretentious realism, its hardworking mix of peoples, without feeling the need to convert the sceptical. As the stories in this anthology attest, droll understatement and unsettling irony, as well as realism, are not unexpected.

Maybe you have to live here to understand the appeal. Most writers have little choice but to write from the place in which they find themselves. And in a city this size there's more than enough 'material'. Birmingham may be a challenge to a writer's aesthetic principles, but the short story form accommodates the city's stories in a variety of genre and theme: a hint of crime or horror haunts the streets; or a memory bites, a childhood rears up into the day; love, mistaken; complicated family tensions; confrontations: every story packs its own surprise.

When Tindal Street Press was started up by a handful of writers from Tindal Street Fiction Group (those keen enough and armed with what would become proper publishing skills), we harboured an indignation that London publishers weren't interested in Birmingham as a setting for fiction, vowing to set the record straight for the city and its writers. We'd begun by publishing a stunning collection of stories by Alan Beard, half of them already accepted for magazine publication, but unaccountably rejected by all the mainstream publishers. *Taking Doreen out of the Sky*, greeted by glowing national newspaper reviews, became the prototype for a hallmark list of regional literary fiction.

The origins of the Tindal Street project go back to 1982/83 when I was a writer-in-the-community at an organisation called TASC (Tindal Association for School and Community), based in the primary school on Tindal Street, Balsall Heath. I worked with children, pensioners and local writers; and I'm proud to say that's where the writers' group Tindal Street Fiction Group was formed in 1983. The model in mind was inspired by what I'd heard of the Glasgow group of Alasdair Gray and James Kelman. Their ruse was to ignore London if it insisted on ignoring Glasgow and to find readers internationally for work conceived within their city, without concessions to RP English. The classic *Lanark* (1981) and Kelman's 1994 Man Booker victory were ample vindication of their stance. The most helpful insight of the Glasgow perspective was, for me, the imaginative mapping of a city, unapologetic about place names and dialect, which enabled citizens to identify more closely and more confidently with their own city through literature, but also created a useful mind-map for outsiders, too. Such a model could equally be applied to Birmingham; and indeed to the writers in this anthology exploring the inner geography of their surroundings.

And so, our group of writers focused on developing their urban fiction. During that time we convened in the community rooms fortnightly, read and critiqued a story each session, taking turns, questioning the work intensively, but constructively, before repairing to the Old Moseley Arms for book chat deep into the night. It's what writers do everywhere. The seminar style is widespread in writing groups all over, especially now at university courses in creative writing. The Tindal Street ground rules haven't much changed: fiction only; equal number of men and women at any one time; whole story read out loud. Though the membership has waxed and waned, the constant flux has flowed around a high-quality core of commitment. As an honorary member for the last decade, I have witnessed the vitality and productivity of the latest formation of writers; I have to say that their work seems stronger, more varied and vibrant now than in all its thirty years.

When we looked down into town from Tindal Street at night the spangling lights used to be the onion globe of the Central Mosque and the upright cylinder that is forever the Rotunda. Nowadays the most iconic skyline sights are the spire of St Martin's in the Bull Ring next to the bluish, illuminated armadillo of Selfridges. The cityscape has changed considerably, but the commitment to city-focused fiction lives on at a new address, in Moseley. 'The Fiction Group' still thrives after thirty years. Such fine writers as Alan Beard, Joel Lane and Gaynor Arnold are its sterling officers of recent years. Among other published novelists are Amanda Smyth, Mez Packer, Annie Murray, Jackie Gay, Mick Scully, Luke Brown and Julia Bell. The twenty-two writers represented here have borne in mind the changes in the population of this cosmopolitan city, now more than half non-white, and appreciated its fascinating and rich mix of peoples: African Caribbean, Punjabi, Pakistani and many more, from the Soho Road to the Stratford Road, not forgetting the long-established Polish, Chinese and Irish communities.

The antennae of short story writers are always finely attuned to cultural, political and historical change in their city.

It's not possible to maintain for long the pretence that this city's miles of canals make it the equal of Amsterdam or *la Serenissima*. And yet the canals are wildlife corridors just as they were night markers for the Luftwaffe bombing the BSA munitions factory in Small Heath. Writers, as well as ramblers, runners, dog walkers and cyclists, are drawn to such places. I fancy the great Italo Calvino would have had a wry smile for Gas Street Basin next to Symphony Hall: Birmingham at its most Venetian, with its bankside tables and its tourist barges; and in Brindley Place there's a postmodern campanile and piazza. Invisible city indeed.

The palimpsest of this city would show that the first city library was a neo-gothic pile, where scholars and dreamers stared through church-style windows, destroyed for a sixties ring road. That was swept away by an eight-storey concrete Brutalist block (loved by its millions of readers, if not by the Prince of Wales who thought it looked 'more like a place where books are incinerated, not kept'), the Central Library, a nonetheless welcoming place inside for students, refugees, office workers, readers every one. But now joined at the hip to the Repertory Theatre is a giant cardboard box covered with chicken wire topped by a golden fez, which is the brand-new Library of Birmingham. And what a brave new shape the Dutch architects have constructed, to address an uncertain future, as we engage quite differently these days with literature, information and music. If this is the city's gesture of literary solidarity then it is a welcome one for its writers and readers now, whose reading habits have been so transformed by Amazon, Kindle, iPad and iPhone, but who still and will always need to read in and about their city. The newly opened Library of Birmingham should be a much-needed site of hope, a gathering place, an arena for diverse voices, for sympathetic polyphony; something to match, we hope, the perfect acoustic of Birmingham's Symphony Hall – and, in bringing those voices together, not unlike this richly textured anthology of stirring urban fictions.

Alan Mahar
Birmingham, April 2013

Mr Spider
MEZ PACKER

During your lifetime you'll swallow eight spiders, or thereabouts. You've probably swallowed two or three already, depending on your age. It's guaranteed. It happens while you're sleeping. They crawl over your duvet in the night until they reach bare flesh. Your neck or your face. Crooked legs test your skin – hesitant at first – but then *pit pat, pit pat* they go in that queasy way they have, all knees, until they reach the curl of your lip.

You? You're dreaming you're in Macky D's or Burger King. You've got your mouth open ready for a feed-up. Your head's tipped back and the way down your gullet's all slippy and easy. That's how come Mr Spider can creep in.

You're soundo, so you don't move as he pokes around your teeth. But soon enough you take a breath and your mouth becomes a wind tunnel and the spider has to cling on to a molar with one foot to stop himself from being sucked down. He can't escape, though. No weight, you see, and he folds into a crumpled star as your breath drags him off. Eventually he hits the dangly thing at the back of your throat and you sit up, hacking in the dark, wondering if that dream burger you were chewing had a bit of fingernail in it or something.

Course, the little ones get right down your pipe before you know it. You don't feel them like the big buggers, and when you swallow they're washed away to dissolve in the acid in your gut.

It's rank, though, the thought of creepy crawlies inside you like that.

I learn all this spider stuff while I'm on a job in Coventry, up near Foleshill. Not my usual patch. I live in Brum these days. Still, I have a soft spot for Cov. My old man would bring me when I was a kid. He knew about assembly lines. That's all I remember about him – cars and engines and the smell of oil when he lifted me onto his shoulders. It's forty years since I've seen him and I can't get a fix on his face. Mum burned all the photos when he left us for 'that tart' (whoever she was) in 1974.

Anyway, I'm leaning inside this porch with a roll-up on the go, keeping an eye on the comings and goings on the street instead of doing the rough stuff inside. I've been up all night with a gippy tum – dodgy curry off Ali Baba's in Sparkhill – and I don't fancy working anybody over while I'm burping last night's vindaloo.

This kid comes along, thrashing at things with a stick. He's about seven I'd say, skinny runt, and he stops in front of me and looks me up and down. He's got a right cocky face on and I'm about to scare him off when he shoots into the next-door garden. The stick becomes a gun and he takes pot shots at me from behind the wall, making all the noises. *Braap braap*. Black gangster bollocks – the way kids do these days. I ignore him and watch the junction where the traffic on the main street's bottlenecking, eyes peeled for trouble or the Bill.

Eventually the kid gets bored and strolls back along the pavement. He kicks an old can a few times. Starts poking in a drain with his stick, fishing for attention. Little brat. His Sky Blues shirt's too big on him. His shiny sports trousers have gone bobbly on the arse. Crack-mum poor I'd say, that or she's on the pop. There's a tidemark on his neck, smudges on his cheeks.

I don't like to judge, but it goes with the territory. You have to be able to size a body up. Even a kid. This one sits on the kerb now and starts chucking gravel at the can he was just kicking – missing and hitting and missing. It goes on like this until he's wound me right up and I can't help myself but tell him to fuck off, and I bare my teeth at him.

The kid's face pinches a bit, flint in his eyes. But he's used to a rollicking and my warning sloshes over him. He doesn't budge.

'Did you hear me?' I put a growl on for good measure.

'I heard ya,' he says. 'But I ain't goin' nowhere.'

'You'd better, else I'll twat ya.'

He shrugs one shoulder and goes back to chucking stones and I feel a narky fist stirring the bad curry round my guts. It's not clever getting distracted on a job, but the kid's riled me and I hoof over and catch him off guard. Grab his shoulder.

Kid twists like an eel to get free, but I've got him. I could squeeze his arm right out of its socket if I wanted. Snap, it would go. My jaw's clenched up with the thought of it.

A *pring-ching* sound, frisky and new, makes me turn and there's a bleeding PC on a bicycle gliding into view, ringing his bell. I freeze up. I mean, I didn't know they still had bicycles. *Pring-ching.* He rings his bell again and comes up alongside us, but it's only the fluff. Chimp, soya, plastic plod, call them whatever joke name you like, but community support officers can be nasty little pricks, giving it all that *bobby on the beat* bullshit, trying to prove themselves. Well, I have to go down on my haunches, don't I? As if I'm talking kindly to the kid. And the chimp leans on his handlebars and makes a face like something's crawled up him. I do a smarmy thing with my mouth in return, but keep a grip on the boy's arm.

'Afternoon.' Fluff nods, checking my face to see if I'm a regular.

I stare right back. 'Afternoon, officer,' I say.

He turns to the kid. 'How's young Kyle?'

Now, I don't want a polite conversation outside this house where something unheroic is going down inside. Geordie, my partner, is in a back room showing a wannabe gangster called Jason Ruby who's boss. But I have to play it all pally. Besides, it's clear the chimp knows the kid, which isn't what I need. I keep the pressure on Kyle's arm.

'I'm fine, aren't I?' says Kyle.

'Where's your mum?'

'How should I know?' he says, then under his breath, 'Stupid.'

I like this rascal's spirit. He's not afraid of the fluff and he's not afraid of me. But he's weighed it all up and decided that, between the two of us, I'm his best bet.

'Who're you then?' asks the chimp.

We don't add up, me and Kyle, and like all them community officers this one's a nosy cunt. But his boots are scuffed, there's a stain down the front of his Day-Glo jacket. The chin strap on his cycle helmet's undone. He's sloppy. Half-hearted. Hundred to one he's got no stomach for adventure. Wanker. I'd have him in seconds if he turned out to be a bother.

'Friend of the family, aren't I, Kyle?' I say with a wink.

Kyle makes the right face.

The chimp scratches his neck and stares off to the snarl-up at the junction, then back to the skinny arm I'm squeezing. I ease off. Pat the boy's head. Kyle rolls his shoulder as if he's been itching to escape and I do a little *heh heh*, and say, 'Kids, eh? Blighters.'

'You're all right then, Kyle?' says the fluff, but he's more interested in the junction where horns have started blaring and a fair old line of cars has built up.

Kyle pushes an empty fag packet with his toe. 'I told you, didn't I?'

Chimp puts his weight on the pedal and says, 'I'll be off then,' but he looks over his shoulder by the Paki shop, still trying to work us out.

I can't help but do a little wave and he wobbles a bit before pushing off proper. Funny.

When I turn round, Kyle's vanished. I look up and down but I can't see skin nor teeth of him. This is a terraced street, all of 'em two-up, two-down, arse end of Cov where Foleshill meets Stoke. Ruby's house has rotting window frames and a front garden full of rubbish. A house further down is boarded up. The one on the corner's burned out. Forty years back, this would've been solid working-class, scrubbed steps and men with pressed overalls, off at 6 a.m. to the assembly lines. Now the factories are closed and people like Jason Ruby live behind fag-yellow nets drinking Special Brew, watching daytime telly, smoking crack.

I call Kyle's name a couple of times, walk up the street and check behind a few bins. I reckon he must have nipped down an alley, but when I get back to the house there he is, kneeling at the letterbox.

'You little sod,' I say, lunging for him.

He sidesteps me this time and hops onto the pavement. Got the measure of me already, nifty devil. I'm used to working with big bastards, men with fat necks and hands like wrecking balls. I know the speed of men like that.

'Look, Kyle,' I say. 'You'll piss off if you know what's good for you.'

'Piss off where?' he says, toughing it.

It makes me laugh to hear a kid so feisty. 'I don't know.' I shrug, going a bit soft. 'Go and play in the traffic or something.'

I remember Mum racked out on the sofa. 'Go and play in the traffic, shit for brains,' she'd say, threads of spit coming out, throwing whatever came to hand. Shoes, ashtrays. She didn't mean to hurt me; besides, you learn to dodge and weave. But just as I'm chewing on that childhood crap a shout comes from inside the house and it's my turn to stick my neb through the letterbox.

Ruby, bleeding from the nose, is on all fours making for the front door, Geordie at his heels. But when the youth spies my fizzog all framed up he's crestfallen. Knows he's done for. Sorry sod. Geordie gets his ankles and Ruby flops out flat, arms stretched in front as if he's begging me to save him.

'Get back in there,' I tell him, my mouth at the slot.

I imagine what my face must look like, all in bits, as Geordie hoiks him back down the hall.

I can feel Kyle staring at my back and I turn round quick, brushing the knees of my trousers as I stand.

'Couple of friends of mine,' I say, pointing over my shoulder with one thumb. 'Now go on, hoppit.'

I make an angry face to show him I've lost patience, but his eyes are big and dreadful.

'You got no home, or what?'

He stands rigid.

'Where do you live, Kyle? Where's your mum?'

No response.

'It's not wise for you to stay here, lad.'

I think he's about to speak but then his mouth goes tight. He knows when to keep his trap shut.

'Is this your house, this one here?' I flick my head towards the peeling door behind me.

Nothing.

It is his house. I know from the way he's scowling at me. But he's bricking it, I can tell. It's like his skull's see-through and I'm watching all the shit-scared stuff inside.

I laugh. 'Aw, come on, Kyle. There's nothing wrong in there.' And I do a jokey little jig. 'Is that what you're thinking?'

The last thing I need is for him to run off and find that community arsehole. It would ruin a day's work.

'Tell you what,' I say. 'Let's have a competition. Let's –'

'Fuck you.'

I force a smile. 'Steady, Kyle.'

'Where's my brother? What've you done to him?'

Okay. There it is. Jason Ruby is Kyle's brother. Now that's a surprise.

'You live here with your brother, do you?'

These families are all the same; mum's some useless bird who can't get a grip. Inflicted a string of uncles, boyfriends, stepdads on her snotty kids. Social services visiting more often than the postman. She's off God knows where – pub, dealer. Left the littluns to fend for themselves. It's no wonder Ruby's already a full-fledged lowlife. But a brother's a brother, I suppose.

I still see mine from time to time. John's a wimp, but he's all right. Got a dry-cleaning business in Hornchurch and a dumpy wife, and kids and that.

Thing is, though, Ruby owes my boss money. He's had a few rocks laid on and he's fucked it up. It's easy to avoid a beating but the likes of Ruby never do. Can't keep their mitts off the goods.

'Listen, Kyle.' I try again. 'Your brother's fine. My friend's teaching him . . .' I'm struggling for ideas. 'He's teaching him to act. Yeah, it's like an acting school. And today they're learning how to do fight scenes. Yeah.'

That bullshit comes out quicker than my brain can think it, but I've confused the kid. He likes the idea of acting fight scenes. It makes sense to a lad like him.

'How comes you're not acting with 'em?' he says, suspicious.

'Me? I can't act.'

'What do you do then?'

'Well . . .' *Give me strength.* 'I sing, mainly.'

'Go on then. Sing us a song.'

A song. A fucking song. What made me say I could sing? I give my jaw a good long scratch and check down the road, playing for time. The traffic at the junction's thinned out, finally. Perhaps that chimp got in there and brought some order to the chaos, after all.

Two women waddle towards us on the other side of the street. The sunset makes their saris glow and the colours look almost cheerful. But as they draw level I can see they're weighed down with bags of shopping. Their saris are cheap and they're wearing plastic sandals. One of them grunts as she passes, red dot on her forehead all smudged from the sweat on her face. But though she's knackered she's got enough juice to give me the evil.

'So, are you gonna sing or what?' Kyle's buzzed up all of a sudden.

I touch my forehead, check my fingertips. 'What? Oh yeah. What song should I do?'

He thinks for a second. '"Incy Wincy Spider" and you have to do the actions.'

Little sod's having fun with me now. It's been thirty years since I've sung a note. Mum used to sing a song; it wrings my insides out remembering. The song was about a new dawn, and a new day. She'd end up blubbing, but still try and push the words out. *Feeling good. Feeling good.* Eyes swollen with the gin and the pity of it all. Eventually she'd quieten down, mouth like a corpse, and I'd roll her on her side so she didn't choke in the night. She's in a better place now.

'Remind me how it goes,' I say.

'You don't know "Incy Wincy Spider"?'

'Course I do, it's been a while that's all.'

Kyle's only a shave over four foot. He's got a serious face and he's standing with his legs apart, concentrating. He puts his index finger on the thumb of his opposite hand then brings the other thumb up to meet another finger. And so he goes, awkward, finger over thumb, until his arms are stretched above his head.

It's a sweet little voice that comes out of him. '*Incy Wincy spider climbed up the water spout.*'

A memory forces its way in, near my heart, bubbling round my gippy guts.

'Come on – you've gotta join in,' he says.

I look at my hands. Grey hairs coiling out the leather of my skin. Huge fingers. Nails tougher than tungsten. God, they've seen some work these hands. I look at Kyle. His head's not much bigger than my fist. I try to copy what his hands are doing but my fingers are too stiff.

'No, here,' says Kyle, reaching out. 'It's easy. Give me this thumb here.'

I let him push my fingers into the shapes and we sing together:

Incy Wincy spider climbed up the waterspout
Down came the rain and washed the spider out
Out came the sunshine and dried up all the rain
So Incy Wincy spider climbed up the spout again.

And that's when Kyle tells me about the spiders in the night, eyes shiny with disgust, watching my reaction. I'll bet he's told this story a hundred times at school. He's grinning as his body goes all *linky-lanky*, acting out the spider's legs feeling for my lip. But just as he finishes off, a dismal sound comes from inside the house. Geordie can sometimes let things get out of hand.

Kyle's face becomes a picture of gloom. He's let his guard down and put himself within my reach without meaning to. It's too bad.

'Let's go inside,' I say softly.

He shakes his head.

'Come on, Kyle, we're friends now. I won't hurt you if you keep quiet.'

I've got him by the scruff and he struggles a bit as we get to the door but, like I said, he's used to a bit of manhandling and knows not to make too much fuss. Turns out worse if you do. I knew that too at his age.

We're about to go in when I see a spider's web strung out between the wall and the wheelie bin and, in the middle, a big fat fucker balancing on the silk waiting for a bite. It makes me feel peculiar, right deep inside, and I pluck the spider off its loops and pop it in my mouth.

Two Parties
ALAN BEARD

Smashed on the smoke they listen to the rain's whisper, set off for the pub. In the Red Lion there's an old-fashioned rock band on; they watch and take pills with their beer. Chris is younger, hanging onto a crowd who mostly ignore him. He doesn't dance, but feels the current rise in him, feels switches going on and off like the lights sweeping the room. The plucked bass settles in his stomach, while his head's a flower opening. Is he pink, is he yellow, is he beaming too much? There's a glass in his hand sloshing, there's a frank heat in his groin, there's that woman in the corner.

A leaning man talks to him and Chris sees the voice like slices falling. He's by the bar and watches the barmaid twitch as she pours; a bead of sweat held by each bleached hair on her lip. How she deals with them all, a long-haired weakling saluting her, another whistling, and others with penis smiles. Chat and music break in wave after wave around him. He's trying to talk but he's slipping in words, buttery shit all around. Wondering how to save himself.

He goes out for air, for relief to trees round the back. There are few stars, but the rain has stopped. He feels infected with bark, leaf and sap. He is stumbling carefully. Images begin to pour out of his head, liquid like milk at first, then gaseous, quickly bubbling and disappearing. Faces and hands clenched with stones, and teeth chewing at trees, wolves and owls stirring. He tries hard to stop the flow, hands to his head, but they continue. Is he spewing them?

He realises he is retching, clutches his stomach. Bright spots dim in the undergrowth, absorbed and gone.

Nobody comes for him. He sucks back the dribble and walks to the pub like a ship landed, brimming with so-so music and light, its roof bouncing, and crowded, the aliens spilling out. His gang, his non-gang, coming out too, the lads a dark knot round her, a flame in the dark, Kate as he finds out later, this thing that replaces everything in his brain is Kate.

He is listening, he hears her speak, like the barmaid dipped in gold, smooth and unbreakable like stars bunched together, he is hearing her say it is her twenty-first and there is a party and everyone is invited; Gleave Road, you know it, Selly Oak, off the Bristol Road, couple of miles away. She is spinning round to everyone, he is included, she is Wonder Woman without the costume, darker and thinner, the woman he'd watched on TV as a kid, not so long ago. She is as shiny, as sparkly, but darker, closer, more beautiful.

So he tags along; she has gone in a taxi but the gang grown large enough to hide in walk and walk down Cartland Road and up along the Pershore Road through the smell of baltis, buses pass like steamships going upriver, belching smoke. Heads turn to see them pass, through windows either side, buses, cafés, there is laughing and jokes he half understands. He is poked in the ribs. 'Righty righty, ole Chris Cross.' 'Chris crossed and final.' He is gently pushed. He has to take a piss in a doorway. 'Chris pissed and crossed the final.'

He had a friend once. He doesn't want another. He wants Kate. From Stirchley to Selly Oak following a slowly disappearing number 11, past a night-shift Cadbury's emitting a faint smell of cocoa and soap, past his own semi-detached (where his mother could be looking out for him and just in case he looks away), past no pubs; he thinks of kidnapping her, locking her in his un-lockable bedroom, his mum mysteriously gone, his dad gone already anyway, six shooter in pocket, off to his own sunset. The dust of him left behind. The entire house his and Kate in his bedroom. He'll feed her, he'll take food up. Bread and soup. Toast and coffee. She'll nibble and sip and later he'll lay his head on her stomach to listen to her digest. His face on her skin, his ear to her belly.

Into the little block of houses behind the shops, the health clinic and patch of concrete playground built on a bombsite. Two of the lads break off to climb the frame and spin the roundabout, clinging on until they shoot off, rolling on the ground. Then into the street where you don't need to know the number, the tight terraced houses huddle together darkly except for one in the middle where the sound and light of the universe seem crammed into it. It beats. People cling to it, to the bricks, the bay window and door frame, or lie across the pavement or prop themselves up against cars parked there.

It is hard to get through the opened door, through the people lined up taking a piece of each person as they pass, a word or a brush of flesh, a shoe on the foot. 'Hey Boy Hey Girl' squeezes Chris into the kitchen up against some pretty boys just out of university talking about the band they're in. Sentences sink into him. For a moment he's upright and sensible, nodding sagely, as sagely as an eighteen year old can. 'We play high-tech, intelligent pop.' Someone laughs, some thirty-odd bloke says to his wife, 'Sounds just like us, high-tech, intelligent.' The pretty boys wear make-up like something out of the early eighties, they are talking OMD and ABC and Chris feels his understanding leave or kneel down at least.

All ages here, well up to forty or is she forty-five, the woman in tight jeans and white fur top? Three Asians of different heights opposite him against a table with a solitary Tupperware dish holding a few shards of crisps, start to perform a dance routine, going up and down in turn to Madonna's 'Ray of Light', coming from the room next door, and singing parts: '*Faster than the speeding light*' . . . '*She's flying.*'

His belly like a brick, his prick a little plastic nub, his eyes like pennies held by children he wants more he wants to unstick he lines up for drink swaying and being asked his age. 'What's my age again?' he asks the man behind him. He wants more than drink he wants Kate he goes into the back room with its red oily light and green mossy carpet where smoke like clouds from a disturbed sea bed swirls up, searches for Ian and Fred, the main men tonight, for more pills that are getting spilled and will make the Hoover sick tomorrow. He slumps, feels six, sixteen, as his back touches the wall, mad music spinning him, people wavering, dancing above him. Too hard to get up, to shift his frame, he lets the clotted air sink him.

He sees her go by, watches the form of her, from her ankles to her shoulders, her half-curled hair, blocks of her forming and re-forming, disappearing and reappearing through the layers of clothes and smoke and music. He lifts eventually, a rush, everything blurs and sings, but people are nudging others as he goes by and the message is going round and round about him about his age about his stupidity about his evil intent about his search for Kate. He doesn't even know if she has blue eyes, if she likes strawberries, if she likes the stuff that's playing now – Primal Scream, he thinks – he wants to watch her sway and dance to check. He'll know if he can see her, he'll know everything.

It is true everybody hates him, wants him dead, because when he goes outside looking and maybe to lie on the cold grass by the child's swing someone slams their fist into his face and busts his lip. The blip of flesh hanging stops him closing his mouth. It feels like a mini-world to him. He thinks he will always have this world bulging, with its own lands and seas, ocean-going liners full of jolly bacteria singing and laughing at him like he is a dangling idiot. There is a pain, a screeching like a fairground ride coming off its rails. Makes him sick again, makes him shutter down and fall on the ground and no one comes to see to him, he half hears the party, half sees it, reaches for it, for her, but it won't come, he can't lift himself again, he is Chris the type that never gets up that is sick and follows people around.

Light seeps in then, he's gone deaf, or the music turned down; there is an empty feel as he lies by the swing and on it is Kate, twenty-one, singing softly, bare-legged, pushing herself back and forth with pointed feet.

She says, 'You're awake.' She speaks to him, actual words fall from her lips and stick to his mired face. She's up like a ballet dancer, her toes touch grass first and a little pirouette round to him: 'You okay?' Her hand like a bird, like a voice to his cheek, the back of her fingers on his cheek, his forehead. 'Think you're okay.' Touches his busted lip, her nails measure the blip, move it around, sending all the world out of its orbit. Her lips are better than Wonder Woman's they are like Jane Fonda's in *Klute*, his father has a book, left behind, Chris once studied the stills nightly. Kate has Fonda's mouth and teeth, dark eyes too, not like WendyfuckingWonder, he has to alter his image of her, the person to whom he'll bring bread and soup. She'll sip it now with Bree Daniel's pout.

'I'm fine.' Chris manages a sentence. 'Someone hit me.' She shifts back, and her movement pulls him up to sitting. Her legs as she stands, her brown legs, the knees like the best things in the world, and above them shining thigh, muscles show lightly as she straightens. He can't look at her face in case he cries or grabs. He tries to make a joke about his own swollen lip – 'like yours' – but he feels her puzzle, move back more.

''s fucking Nige.' She has a soaring Brummie accent, the 'g' of 'fucking' strong. 'Gone do-lally again. Virtually cleared the place.' An angel too brutally there to be an angel, the marks of the swing on her under-thigh, her feet flattening grass, she says, 'All okay now, though. Everything shipshape.'

His eye level with her knees, he can't look up. He's entering some new world, he can feel time, minutes and hours shed, like rain might bounce off him now, he is in some un-wettable element now, air touched with her lightness, her brownness, her mouth talking to him.

His face tingles from where she touched it as she moves away. He can feel the air change, suck away, as she joins others in the garden that reassembles, dawn broken fully. Selly Oak Hospital buildings loom over the wooden fence at the end. The gardens each side trying to enter Kate's, flowers and weeds along the path, a patch of garden not touched, a student house now, once a family one.

All, even Kate, especially Kate, look isolated, a fat black line drawn around them and they are flat against the soft banks of roses tumbling in from next door. Chris is silent and ugly and bust open. He tries to curl around himself. Kate flattens herself, away from him.

He slinks away, sidles, hurt, down inclines, getting out of there, out of a cold heat, and stumbles to the sanctuary only a mile away, his mother surely in bed, he'll sneak in and up swaying stairs and hide in his room until kingdom come.

*

His wife is pregnant, and sends him to get a 'meal for two, a nice one' and wine to celebrate – 'Only one glass for me,' she'd said. 'My last for a while.' Chris feels sick, turning into a garage on the way back, the shopping sliding on the back seat. He feels wounded. It isn't what he wants, he realises; he feels too young.

He's paying for his petrol when he hears the unmistakable voice. 'These cards too, oh and a pack of Kings.' That strong 'g'. He didn't know she smoked. He turns, putting his wallet away and bumps into her deliberately. 'Sorry,' he says, taking his time to look at her face, her mouth, taking his hand off her bare arm slowly, but not so slow she'll notice. She's not looking properly anyway, not like she did that once to ask after his smacked face; she's too distracted with paying.

He steadies himself. She's dressed up, a thin-strapped black dress. He steps back to take her all in. She's more golden, five more years of burnish make her flaws, the breaks, the lines, the curls lustrous. He feels it again, a hot shock, her allure intact and magnified from the time he saw her last with roses behind her. He is buckling.

Outside the door he blocks her way, fiddles with his mobile, steps again into her to feel the heft, to smell her, some flowery perfume that makes him sway. She is different, she is better. She barely notices, gets by to the waiting husband pointing at his watch, a pair of sunglasses perch on his pale jumper like a black insect landed. Shows him the card, he shrugs and they get in the car, the sort that purrs.

Chris is off to his own car, luckily at the nearest pump. He tries too hard to get started, can't get the key in the ignition, he is still stupid. But they are stuck at the lights, out on the dual carriageway and he pulls in behind them.

Many times through the south of the city, through the houses and shops lining up to clap them through, and on to the suburbs, and further, Shirley, Solihull, Knowle, he thinks he's lost her, and every breath is a little pain. He thinks he'll have to stop and maybe spew again in some side street, maybe that will get it all out of him and he can go back to microwaved noodles and toasting the future with his wife.

But then he spots them two cars ahead, overtakes to get behind again to see her silhouette in the lights of the oncoming traffic. The shape of her head pulls him on. Out in the country they suddenly turn left through gates that he overshoots. He parks on the side of the road, drives into the soft and scratchy hedge to get the car off the tarmac, and walks back.

He turns through the gates flanked by columns through rain suddenly slanting into his face and down to the lit-up house at the bottom where music comes through open windows. His shoes crunch as he passes someone directing cars, people float in and out of the house, under porches smoking. As he walks in he is given wine and the music jumps into his head and Kate is nowhere.

Into a room, the main one, a chandelier shedding petals of light over all the dancers and guests lined up around the room, glasses in hands. Three men in bow ties sit in a row on a sofa. Greetings, shouting and arms flung about one another around him. A tall blonde in black, nose like a boxer's, dances by with a smaller man in white with white hair one side of his face, black the other. Another blonde, hair piled up, green velvet dress, takes Chris's glass from him, gives it someone and pulls him out into the dancers. 'Didn't feel like dressing up then?' she says, swinging her eyes up and down, moving him about like a marionette. Eventually she dances away and leaves Chris stranded and pushing his way through the crowd pumping and grinding ironically or sedately swaying to 'Hey Ya'.

He looks, looks, goes from room to room along corridors where framed pictures hang like a gallery and past a sweep of stairs occupied by couples sat together, the women in big dresses or little ones and into a room where a German professor of astronomy – he says as much – talks of his position, his accumulation of atoms in the universe, while a man behind him strips to the waist and beats his hairy chest.

He has to go to the toilet and searches through rooms getting smaller and bigger, has to ask directions. The toilet is full of plants and lined with books. He could bring her here. Invite her politely, 'You may come to my den.' She could sit in the chair there and he could just look and look until he did more. Have they put something in the drinks because he feels shimmery, as if on the edge of fever, although the cock in his hand hasn't drug-shrivelled.

In a room of tables of food, pâtés and whole roast chickens and other fowl, many different kinds of bread and a terrine, a cake and more bottles, he drinks, stands still. Perhaps that will be best, not moving, eventually she will come through. He listens to the voices around him:

'No front or back to that dress, is there?'

Not Kate then, a plunge at the front, but not at the back.

'A knife, a fork, a bottle and a cork.'

He wants to hear Kate sing, he wishes he could remember the song on the swing, he wants to come home to her, not the one waiting for him now, instead he wants to see Kate slowly accumulate the years in her eyes and in her stance. Send him out for wine.

'I'm from Hong Kong originally.'

Isn't that her husband, her stupid twat husband, not dressed up either, is he, not much. He could follow him, the pastel jumper his lead through the crowds to his treasure. But his way is blocked by a fat fart who talks through drink, a little gurgly voice of protest about a girl who changed overnight. The next time he saw her he only recognised her by her voice. Is he talking to himself, is he that fat?

He glimpses Kate, her face, behind this man, to his right. She is in the room. Why isn't everyone turning to bow and curtsy, to strew flowers before her? But he eases too, relaxes. He has the world now, the world has just walked in, he breathes out. He sympathises with fat fuck, his chins, his nodding wispy head, baldness corrugated, all the while watching his future woman expertly slip away from people, slip the clutches of men. Now she is leaving and he bites his tongue, stays polite, she is around, she is a room away, but it is hard not to shove baldy aside and run to her.

But he takes his time now he's on the scent, sees her with this group or that, always in the corner of his eye, watching the light sway of her movement: that hasn't changed. He drinks more and accepts a joint as he goes outside and watches a man with a rose between his teeth climb a trellis, and others re-enact scenes from *La Dolce Vita* in the small fountain.

Light rain now and then, no one seems to mind. He goes in slightly wet, and there she is, stops to talk to him in a utility room, wellington boots and freezers around, pipes and further plants growing in pots along the sills and in the corners.

'Everything shipshape?' he asks her.

'Do I know you?' she asks and he shakes his head, can't tell her, her face like a face on a cinema screen, he could climb it.

'Don't you agree I'm too young?' he asks, the glow from her has dimmed everything in him.

'For what?' She laughs. Her first full laugh for him.

'For stuff.' He gives a twirl. He is an idiot. He does not know what to say to keep her there. 'Music's good. Are Primal Scream your favourite band?'

He wants to tell her how upset his mother had been, who had waited up and said there was only him and her now, he was like his stupid father, off wrestling cows elsewhere, and about his frantic wife, his phone shut off and not to be looked at, except if he could have Kate's number. How he'd put them all on a raft, a rickety, strung-together raft, wife and bleating mother and future son or daughter; he'd push them off from the bank and watch them, no not even watch, as they cling and shout and go over rapids and out to sea, if only Kate will keep smiling at him and raising her eyebrows and keep talking, with her new shoulders and arms showing and the plunge of her breasts always there below her talking, full-lipped Jane Fonda mouth.

'No, the Beatles of fucking course, but I do like MIA, and a bit of dubstep now and then.'

She looks like she's not sure if she should go.

'How's Nigel these days?' he says before he can stop himself.

Her face loses the quizzical look. 'Of course! You know him. That's where I've seen you. I'll go get him.' He sees at once she has married the bloke that hit him in advance, years in advance, for the abduction/seduction he is going to carry out. Trying to ruin his lip that will touch and taste her.

She goes before he can stop her, off to get her husband, who'd had more intimate contact with him than her. His blood and spit on his fist.

As he makes his way after her, he is ushered through to the hall. Someone is coming, something is happening, some grand entrance to be made. Chris sees Kate and husband further down and starts to manoeuvre through the crowd to them. He gets closer but it's difficult due to bodies streaming in from doors all around or coming in from outside, squeezing in, filling up like the house in Gleave Road.

He manages to get behind her, the husband in front. A Kate sandwich in the middle of everything. The bodies keep coming in and reeling past, pushing them closer, the fat man looking for his girl, the two-faced joker, the green-dressed woman doing a little dance when she sees him, hands above her head. He moves smack into Kate and she smiles back at him, nods her excitement at what's happening. But he continues to press against her, body against body, touching at vital points, the electric running up and down, head to fingers to cock to feet. His knee slots into the back of hers, he puts his palm on her hip, feels the bone jut precisely into it, his fingers press on the flat flesh below. She squirms and turns, her smile gone. She taps her husband but Chris squeezes tighter as the celebrity walks in and cheers go up and clapping starts as if celebrating his moves. He pulls her tight into his opened up body. His maw. Chris covers Kate with kisses.

The Way of the World

KIT DE WAAL

Skip would walk the length of Springfield Road, past the castellated Victorian villas with ornate railings bent and rusted, past the skinny trees hard pruned to allow the buses to pass, through a flat field of allotments, and come eventually to the wild end of the road where Moseley bled into Sparkhill, shabbier and poor.

Skip would walk all that way to our house, but he when he got there he didn't knock. He would rattle the handle of the front door by way of a warning in case anyone was arguing, kissing, indecent or otherwise unprepared, and just walk in. He'd come strolling into the back room with an extravagant block of pink and white coconut ice for me and a couple of bottles of treacly beer for my mother.

'Now,' he'd say. 'I've got sweets for the sweet and stout for the stout. Who's having what?'

She would look up from the paper, feigning disgust. 'You'll need more than Mackeson if you get him drunk again, you idle sod.'

He would land the bottles on the table, pass me my sweets or a sixpenny bit and slip away into the sitting room with my father to open up the cocktail cabinet and West Indian rum. They would singe their socks at the electric fire and talk about cars and strikes, wars and astronauts, men on the moon.

More often than not they had the same shift: Skip as conductor on my father's bus, the number 8 that crawled a wide circle around the city centre. So their days off were the same, midweek or weekends, two days together. Apart from Christmas, when Skip arrived with the snow and seemed to stay for ever, apart from those times when Skip would struggle in with a Wendy house for me and a baby doll for my little sister, apart from those times, it was always summer when Skip came and the sun would always shine. Dad would be in a good mood and my mum would be singing and reading the paper and washing up all at the same time.

Long before I understood anything at all about the way of the world, I knew Skip was different. I could see it with my own eyes. Skip was a white man. White women we saw all the time in our house: my mother, her sisters and the next-door neighbour. But white men, never. Skip was like a cartoon, with crayon-blue eyes, ice-cream skin and thick, yellow hair that rippled in waves on his collar. He was as tall as my dad, way up there near the tinkling, plastic chandelier and the picture rail in the front room. He wore a navy blazer with gold buttons that he never fastened, so it flapped open showing a Persil-white shirt over his massive chest. His tie was navy, too, with a cream stripe - and, at the bottom, embroidered in a fine gold thread there was a tiny golden cricket bat and a red ball.

When he settled himself on the good sofa with a glass in his hand, I was sent in with nuts or crisps and I would tiptoe up to him with the tray. Sometimes, if he wasn't too far gone, he would grab me, balance me on his thick knee and ask me ridiculous questions like, 'Who ate all the numbers on the clock, Patches?' or, 'Where's the off switch? Come on, what's your answer?'

I wouldn't speak. He would look and look with his watery eyes and very soon he would forget I was there and I could slide away back to Mom or the telly or to my sister and our games in the garden. But there were times when I ran off too soon and he would chase me, squealing between the sheets on the line. When he caught me, he would spin me around and ask the question again, roaring with laughter at nothing at all. 'Patches!' he would bellow. 'How long is always?'

Skip seemed to fly. He seemed to take up all the space, all the air wherever he was, his arms wide open, fingers splayed, his chest pushed out. Always gathering things, inviting, shaping, describing, throwing his hands up in horror, in jest, in supplication. He was, people would later say, larger than life, bigger than the bus depot even, conducting the passengers, on and off, round and round, tickets for tuppence, clickety click. Of course, as a child, I had no thoughts about life, so no idea that there could be more than one way to live it or that people like Skip tried to get hold of it and wrap it around their dreams.

'Life,' he once told my mother when I was colouring in and he was chatting to her in the back room, 'Life, darlin', is a bully boy flexing his muscles. It takes grit to stand up to him. You have to stay awake, catch him at it and do him down.' He took his cigarette and stood at the french windows. 'Otherwise, love, the arrogant bugger will tear off, lead you a merry dance and get away with murder.'

When Skip was dying at Selly Oak Hospital and the matron let in the evening visitors, my father would stride the length of the ward looking for his friend. Skip would struggle up, even then, to catch a glimpse, put a face to the footfall, start the visit early, squeeze the very marrow out of the time he had left. He didn't see that all the other eyes were upon my father as well.

My father told me once the trouble he took over the pressing of his visiting suit, riffling through his tie drawer, matching and discarding handkerchiefs until exactly the right one was selected. 'And a tie-pin, yes. I knew everybody was watching to see where the darkie was going. Is all white man on the ward so I dress myself right. Just to say, look! Yes, we can dress up good and better than you lot.'

He clenched his teak fist and spoke with bitterness, having known the truth about Skip for a long time by then. 'When I get myself ready in all that stuff and I see your mother watching, I did believe she was jealous like I had a fancy piece or one of the nurses was a looker. Stupid, eh?' Then he closed his eyes. 'Ah, Skip, man. Skip.'

And when Skip saw my father, he would wave his two-armed wave, gesturing to the seat next to him. 'Come on! It's not catching!' And all the white people must have seen my father slap hands with Skip, laugh and joke and embrace him like a brother.

After many months of his absence in our house, when the rum

bottle remained untouched and the cabinet doors hardly opened, Skip got into his final scuffle with life, but he didn't have the strength to hold on. Apparently he died right after lunchtime, mid-sentence, telling one of the nurses that it was no wonder he was the worse for wear when his phlegm had more substance than the custard. He started laughing at his own joke and the laugh turned into a cough and the cough turned into his farewell.

A prickly hush came into the house when my dad came back from the hospital. He shut the door to the kitchen so we knew there was a secret in the house. My mother went to the front room and poured him a rum deep enough to show she understood, that tonight he would be drunk and a good thing it was too.

'He'll be surely wearing a smile under that coffin lid, George love,' she said. 'You mark my words. Smiling, he is.'

Dad sat a long while by the coal fire in the kitchen and we weren't allowed to disturb him. We couldn't even go in for our cocoa, so we sat on our beds with our plastic mugs. The extra sugar told us to be quiet.

A week later I sat on the sofa watching my father tackle the crease on his best black trousers. He stood, six foot four, bent over the ironing board with grim concentration, grief and sweat mixed across his wide brow. In his hand the iron looked like a toy, but when he planted it on the sheet of thick brown paper it curled up at the corners and a burning smell filled the room.

The trousers tamed, my father started on his jacket in the kitchen; a jacket was never to be pressed, never. It was coaxed into obedience with steam from a constantly boiling kettle. Holding it high over the stove, my father brushed the cloth with his asbestos hands, whirring it around like he had a motor for a wrist, smoothing the front, tugging the back, folding back the lapels again and again. After ten minutes, the thing looked new.

My mother was entrusted with the shirt which, after all, would spend the whole of the funeral under the perfect jacket, so it could bear the few mistakes she was bound to inflict upon it.

He took the pile of clothes carefully upstairs and emerged half an hour later, the black prince, smelling of Bay Rum, immaculate.

Just before he left that day to carry the coffin, hold the rope and lower Skip, smiling surely under the coffin lid, into the cold February mud, I ran up behind my father and said – because I wanted to say something important on this important occasion – 'Why did Skip die, Dad?'

He didn't answer me and I wondered if I had finally caught Skip's habit of asking a stupid question.

'Stella? Stella?' he called upstairs to my mother. 'I'm gone.'

He opened the front door and, because I stood in the way, he couldn't shut it and had to say something. He looked down and I thought I would hear something from my father about the specifics of Skip's disease but I only got the usual.

'That's the way of the world, Patches. That's the way of the world.'

It was many years later, a long time after my father had left us for the last time, that I remembered Skip and my mother in the garden that hot summer before he died. We were lying on the grass, the three of us, on the carpet-runner lawn, close together. I was between them, slipping in and out of sleep. A shift of tone in my mother's voice brought me awake. 'I don't know, Skip. I really don't.'

'Try,' he said.

'No,' she replied.

I sat up and he spoke to me. 'You can spell, can't you, Patches? How do you spell "man"?'

'M A N,' I said.

'How do you spell "woman"?'

'W O M A N,' I said.

'So what do the "w" and the "o" stand for then? Come on. Your mum said she doesn't know.'

I looked at her, but she looked away. It was a test and she wouldn't help me.

'We . . . When . . .' I faltered.

'How about Weak and Obstinate?' he offered, looking away past me towards the playing fields and the secondary school beyond, towards his own home somewhere at the edge of the city with more trees and less concrete.

I said nothing.

'Or Willingly Open?'

I felt the wind of the slap my mother gave him, and she stood up suddenly, straightening her skirt and trying to smile. But the smile crumpled on her face and she told me to get up and go inside. 'You've had enough sun for one day,' she said. 'You'll be as black as your dad.'

'Or White Only?' Skip asked, looking straight up at her.

As I walked back into the house I knew I had failed the test and made my mother angry. I looked back and saw her stand over him, her hands on her hips. 'How about We're Over?' she said.

She saw me looking and shooed me away. I went inside and straight to the french windows where I watched her sit down again, next to him.

I thought and thought, but dared not disturb them. When I looked out again I saw my mother laughing, Skip on his back, his face to the sky, his hands knitted together over his heart.

Go to Sleep, Lobster

JULIA BELL

They stood like penguins at Euston, necks craned at the departure boards. All trains north of Watford delayed because of a person under a train. Kirsten waited another ten minutes until it was obvious that no one was going anywhere, then went and bought her second coffee. Outside the concession a poster advertising the benefits of the brand mocked her with its jaunty inscription: *The perfect start to your day!*

Fuck off, she mouthed back at the pearlised woman who seemed to be making love to her cup.

It wasn't even as if she wanted to be here: she was doing this instead of Fabien, because he had phoned in with a family crisis and everybody knew that she, being single, was the only one who would be available at such short notice. She had the laptop, a bunch of briefing notes to read and the address of a chain hotel, which was, according to TripAdvisor, rated 30th out of 137 hotels in Birmingham.

A pitch for one of Fabien's contacts: a website, a brochure and an identity for a new restaurant. She would have to present it to a roomful of Brummies tomorrow, go through the thinking behind the layout, explain the reasons why they had taken out the Os in 'Noord Oost' and turned them into pencil-drawn balloons. Why they had chosen a chunky typewriter font and not something more elegant like Nexus. Probably they would look bored, demand changes. She would go back to the office, work on it some more and the client would eventually settle on something very similar to what they had started with. As Fabien always said, designing an identity for someone means you are showing them who you think they are; they will always look in the mirror and get fussy about the reflection. Kirsten had only glanced at the documents, but they should be happy: it was a solid bit of work; the logo was quirky, touched by a kind of homespun, high-end boot sale chic, a look which was hot in London right now. She had packed her Stella McCartney trouser suit especially.

Maria used to laugh at her attempts to femme herself up for work, and it was true she did feel fraudulent in heels and make-up. Her usual look was casual, sporty, hipster even, with the right T-shirt. But since Identity had taken off, she was obliged to turn on the designer suits in line with the expectations of their increasingly corporate clients. Bored, she wandered around a cosmetics stand at the station, fingering the products, testing the hand cream. Maria used to say testers were unhygienic, full of germs. But that was Maria all over - a snob and shit scared of other people, in case they wanted something from you. How long since she'd heard from her? Seven, maybe eight months. It surprised her quite how much their break-up still hurt. She had failed, after all the years of trying to make it work, not just at her relationship, but at life, too. At thirty-eight here she was, still single, still trying, still confused. For all her career success, the lack of a lover bit deep and, worse, she had a niggling feeling that it was her fault. There was some devil in her that meant when someone was too nice to her she was overwhelmed with an urge to be mean. And she always regretted it, almost as soon as the words had flown out her mouth. As if she were saying *come here* and *go away*, both at the same time. But some words can't be unsaid and it was this, she knew, more than anything that had killed the relationship.

By the time she boarded the train it was past two, and then they were kept waiting in the station for another half-hour. The train was packed; people standing in the aisles and in the vestibules. She got a seat next to a man who couldn't settle. He wriggled in his seat, constantly fiddling with his magazine, pulling on the tray table, crossing and uncrossing his legs, until it got to the point where she put her hand firmly on his arm.

'Tranquilo,' she said, although she had no idea why she'd resorted to her smattering of Spanish to try and calm him down. He looked at her and grunted then continued to rock in his seat for the whole slow three hours of the journey. Nightmare. And all for the sake of someone else's suicidal feelings. The thought that someone had ended their own life by getting mashed up beneath the wheels of a train was at once so gruesome and so melodramatic that being annoyed and then slightly depressed seemed the only decent response.

When the train finally arrived Kirsten was so desperate for air that she walked from the station to the hotel on Broad Street. Her room was compact, featureless, with a brown and cream bedspread and a kind of hard, plasticised sisal carpet. She dumped her bags on the bed and looked out the window at the narrow street outside, fought off a familiar despondency. If she were ever going to kill herself it would probably be somewhere like this. She could hear the thump of music, the clatter of passing traffic. It was a street that had once been warehouses, now turned into bars and restaurants. The kinds of places that projected an image of the future that was starting to look dated. The glass and chrome, the funky minimalism. It was too studied. What was cool now was more low-key, bohemian; antiques thrown together to look like a house of curiosities, more romantic, earthy. God, you could tell you were in the provinces, she thought, bitchily.

The phone startled her. She looked at her mobile but then realised it was the grey handset near the bed that was ringing. Reception: apparently there was someone in the lobby who wanted to talk to her. No one had mentioned that she would be met. She had the address of the office where she would make the presentation tomorrow morning and a taxi booked to take her to the station in the afternoon. This was the extent of the contact she was expecting to have with the city. In the lift she had a fleeting fantasy that Maria might have tracked her down, had come to say she was wrong, that she was sorry and could they work it out? She had a sudden physical flashback: the soft weight of her hands, the way she always paused before a kiss. But the receptionist pointed to a man sitting on one of the sofas in the lobby. He was wearing a dark suit and was tall, and weirdly flat. Broad from the front, but when he stood up to greet her, she saw that he was actually very thin, like an animated cardboard cut-out.

'Hi, hi, *hi*. So sorry to bother you.'

He stuck out his hand; his grip was limp and clammy. But she was more wrong-footed by his broad Black Country accent.

'You're from Identity? You work with Fabien, right?'

She nodded.

'Right, right, he's told me about you. So, he's not here?' His face was bloated, stubbled. He looked hungover.

'He had to stay in London. I stepped in, a last-minute thing. Can I help?'

'Well, you know Fabien and I, we go *waaay* back. Anyway, I've got these reservations. I was supposed to pick him up; we were going to go together. I thought he would be here. I guess he forgot to let me know he wouldn't be coming.' His eyelids fluttered while he spoke.

'I think his eldest broke his arm playing football. Had to go to A&E with him.'

'I'm *so* sorry to hear that,' he said, with exaggerated sympathy. 'Terrible, *terrible* news. It's awful being a parent . . .'

'Do you have kids?'

'No . . . but you know, I have friends who do. Fabien . . . other people.'

He seemed so nervous it was making Kirsten itchy. 'I'm sorry but I don't even know your name.'

'I can't believe – sorry, sorry. It's Rich. Richard Jones. I work at Marque. In accounts. I'm not a creative like you guys!'

Marque was a bit player agency, one which focused on local TV adverts, downmarket weekly magazines. Fabien was always laughing at them for being stuck in the nineties, for producing static, airbrushed work that made the models look like aliens or dolls.

'Well, here's the thing . . . now that Fabien's not here I've had to recalibrate my plans but I'm thinking, why not just be *spontaneous*?' He giggled. Kirsten had no idea what he was talking about. 'You're here for Noord Oost, right?' She nodded. 'You know it's going to be the best place in the country to eat? They're making a real statement by launching it in Birmingham and not London. Head chef comes from the French Laundry. Fabien and I were going to go tonight. They're doing a menu test ahead of the launch. I've got reservations if –'

'Fine,' she said; she just wanted to put him out of his misery. His discomfort was painful. 'It would be good to check them out.'

'Great! Fantastic!' He looked delighted. 'Oh, that's great!'

'What time?'

He shrugged. 'We could go now.'

'I thought you had reservations.'

'Oh, I do. But we could go and get a drink first. If you like.'

He was pushing his luck. She shook her head. Told him she needed to get changed, do a bit more work, suggested they meet again in a few hours.

'Oh, yeah, yeah, *absolutely*, of course.' He held out his hand and dipped his head in an attitude of supplication, which really irritated her. She wondered if she should have politely knocked him back; spending an evening with him was likely to be a complete chore, but it would be useful to get a heads-up on tomorrow. She didn't know who else was pitching for the job, but her competitive instincts meant she didn't want to lose it, even if it wasn't her client.

She stood up. 'Okay. I'll see you at eight.'

He didn't make any effort to move. 'I'll be right here.'

She realised as she walked back to the lift, aware of his eyes following her, that he was going to sit on the sofa in the lobby and wait for her. She found it hard not to think about him as she went through the details of the presentation. What the hell was she going to talk to him about? She should have said no. And she didn't *need* to scope out the restaurant either; this was a small job in real terms. By the time they'd factored in the cost of her coming to pitch for it there would be at best a marginal return. And that's if she won the pitch. She didn't understand Fabien's business choices. Of course, it was sometimes better to do small jobs if they offered a useful affiliation – a cool product or service that would give the agency a lift – but this was obscure fine dining in Birmingham. Or at least that's what she assumed, there seemed to be very little information in the documents Fabien had sent her. *Noord Oost is a new kind of dining experience for the discerning citizens of Britain's second city* was all she had to go on. Surely there were local agencies that could handle the job just as well? Even Marque could have pitched for it. Perhaps Fabien was intending to open an office here or something.

When she'd first met Fabien nearly seven years ago, he spent the whole of her interview playing with a wind-up robot, setting it in motion across his desk. It held out its arms like a zombie and had a smile that she supposed was meant to be friendly but which actually seemed malevolent. It waddled despotically between his keyboard and coaster.

'What does it make you think of?' he asked.

Kirsten shivered. 'It's scary. It moves but its expression never changes.'

'Yeah! Totally! What if there was, like, an *army* of them?'

She wasn't sure whether to agree or disapprove, so as a compromise she laughed. He offered her the job the next day.

Now he was forty and divorced and had two kids. He had started to soften around the middle and his hair was receding. He'd stopped riding a scooter to work, buying instead an Oyster card and a set of Dr Dre headphones. But he still lived inside a universe of restless cool: he thrived on a combination of nostalgia and novelty which currently meant seventies print jumpers, a greying beard and big glasses, and obscure Japanese toys. It was odd that he should have a friend who was as utterly uncool as Rich.

Kirsten really wanted to stay in her hotel room, watch some TV, drop a sleeping pill and get an early night, but there was something about Rich that was so pathetic she felt sorry for him in spite of herself. She wondered if this was how he made Fabien feel, too. She put on her suit but took it easy on the make-up; she didn't want him to think she was in any way into him.

She got down to the lobby ten minutes late. He was sprawled on one of the sofas, looking even less composed than he had done two hours earlier. His face was red and his eyes were drooping. She wondered if he was drunk.

'Hi.' He giggled and puffed out his cheeks. 'Sorry, I had a cheeky spliff.'

'Right.' Inside her trouser pockets she clenched her fists. Why had she agreed to this? She was now going to spend the evening babysitting Fabien's weird and very stoned friend.

'Me and Fabien always go for one, it's like, *man* . . . d'you want some?'

'No thanks,' she said primly. 'So, you live here?' she asked, neutrally.

'No, I live in Wolverhampton. But I always get the Metro in if Fabien's here on business. He just gives me the call and here I am! It's a kind of thing we have.' He looked at her, but his gaze seemed to go right through her. 'I texted him and told him we were meeting. He says hi.'

This was far too intimate. She didn't know this guy well enough for him to be relaying second-hand messages from her boss.

They walked out into the evening, which had turned to drizzle. Rich at least was quiet for a few moments. He led her towards the canal and past a cavernous Wetherspoons which had loud, drunk people spilling out onto the steps down to the canal side. The air smelled of stagnant water and chips.

They turned into a narrow street that fronted onto the canal, lined with what were once Victorian factory buildings. She supposed the restaurant was going to be in one of them, imagining creaky floorboards, a dark interior, antiques. But instead they walked the whole length of the street, crossed another bridge and suddenly she found herself in a throng of men queuing outside the Pocket Rocket, a venue advertising itself as an Exclusive Gentleman's Club.

Two bouncers stood like statues, their hands clasped in front of their balls, staring at the men as they passed through into the lobby, which looked to be padded with thick black and red plush, presumably to give the impression that one was stepping into a boudoir.

Rich hunched his shoulders in an expression that was half apologetic and half naughty boy. 'I've got vouchers for free drinks,' he said, as if by way of explanation.

'Right.' Kirsten didn't know what else to say.

'You don't mind, do you?'

She looked at a poster on the wall of the club, which showed some airbrushed glamazon in a slashed jumpsuit that all but revealed her nipples. She couldn't quite believe that he was serious.

'I thought you were . . . you know . . . Well, Fabien said you were . . .'

She saw he was blushing, squirming even.

'What?'

'*Gay.*'

'So?'

'I thought you'd be like, er, you know, down with it.' He made a gauche hip-hop hand signal. She pretended like she hadn't noticed. 'There's quite a lot of women that go.'

She glanced sceptically at the queue of male faces. 'Are you *serious?*'

'Why not? We're all adults, right? You're not a prude or anything, are you?'

She stared at him, the nature of his relationship with Fabien revealed. So *this* is what they did together when he came to Birmingham. Got stoned and went to lap-dancing clubs. That explained the cheap clients, the unnecessary business trips. She would be sure to let Fabien know she was on to him when she got back. She clenched and unclenched her fists again. God, she was so mad, she wasn't sure how she was going to sit through a whole meal with this guy. Maybe she should make her excuses and leave.

'Just the one drink?' He seemed to pleading with her. 'It's all quite tame, you know. The women are just the decoration, like.'

'*Decoration?*' Kirsten was sure that, whatever else she might have to do this evening, she was not going to go into that fucking club with this wanker.

But as she opened her mouth to tell him this, he turned away from her, distracted by a woman in vertiginous Perspex see-through heels and a clinging white dress that showed off the curves of her breasts. Fake, Kirsten thought, looking at the perfect circular shape of them; they were like round cushions or pillows that had been attached to her chest as a joke. Like she was trying as hard as possible to resemble a blow-up doll.

'*Heeeey*, Richard,' the woman said, cupping his face in her hands and giving him a big kiss. 'You come to see me with your new girlfriend?'

'Ah.' He looked embarrassed, took a step back. 'No, this is Kirsten, a – a colleague. Remember Fabien? She works with him. Kirsten, this is . . . er . . .'

'Beti,' she said, touching Kirsten on the arm, the warmth of her hands through Kirsten's thin shirt making her shiver. She had an Eastern European accent, maybe even Russian, and her skin was the colour of a tangerine, her make-up so thick it made her look like she was in drag. She gave Kirsten an appraising glance then looked back at Richard. 'You come to see me now I start my shift?'

'No,' Kirsten said, more definitively than she meant. 'Sorry.'

'Of course,' Beti said, tilting her head like she understood, a gesture that made Kirsten angry. She imagined paying Beti to dance for her, how she might look as she slid her body up and down a pole, the pornography of her ridiculous breasts, and then, realising she was staring, succumbed to an uncomfortable throb of power and shame.

'I'll be back in a couple of hours,' Rich said.

'Okay, baby, love you, love you,' she flirted, blowing him a kiss.

Rich started to walk away, looking back at her over his shoulder. 'She's so cool.'

Kirsten said nothing, not wanting to give him the satisfaction of her disapproval.

'Where is this Noord Oost place then?'

'Just here.' He pointed to the neighbouring building that had two heavy red doors, propped open with fire extinguishers. There was a smell of garlic and fresh paint. 'Used to be a machine shop for rivets, once upon a time.'

Inside, the space was huge, broken up by cooking stations around which people sat at bar stools, watching the chefs. In the middle was a giant fish tank, the size of a partition wall, teeming with fish. At the back was another tank full of lobster and crab. The décor seemed to be deliberately brutal; the air conditioning ducts and lighting rigs exposed against brilliant white walls. With the watery shadows from the tanks it created the effect of a laboratory and Kirsten realised almost immediately that Identity were not going to win the contract. This was high-class techno-dining. Not some kind of nostalgic hipster venue with scrub-top tables and old church chairs. The branding needed to be futuristic, industrial, not poetic and sincere. Why had Fabien not briefed her properly? This whole trip was a clusterfuck of false intentions. The lap-dancing was clearly more important than business. She fought the impulse to ring Fabien and give him a piece of her mind.

'Welcome!' A voice boomed out from behind her. She turned to see a man dressed in lab whites, over which was tied a thick blue apron. 'You are here for the tasting menu?' He had a Dutch accent that made him sound as if he were speaking through a mouthful of marbles.

'Yeah,' Rich said, 'we're here from Identity.'

The man with the blue apron told them his name was Jaap and that he was to be their chef for the evening. 'We are bringing you a totally new food experience,' he said. 'We are taking a holistic approach to your food. And we are, of course, serving only sustainable seafood.' He pointed at the fish tanks. 'We have twenty chefs here and each night they will prepare your food in front of you while you watch. So you can learn the cooking but also see how your food is prepared.' He handed them both a menu, which was a simple printed sheet of paper. The food was surprisingly unfussy – prawns in garlic, mussels in wine, a salad with cheese and pears, and for the main courses, steak tartare or lobster cooked in butter and shallots.

'You want drinks?' He held up a bottle of Chateau le Moulin Merlot.

'Yes please.' God, she needed a drink. Rich had turned surly; he hadn't said a word to her since they stepped inside, and when she looked at him he was staring at the fish tank with a bored glare. They took their seats at one of the stations on high bar stools, which meant they were sat up at a counter overlooking a small kitchen – complete with range, oven and a salamander grill, almost like the set of a cooking show.

'If I can please take your order?'

She ordered the salad and the lobster; Rich, the prawns and the steak.

They sat in silence, Kirsten sipping on her wine, watching the fish shoaling against the current. Rich looked at his watch.

'How long do you think this is going to take?'

'I've no idea, but don't worry I'm sure the Pocket Rocket will still be banging on into the night.'

He laughed. 'You're funny.'

'Thanks. Can I ask you something?'

'What?'

She drank her wine and looked at him, impassively. 'You're single, aren't you?'

Before he could reply, they were interrupted by Jaap who had returned, carrying with him a plastic box of ingredients. In one box, which was full of water, was a lobster, its claws bound with elastic bands. The arch of its back, which was out of the water, was glistening wet, its tentacles moving like fingers. She could smell it too, a whiff of fishiness, reminding her of the seaside, of that holiday in Camber with Maria. Jaap nodded at them curtly, then set to work, chopping shallots at a showy speed.

'I was married. We were together for five years. But . . . she . . . a car accident.' He cleared his throat, and for one awful moment Kirsten thought he might cry.

'I'm sorry.'

'It's okay.'

'So you come to see Beti?'

He shifted on his bar stool. 'It helps.'

Maria would have given him a hard time about it, would have told him he was selfish, patronising, a misogynist. She would have picked a fight. Thinking about Maria gave her a pang of remorse. Love was such a bitch. Jaap looked up at them and smiled; she wondered if he'd been listening to their conversation.

'Is everything okay with your experience?'

Kirsten wondered what she should say to this. No, actually, your restaurant is weird. It's like being on a TV set without the cameras or the interest of a presenter; it has the atmosphere of a morgue and the food is boring. But she didn't say anything, just nodded and slugged more wine.

'Here are your starters.' Jaap presented them with two plates, pretty salads, finished with drizzles of oil and vinegar.

Kirsten took a forkful of her salad.

'You are having the lobster, right?' he said, looking at her.

She nodded and looked over at the lobster, still sat in its watery box, watching her with the beads of its eyes, and she wished she'd ordered the steak.

'Let me show you something I learned from a chef in France,' Jaap said. 'Before we cook your lobster first we have to make it go to sleep.'

He took the lobster from its container and upended it, so that it was doing a kind of headstand on its claws. Kirsten could see its antennae moving. He stroked its back, gently.

'In this position the lobster is relaxed and soon it will be sleeping,' he said. 'When it is sleeping we can cook it and the meat is lovely and tender. It makes the lobster very hypnotised then it does not know it is going to die.'

Rich laughed. 'Well, what d'you know?'

'Would you like to try?' Jaap offered.

'No thanks.' Kirsten wasn't sure she would be able to eat it now. There was something sinister about the whole idea. The lobster was magnificent in its complexity, the way the exoskeleton articulated to allow the tail to be tucked under, the proud menace of its giant claws. It was like an armoured vehicle, she thought. Giving it a false sense of safety before flinging it into a pan of boiling water seemed like such a cheap trick, and she watched with a growing sense of alarm as Rich reached over and touched the lobster, carefully cupping his fingers around its back, stroking it up and down in a gesture of tenderness.

'Stop!' Kirsten elbowed him out of the way and scrambled to grab the lobster, at the same time pulling some notes out of her pocket, which she threw down on the counter. She took the plastic tub, still half full with water, and plunged the lobster back into it. Jaap and Rich were both staring at her.

'I can't deal with this,' she said.

As she walked out of the door she formulated a plan: tomorrow she wouldn't go to the presentation, instead she would take a train to the sea, put the lobster back in the ocean where it belonged. Out of all the wrong that had happened in her life, this at least would be something she could do right. She stroked its back as she walked down the street, feeling the hard crust of its shell with her fingertips, whispering small reassurances – *It's okay, I'm here, you're safe with me now, I won't leave you* – and the lobster seemed to respond, tentacles quickening as if it were listening and alive to her touch.

Waiting

AMANDA SMYTH

Sam and I went into the Odeon cinema.

'We shouldn't be in here,' I said. 'We might see someone.'

'Don't worry; Jews don't come here in the middle of the week.'

'Where do they go?' I unwrapped my long scarf and checked myself in a nearby mirror. The wind had blown my hair about; I took off my gloves and patted it down.

I must have looked confused because Sam said, 'Don't worry; you don't need to know about that.' Then he walked across the foyer to where the ticket man was sitting behind a glass panel. The film had been running for a while, he said, but if we wanted to go in and see the end, as long as we paid full price, we could sit where we liked, there were plenty of free seats. There was something in the man's eyes that seemed to say, *I wasn't born yesterday*.

Sam slid his credit card under the glass. 'You've made my wife very happy.'

I pulled Sam by the hand and next thing we were running up the steps. I was clinging onto the gold rail and suddenly he was at the top, looking back at me as though I was a brightly coloured bird, something he had imagined or invented; something he was amazed by. And I did what I always did when he looked at me in that way – I stopped right there and looked at him. Then I wondered what he saw.

One day I'd asked him, because he'd happened to say, 'You are the same now as you were on that first night.'

I'd said, 'In what way?'

'I don't know,' he said. 'I really can't explain it.'

We'd been standing outside New Street Station and I was rushing to get my train back to Leamington. It was very cold and dark. Some people had to walk around us. 'Beautiful,' he said. Then: 'Seductive.'

I said, 'You can't put the two words together. Beauty is one thing – beauty transcends sexuality.' Even as I said it, I didn't know if it was true. I ran through the ticket barrier, into the hard yellow light of the concourse, then hurried down the narrow steps to the platform. It was empty, ghostly. I didn't care; my heart was light as a balloon.

We found two seats at the back and in the corner. I couldn't remember much about the film; there was a ship tilted on the sea in a storm. I knew the music was loud because he was trying to tell me something and I couldn't hear what he was saying. I remember his minted breath and thinking, Don't do this. I also remember his hand and how it pressed my legs apart, how I angled my hips so he could find his way. And then weeping at the end for no real reason at all.

When I first came to the Midlands I took a job at the Loft Theatre in Leamington. On the weekends, I had to open up before the show. If there wasn't a show, Della and I would go inside. Della worked part-time in the box office and she was also studying painting at Birmingham School of Art. She would sit in the lighting box and fool around with the switches and when I shouted 'lights' the set – the clouds or the forest or the inside of a house – suddenly looked alive, warm with yellow, or a cold, cold blue, a spooky green, or red like in a bloody thriller. If I didn't like them, I'd say, 'Change the lights!' Sometimes, I stood in the centre of the stage and did Desdemona before she dies, or a burning Saint Joan, or I did Alice and the bit with the caterpillar, while Della followed me about with a bright spot.

We had this saying when things were going wrong: *change the lights*. And that meant you had to look at something in a different way. For instance, if Della's grades were disappointing, she'd 'change the lights', and instead of feeling unhappy, she might reassure herself by thinking that she had passed, and that's what mattered. Or if I went into town to buy a dress I'd been saving for and the dress was gone, I'd 'change the lights' and say, 'I'll find a nicer one.' Of course, it wasn't always that easy; usually we had to remind each other of our mantra. Also, if something really bad happened, you'd never say 'change the lights'. I remember when Della's mother had a blood clot and the doctor came into the special care unit at Warwick hospital and told her it was over. Della turned white, and someone brought a chair. I remember holding her hand, and thinking, Christ, if you could really change the lights then life would be very different.

Sam and I saw Della one night when she had just finished work.

I said, 'That's my friend, Della,' and pointed through the window of the wine bar. We watched her cycle away from slow-moving cars towards the busy roundabout, her fair hair blowing behind her like a pale banner, her reflective jacket shining in the twilight. I worried about Della on her bike and imagined her vanishing for ever in the tangled city roads.

I couldn't imagine driving in central Birmingham, far less cycling. 'She's an amazing, brave woman,' I said.

Sam said if she was a friend of mine, she'd have to be pretty special.

'Her mother died, from a blood clot, last year. And look at her now.'

He said he was sorry to hear that; you never know what life will throw at you. Like his dad – just before Sam's wedding – having a heart attack. They hadn't known if he was going to make it.

'Maybe that was a sign,' I said.

'You could be right there.'

That night we went to the Hotel du Vin. I had always liked the look of it when I passed on my way to the office. It was red-bricked and grand, with flags outside the entrance. Sam said it was part of a chain, but I'd never heard of any others. We drank hot chocolate in the reception room because we didn't want the concierge to think we were desperate. The bedroom was big with dark wooden furniture; there were white sheets and white pillows on the four-poster bed. I had never slept in a four-poster bed before, and Sam said it was mahogany. 'I only like white,' I said, my arms stretched above my head and my legs taut – like I was about to dive from a high board.

He said, 'That sounds like a race thing to me,' and for a moment I thought he was serious and I didn't know what to say. Then he smiled and said, 'You're not in a hurry, are you?'

We kept the lamps on, and I was okay with that. I was glad of the sheepskin rug on the floor and glad that when I went into the bathroom, I didn't look as pale or as tired as before.

'Don't go yet,' I said, when Sam sat up and looked at his watch. I hooked my legs around his waist and said it again, but this time in my baby voice, which made him laugh, and he rolled back on the bed towards me and suddenly we were very close, looking at each other, breathing in the same way.

It was strange waking up alone in a hotel room. I didn't bother with breakfast, just a cup of coffee while the bath filled.

I wanted Della to meet Sam, but she said she really wasn't up for that. She was too busy right now, maybe at the end of the summer. I said we could drop by one evening at her studio in the Jewellery Quarter, but somehow it didn't seem to work out. Once we took a chance, but she was gone. 'I think she's left,' I said, pressing the buzzer, again, in the shadowy street. The thing is, I explained, she doesn't like to hang around when she's finished working. She's like that, independent. Sam said it didn't matter; maybe it was just as well, because Della sounded like a tough nut to crack, and no doubt he wouldn't be good enough.

When I told Sam about the time Della went to India on her own, he said, 'God, whoever does that?'

We were sitting in Filini's restaurant in the Radisson. It was dark, elegant; the city was hidden away behind sheer gold curtains. Sam liked it at Filini's because you could be there for ages and they left you alone. The food was expensive and delicious; the ingredients flown in from Sicily. For some reason Sam wasn't wearing a suit that day, and his dark hair was away from his face. 'You don't look like a husband,' I said. 'You look like a boy. A boy of twelve or thirteen.'

'Good,' he said, and reached across the table. 'Does that mean you'll take care of me?'

'Maybe.' I put my hand on his and looked away at the bar where a crowd of young people was gathered.

'Why does the idea of that make you sad?'

'I don't know,' I said. 'I really don't know.'

Then I told him about the things Della made: the installation pieces for organised events and large-scale parties; about the transformation of Victoria Square in the spring with huge bright flowers, butterflies as big as people, enormous birds flying through the scented air, giant rabbits jumping on mushroom-shaped trampolines. Della had a team of twelve making props for three months straight, I said. 'Can you believe that?'

When I told him about the swimming pool she put in the park with fake fish and little coloured boats you could row, Sam said that Della sounded like a 'real pro'. Then he said, 'Maybe she could do something for us. Maybe she could make a little island, with palm trees and blue water?'

That Sunday, we met in the Bullring and walked through the shops. There were so many people it was easy to disappear into the crowd. Sam said his wife liked to do her shopping in Solihull; Touchwood was right on their doorstep. Suddenly, we were looking at books in Waterstones. It was like that with Sam; one minute you were driving through fields in a silver car, and the next you were looking at Jesus on the ceiling of a church, or samba dancing in the basement of some seedy club, or having tea in a hotel lounge overlooking the park like a proper couple on a proper holiday. Sam said, 'Let me buy you something,' and I was about to say no but it was too late; he'd bought me a book of love poetry and written inside.

In Selfridges, we glided up to the third floor and looked at shoes for his New York trip, but there was nothing he liked in his size. He bought two cotton shirts, and I thought they were expensive, but he said you can't go wrong with that kind of cotton. We couldn't make up our minds about the jacket. I said there was something about leather jackets that I wasn't sure about, especially on men. Like leather trousers.

'I don't like leather trousers,' I said.

Sam said he thought they looked okay on some people.

Even though it wasn't that warm on the restaurant patio, the sun was bright, so we could sit outside. We could see St Martin's Church, the market place, the silvery blue Selfridges building I had come to love. For me, it was the best thing about Birmingham; strange and swollen and beautiful; good enough to lick.

The waiter said, 'What can I get you?'

Sam said, 'I'd like some sparkling water and my wife would like a glass of wine.'

I gave him a look, but he smiled and I thought, so what? I said, 'I can't believe I'm seeing you at work tomorrow and I saw you today.'

'That's how it should be,' said Sam. 'That's how it's going to be.'

From the moment I met Sam, I was aware of something necessary and unavoidable. I didn't know he was about to be married, and I also didn't realise I was the sort of person who could be with someone who was married. Maybe that's the point. You find out things about yourself you didn't know and perhaps you shouldn't punish yourself for loving someone and not loving someone else the way you are supposed to. These were the things I said to Sam when he was feeling particularly sad or guilty.

Like that time we were lying on the grass outside the Pump Rooms, near the old bandstand, and it was sunny and warm and we were making shapes from clouds. 'There's a witch with a bent hat,' I said. 'Look - number eight,' and Sam didn't say anything. I pointed at two high, well-proportioned clouds. 'That's us. We're moving in the same direction.' Then I saw his eyes were closed, and I knew he wasn't thinking about clouds.

The thing is, I soon realised, you can do it for a while. You can meet up, go to fancy restaurants, or a gallery somewhere and walk about looking at pictures and saying what you like and don't like. You can talk on the phone for hours, about anything because she's not there. And while on the phone, you can have dinner at the same time, and watch the same TV channel or read from the same book. But then something happens: a birthday comes and you want to spend the day with the person, or you have some good news and you want to call and say, *How about that?* Or you're lying in bed with a high fever and you want their hand on your forehead; you want them to say, *You're burning up, sweetheart*; or to come to your brother's engagement party; to babysit on Saturday night and pretend the little baby is yours. And when someone asks, *How's your love life?* you can say, *Wonderful, he's coming over in a little while and you can see for yourself.*

And it's not that you are demanding, or difficult; it's just that you want to be able to do those things, some of the time. And you imagine that one day you'll be able to do them. Then something happens and you know why you can't. Like one Friday afternoon when a young woman walked up to my desk and said, 'Is Sam here?' And she was tall and dark, and I knew at once – because I had seen a photograph at the beginning – who she was. (In the photograph she was wearing a bikini and holding up a drink in a pineapple, a cocktail of some sort. She was smiling, making a toast, perhaps; I don't know. And I wasn't sure if it was her tan, but I remember thinking, what white teeth – like in a toothpaste ad.)

A voice I didn't know said, 'Yes, he's just in there,' and a hand I didn't recognise pointed at the office on the far side. I watched her walk across the room, her hips small in brown leather trousers, and open his door without knocking.

Back in Leamington I took the phone off the hook, opened a bottle of vodka and drank a full glass. Then I went to bed. When I woke it was still dark, so I got up and went into the living room and, for the first time in weeks, turned on the television. I lay on the sofa and looked at the ceiling, watching the flickering light. I drank some more vodka and went back to bed. By then the birds were making a lot of noise. I sat up and looked out of the window, the houses across town seemed to me like huge graves pushing up from the earth.

Soon the neighbourhood would be waking up. I felt exhausted and wondered if I should take a couple of sleeping pills. I remember thinking, this is how it happens: you feel unhappy so you have a drink or two. Then you take a few tablets and next thing you're lying in hospital with a tube down your throat and they're pumping out your stomach and trying to find your next of kin.

Della couldn't understand why I was so upset. She said, 'What do you expect? You can't fall in a sewer and come out wearing a new dress.'

On Sunday night, Sam drove over to my flat. He looked scared. Even though I wasn't sure it was a good idea, I told him to come inside. 'I'm sorry,' he said. 'I'm really sorry.'

He sat on the sofa and covered his face with his hands. He said he didn't know what to do and everything was in an awful mess. His eyes filled up as he talked. He didn't think he could cope any more, he felt like driving off a cliff or throwing himself under a train. Why are you so weak? I thought, and I stood up and went to the window. Below I could see his silver car, and two young people under a street lamp, leaning up against the wall. They looked like they were having an important conversation; one of them, the boy, was kicking the base of a post and the girl was looking at her fingernails.

I told Sam to sort himself out. I talked in a loud voice, listing everything that was making me unhappy, and I explained all the reasons why we could never work. I said he was just too scared and that this was the end of the story. 'I can't take care of you,' I said, 'because you're not mine to take care of. What do you think it's like for me?' I said. 'At least you have someone to go home to.' Finally, I put my hands in the air and shouted, 'Why the hell don't you say something?'

Then tears started pouring out of my eyes, and he got up and pulled me to him. Soon I was crying so much that Sam said, 'Hey, you're soaking my shirt. If you keep this up you'll have to lend me a blouse.'

The idea of Sam in a blouse made me smile. I said, 'How about a dress – you can go home in a dress.' Then we both started laughing. Next thing, we were naked, moving swiftly. For the first time in many months, it felt like we were actually going somewhere.

The summer passed slowly. I found another job in a restaurant near home. Although the work was hard and tiring, somehow things felt easier. The restaurant was in a basement with a wine bar and cavernous ceilings. Sometimes it felt like a jail and I couldn't wait to get out at the end of a shift. Della wasn't around because she was working on a large project in London. Apart from that, she didn't have much time for Sam. Whenever she called, she never asked how he was, or if I had seen him. She was more interested in my plans. The truth was, she didn't seem to think he was worth talking about.

I didn't see much of Sam. Sometimes, when I had a night off, I took the train into New Street and we met for a drink or a movie, but he always left early. He said it was important that he didn't make his wife suspicious; that way he could ease out of his marriage without too much trouble. Now and again he turned up in Leamington on a weekend when she was out shopping or having lunch with a friend. But he never stayed for long. Just long enough to have a cappuccino and wander through Jephson Gardens. We walked over the bridge and looked down at the River Leam and it always seemed, to me, to be brown and in a hurry. Whenever I complained about our situation, he said, 'Be patient. I'm going as fast as I can.' I wanted to say, as fast as you can isn't fast enough for me, but I knew there was no point.

Once, when we were lying on my bed, I said, 'Look, just stay here, don't go back home. You can write to her.' Sam said, 'Why didn't I think of that?' So, we wrote his wife a short letter saying how sorry we were for causing her pain and that we wished her every happiness the world could offer. Then we signed it and put it in an envelope.

Sam said, 'God, if only things were that simple.'

When Sam was there, I was mostly okay. But when I was alone, I felt myself slipping into a dark, fearful place where I couldn't stop thinking about his life with her. I wondered how they slept. And what they wore when they slept. And what they said to each other when they woke in the morning. Did they ever make love, even in a haphazard and unsuccessful way? Did they hold hands when they watched TV? What colour was their sofa? Did she ever run him a bath and, while he bathed, did she sit on the side and talk? Did she climb in the bath with him? Did he watch her put her make-up on? Did she call herself Mrs Goldman?

Sometimes I asked Sam these questions as a way of exorcising them, but I wasn't always sure that he was telling me the truth. Della said, 'If he can lie to her, he can lie to you.'

I knew that unless I had something to look forward to, or work towards, it would get worse. Like Della said, it had been going on too long; nothing was about to change. 'Summer is nearly over,' she said. 'Do you want to spend another winter waiting?' She said I should go away, somewhere warm, and think about things. 'Change the lights,' Della said. 'Go and swim in the sea, get out of this place for a while.'

When I told Sam I was thinking about a break, he said, 'That sounds like a good idea. We could leave after the Jewish holidays – when my wife is away on a business trip.'

The travel agent gave me several brochures, which I brought home and looked through. There were package holidays to various destinations in the Mediterranean: Greece (the Islands), Morocco and Turkey. There was a Caribbean break in Antigua, which seemed to have all sorts of extras thrown in. Short breaks in Barcelona, Madrid, Antwerp and Venice. In France, there was a holistic hotel with Eastern practices. It looked like something else, with glass walls and ceilings and an enormous glass Buddha in the gardens. We could always take the train and go to Paris. I had only been to Paris once, a rushed trip, a fly-by-night on the way to somewhere else. For two weeks, or ten days, or even a long weekend; there were all kinds of options.

That evening we talked it over in a restaurant near the station. I showed Sam the brochures and he said they looked really great. The only thing – he didn't want to go too far. It wasn't going to be easy, and – I must try to understand this – even if his wife was away, she would be phoning him at home. Where would he say he had been? How would he explain a suntan? I told him he was being ridiculous, nowhere was going to be that hot. But what about his father? he said. It was likely that his father would drop by one evening. And if his friends called and he wasn't there – where would they think he was?

I got up from the table and said, 'If you don't come on this trip I never want to see you again.'

*

There were regular flights from Birmingham airport, and Sam had made sure our tickets were flexible. That way, if for some reason one of us was late, we could get on the next available flight. I told him to pack sweaters and something waterproof because according to the guidebook it rained a lot in Dublin. 'Bring some walking boots too,' I said. 'We might hire a car and drive into the Wicklow hills.' I packed my book of poetry and remembered my bathing suit. If it was warm enough we might swim in the Irish Sea. We might even go horse riding out on the sand dunes. And, if there was time, we might drive up the west coast and visit the town called Sligo, where I was born.

Sam said, 'Slow down, we're only going for two days.'

'Aren't you excited?' I said.

He said, 'Of course.'

There was a meeting point at the terminal. I waited for a while before making my way to the check-in desk to see if Sam was there. I knew I was early; there was plenty of time. There were so many people I wondered if there was some kind of sporting event going on, or an Irish public holiday. Then I thought, perhaps this is how it is every weekend.

The woman behind the counter said it might be best to wait until my friend arrived before checking my bags onto the plane. I must have looked concerned because she said, 'Don't worry, if the worst happens, you can change to a later flight.' I found a place beside a pillar, sat on my suitcase and waited. I took out the book of love poems but I couldn't read any of them. I read the inscription over and over, and I thought, you don't call someone your beloved if they're not.

When the flight was called, I tried to reach Sam on his mobile but the voicemail came on. There was no point phoning the office; he would have already left. A young couple watched my bags while I found a kiosk and bought a bottle of water and a newspaper. They were going home after a fabulous holiday in Tuscany. They asked me where I was staying in Dublin, and I said I didn't know.

Two more flights were checked and boarded before I finally rang the office. The new girl answered the telephone. When I asked her what time Sam had left, she said, 'Mr Goldman is in a meeting.'

I said, 'What are you talking about?'
The girl said, 'Would you like me to give him a message?'
I said, 'You don't understand.'
She said, 'Is that you, Mrs Goldman?'

Della said it would take time and there wasn't a quick fix. You just have to leave things alone for a while. In the meantime, she told me to cash in the tickets and go somewhere else. That night, when I called, she left work early, picked me up from the airport and drove me back to her new house in Kings Heath. We drank a bottle of tequila. Three or four quick shots with lime and salt, and the rest in tall glasses with ice and Coca-Cola. Sometime after midnight, I looked out and saw the moon was like a big white plate; we took a mattress and some covers outside and, under a clear sky, we fell asleep in Della's little garden.

In the morning, although I was tired and wanted more than anything to climb into a proper bed, I went with her to London and spent most of the day tying streamers on the rail of the enormous ship she had built. It took a thousand yards of red and blue and gold ribbon. When the wind machine blew it looked like the ship was moving.

Careless Green

ROZ GODDARD

To Lizzie Turner, the delicate curve on the great wall of Wormwood Scrubs was a surprise. It seemed to heave in its grey-blackness like a malign belly. She had a great vantage point up in the day room of the hospital. One might glimpse a prisoner, carrying all that unknowable badness – it made your mind whirr thinking of the awful things they had done.

Lizzie had come to visit her mother, Sheila, now sipping chicken soup from a tray in the day room. She had been rushed from the hospital housed at the old army barracks in Worcester down to Hammersmith where the doctors were as serious as composers and the best in the country. Lizzie and her father Tommy had come to visit for the day. It was an occasion when the right words would have been a comfort, but they were a family who could languish for hours in silence. Lizzie wanted to ask if her mother would be all right but there wasn't enough history of conversation to make such a question viable.

It had been a dark summer for Lizzie, filled with sudden, troubling incidents – small whirlwinds that lifted her then dumped her back, unceremoniously, into regular life. The house had more sharp edges since her mother's hospitalisation, colder too, with uncertainty gathered in the grey, untended grate. And there was Jennifer, the girl who could conjure a storm just by talking.

The family had come to the Black Country from Merthyr Tydfil.

The house in Lye was cheap; the previous family had done a flit in mysterious circumstances. Forbidding and chocolate brown inside, it was a cave home in a strange town; the faded blue one in a terrace, a thin line of paint along its face dividing it from its neighbours. The Turners arrived as intruders, walked into another family's life – a family who had long gone but who had left tins of peaches on the pantry shelf, a woman's coat pegged on the door and chairs roughly pushed from the table. For years they would find evidence of the ghost family, little glimpses of their lives and peculiarities: a pair of false teeth in the coal house, a violin with its strings cut.

The first Saturday after they moved in, Lizzie made her way to the library, dodging the random, glistening pools that studded the landscape. She sat in a corner beneath the stained-glass window reading about Lye's wild history. Lye grew on the flatlands between Colley Gate and Stourbridge and had, from the beginning, attracted all manner of barefoot outliers who threw up the mud houses of a shanty town on the windswept wastes from the Cross to Careless Green. That day's local paper was full of outrage about the local resettlement centre that had been built at the end of a dismal semi-industrial road on the rim of the town – it was for men who carried tragedy around and who had run out of options. It sat on a small rise; you could see it from the road, squat and long, with a roof pressed iron flat. Lizzie had seen the shadow men; they were easy to spot, always alone, wearing long coats and trudging under heavy skies, slowly, slowly eyes on the ground. The folk of Lye didn't want these suffering types polluting the place with their sadness and unpredictability. Lizzie thought they were like the drifters who wash up in the dusty staging-post towns of the Westerns she'd seen on television, where shop fronts are heaved up with nothing behind them but fresh air. In Lye everyone had drifted in from somewhere else.

It was there, in the library, that she'd met Jennifer Evans.

'You're the girl who's moved in next door to us,' Jennifer said, looking up from the book she was reading about childbirth. 'Have you ever seen anything as vile as this?' She thrust a double-page illustration of a womb at Lizzie. 'It's purple – look. That's what we're carrying around. All that purple stuff, with tubes and holes.' She stared at Lizzie. 'It's disgusting, isn't it?'

Lizzie was taken aback; she had never seen anything like it.

'I know. Revolting,' Jennifer carried on. 'I'm not having kids. No way. Even if I marry someone really handsome.'

Lizzie stared at Jennifer's hair as she tossed it about and extravagantly thumbed the pages of the strange book.

'Call for me one of the days and I'll show you where someone died,' Jennifer said.

With that Lizzie understood she was dismissed, without her having said a word.

Lizzie's mother set to work in the strange territory, bustling through rooms, sweeping the cave floor to make it home. The exertions made her tired and she often sat in the back room, her head against the sofa to catch her breath.

Lye was grim, but it sang: huge trucks laboured in and out of the brickworks sending up clouds of terracotta dust; the ferocious iron-stamping forge never slept, exposed to the elements, mesmerising as it smashed on its flat plate. A sprawling warehouse opposite was full of galvanised buckets and stiff brooms – silver objects glinted in its dark interior as the shutters rolled up every morning. Lye shuddered with anvils singing out of iron being shaped, of chain being dragged over mucky yards and nails shuffling in their rusty bins. Incredibly, the town floated on a submerged lake, a mile wide and a thousand feet deep. Miners talked about feeling its weight alongside them as they worked, and the hated sheen of wet coal, a reminder that water was near, threading its way down the seam to where they stood. It had its own sound, too; you could hear it on still nights – a bass note, swaying low and constant as if it had pain right in its heart. There was a family who lived in the railwayman's house that faced the tracks and whose windows shivered when a train passed by. Their cellar brimmed with brackish water – there it was when you opened the door, cool and alive, going nowhere, a perfect table that didn't rise or fall, simply lodged there as if inviting you to step in.

Lizzie eventually plucked up her courage to go round to the Evanses'. She had introduced herself up and down the street, but was leaving Jennifer and her frightening sophistication until last. This was the sixties; people didn't have much use for keys, back doors were always on the latch and Lizzie would step over unknown thresholds and be assailed by peculiar new smells so unlike the smell in her own house. The common vegetables boiling away all over town smelled different when they were mixed with the suds of an alien soap, or the swaying pee in the toilet bowl that held traces of serious medication. There was the arrangement of private things, too – the overwhelming surprise of a dark sideboard rising up in a passageway; a door ajar giving way, beckoning you to who knew what.

Everyone called Nell Evans 'The Queen'. Her husband Claude clocked on and off at the furniture factory down the road. He brought sawdust in golden sprinkles onto Nell's carpets and she was sharp with him and told him to take his shoes off. Jennifer had passed her eleven-plus and so she caught the bus to the grammar school in Halesowen and wasn't approachable in the street, having a sheen that seemed to repel ordinary people. She acted as if she was the only girl in Lye to go to grammar school, which might have been true; it was as if her trajectory was towards the stars or at least out of Lye. The first time Lizzie went round to the Evanses', Nell was standing at the kitchen sink washing light bulbs. The fragile grey shapes lay on the draining board drying off.

'I do this once a week. They get dusty,' Nell said by way of explanation. 'How often does your mother wash her bulbs?'

'I've never seen her washing them,' Lizzie replied.

Nell swivelled round and stared at Lizzie. 'What does your father have to say about that?'

Lizzie shrugged. She didn't know if her father had words with her mother about not washing light bulbs. She thought not. Her father didn't say much about anything, but Lizzie had caught him looking at her mother, a narrow, concerned look, particularly in the mornings when Sheila found it difficult to get going and sat on the edge of the bed, her chest heaving under her pinny.

'The man's a saint,' she muttered as she unleashed a tea towel. 'Your father works hard. I see him go off in the morning when it's still dark.'

Lizzie said nothing. Nell held up a bulb and twisted it in the light.

'What sort of work does he do?'

Lizzie had no idea. She knew her father drove a van cold as a fridge that smelled of oil and metal, just like Lye itself.

'My father was a businessman – had his own factory. We lived in a house with six chimneys.'

Nell looked at Lizzie. 'Six,' she repeated.

'Fresh flowers in the parlour every day,' Lizzie continued, 'servants' quarters, swirling staircase . . .'

Nell settled her bulbs on the side and stared at them. Jennifer appeared unsmiling at the kitchen door.

'Come on.' She jerked her head towards outside and said nothing to her mother as she led Lizzie away into the afternoon.

Lizzie had been flattered that Jennifer, a long-haired beauty with perfect white teeth that ran way back into the cave of her mouth, was willing to spend any time at all with her. Jennifer had promised an adventure over to Bing's pool, an area of black, fenced off water that thrillingly had four sloping sides, so you were only a rusty wire-gate away from death. Raggedy plants had grown up around the edge; there was no path and no one seemed to know why the pool was there. Jennifer told her how a local girl, Bella, had drowned there years ago. 'If you look carefully,' she said, 'you can see the edges of her petticoat floating up from the depths.'

Lizzie would remember what she was wearing that afternoon: sandals and white ankle socks and a blue dress with a yellow stripe. They took a familiar route – down the long garden, out through the tangle of trees at the bottom and across the factory estate where buildings rose up, some with low roofs you could hitch up onto and see into the spread of gardens below. Most of them were divided in two: strung-out washing lines sagged on wooden poles near the house; at the bottom, in the wilderness, high grass and honey-smelling thistles crowded everything else out. It was a place for surveillance.

A few hunched outhouses squatted here and there – the old chain-makers' shops, where lone men and women 'messed' to forge a living. Jennifer liked to stop and stare at pictures of half-naked women on the factory walls, with their bouffant hair and glossy lips.

'Does your father have pictures like these?' Jennifer wanted to know, not taking her eyes off the women's bodies.

Lizzie said she hadn't seen any on the walls at home.

'Mine does,' Jennifer said. 'In his wardrobe. I bet yours does too, all men have them. Have you seen your mother naked?' she persisted. 'What are her breasts like?'

'I've seen her knickers on the line, they've got daisies on,' Lizzie said, keen for both engagement and an end to the conversation.

Jennifer gave her a cool look.

'Well, you'll never see her naked now, will you?' She stared hard at Lizzie. 'She'll be dead soon.'

She turned and headed for the inky water, leaving Lizzie to stare at her sandals and the tips of her socks that were black now and spoiled.

While her mother was in hospital, Lizzie's grandmother Cilla was drafted in to help. She arrived by coach from Merthyr, hung her fur coat on the back of the door and asked where the moon came in. She took the net curtains down in the front room and set her crystal ball on a piece of black velvet on the sideboard 'to breathe'. To Lizzie it didn't seem benign, sitting there collecting light and shadow, holding all their futures. She expected it to erupt at any moment with colour: swirling indigo for bad news, yellow for something happy. Either way, she didn't like going near it, afraid she might see her mother's face distorted in its smoky depths. Her mother was everywhere – her pinny hung limp on the pantry door, a bag of unfinished knitting lay next to her favourite chair, needles poking out in a spindly V shape. Lizzie found the reminders unbearable and pushed the knitting bag into a corner out of sight.

Her grandmother had been telling fortunes for years. She charged a half-crown for a sitting and had plenty of takers who wanted answers. Her line was: 'Like weather, fortunes can change by the evening.' Hers had. Her husband had died in a pit accident. She calmed herself each morning by going into the garden and sitting for long minutes on a stool, gazing down the scrubby lawn. Sometimes she'd turn to the sky, close her eyes and take deep breaths.

'What do you want to know?' Cilla said the crystal ball always had something to tell you.

'Can you see dead people?' asked Lizzie. She wanted to know how death looked but didn't want to see it for herself.

Cilla smiled. 'Yes, and they're usually happy.'

Lizzie swallowed the question she most wanted to ask.

As a treat and distraction, Lizzie's father took her for Sunday morning swims. He'd bought a new Renault Dauphine in almond green with soft leather seats and he enjoyed driving Lizzie and Cilla out to Kinver and Clent on the odd day he didn't work. The pool was empty and startling at that time of day, its blue surface still and unbroken. The two-tier diving board with its bendy lip stood prehistorically perched over the deep end. Lizzie splashed about in the shallows while Tommy made for the board in his skinny trunks – bouncing a few times on the tip before spearing down to break the water.

One Sunday, Nell and Jennifer went too. There was a smooth bulge around Jennifer's waist where she had rolled up her skirt to make it shorter and her brown legs scissored out over the back seat.

'Nice car,' she said, stroking the leather, 'better than the heap of junk on our drive. Why can't Claude afford a car like this?' she wanted to know. She looked out of the window and Lizzie could smell the apple scent of her hair.

'Your father does his best,' Nell said.

Jennifer let out a sharp breath and looked at her mother in the rear-view mirror. 'That's not what you screamed at him last night.'

'We'd better get a move on to beat the crowds,' Tommy said and, exchanging a glance of his own with his daughter, he put the car into gear and moved off.

Nell, wearing a red strapless bathing suit and with her hair lacquered into soft waves, sat on the side of the pool circling her feet in the blue and looking around like she was waiting for someone to serve cocktails. Jennifer circled on the bottom of the pool like a shark, rising occasionally to pull at her mother's feet to bring her down. Nell would scream and tell her to stop. When Jennifer got bored of tormenting her mother she swam over to Lizzie.

'Come on, let's have a race.'

The pool was still empty. Jennifer dared Lizzie to steam down the side of the pool and take a running jump. Summoning as much speed as they could they breezed past Nell and launched into the water with a screaming splash that showered her from head to foot, making the waves in her hair ebb away. She acted as if she'd been shot. Tommy made his way down from the deep end and laughed as he threw her a towel.

To Lizzie, time was glacial. She read comics in her room or climbed out of the bedroom window onto the flat roof of the extension her father had built. Lay on her belly and threw things into the Evanses' garden: potato peelings, slivers of soap, egg shells, bits of paper with cryptic messages on; adding to the map of debris on their patio – until Nell came out one morning muttering to herself and swept it away.

At some point, Nell came round to see Cilla with a half-crown and lots of questions: could Cilla see a house in Racecourse Lane somewhere in the future? Would Claude be promoted? Would Jennifer become a doctor? Was there a change coming in her life?

'Whoa,' said Cilla. 'What is it you want to know most?'

Nell said she could feel a change coming, something big, something that would propel her out of the noise and damp of Lye. She imagined living on a wide avenue, so quiet you could hear leaves falling; she saw a balcony that jutted out from the upper floor, golden fields rolling out below. She wanted to know if those scenes were there, vivid in the crystal ball.

Cilla said there was movement certainly, and an upheaval that would shock people and alter the course of their lives and that Nell should be prepared. Lizzie caught Nell's rapturous expression through a gap in the door as if she had been told exactly what she wanted to hear.

One afternoon in late autumn Lizzie was standing by her father watching him fix a tap. The water had been dripping for months, leaving a deep, orange stain down the enamel bowl. Tommy's tongue held up his top lip as he wielded the spanner. They heard a scream from next door. Tommy downed his tools and inclined his head for Lizzie to follow. They nipped over the low fence and found Nell standing at the kitchen door, flustered, in her tight jumper, broken crockery strewn over the floor.

'The shelf collapsed,' she wailed. 'My best china.' Her lips were shiny coral. Jennifer was nowhere.

'I don't know where Claude keeps the broom.'

Lizzie was told to go and fetch one from the garden shed. She was not wild about leaving the scene; something didn't add up. Kitchen shelves don't jump off the wall of their own accord, and why was Nell wearing high heels? When she returned, her father was laying broken china onto newspaper. He took the broom and handed it to Nell.

'I can't manage to put the shelf up on my own. I don't think Claude has the tools.'

Lizzie helped her father pick up the scattered blue pieces.

'My best china,' Nell said, sniffling.

'Crockery's easily replaced,' said Tommy, handing her a plate that had survived the fall. He took Lizzie's hand and they left Nell in her high heels, holding the broom.

Lizzie was watching Jennifer from her bedroom window. She knew that she was going to meet a boy who wore a fringed leather jacket; they disappeared together down towards the old railway line, where there were notes to the milkman caught in brambles and secret flattened pieces of ground where animals or people had lain. Her skirts were shorter now and she had bigger, wavier hair. It was as if she wore her grey grammar school blazer and purple tie only for her old self, she walked easier in her tighter, more colourful garb.

After Jennifer had left, Lizzie saw a police car pull up outside the Evanses'. A dart of white with an orange stripe down the side. Two sombre men clicked their way up the drive in their shiny black shoes. They were inside for ever. Jennifer came sauntering up the street, swinging a red suede bag. Lizzie saw her freeze when she spotted the car and then break into a run as she belted away in the direction she had come, her lovely bag flapping at her legs.

It went quiet next door, as if they were hibernating. The curtains remained drawn well into the morning and Jennifer was nowhere to be seen. Claude went to work, keeping his eyes on the ground like one of the shadow men from the resettlement centre. Lizzie thought that perhaps Jennifer had strangled someone or stolen cigarettes or cut out pictures from library books or run naked down the high street – she was capable of all of these things.

*

A few days later, Nell appeared at the kitchen door carrying a fruit pie cooked on a plate. Her jumper seemed to have stretched in the wash and she was wearing slippers. Cilla invited her in and she sat heavily on the sofa. Lizzie hid behind *Treasure Island* in the corner, hoping to remain in the room, skim the dull story and be treated to an update of life next door. But faces were too serious, the freight of unspoken, carried woes too heavy, and she was asked to leave.

The crying that came from the living room that morning was theatrical. Tears bowling down and splashing into the saucer. The story was all about Jennifer. If you were to cast it in a positive light, she was now something of a clothing entrepreneur, had spotted a gap in the market and was making money. Her business involved taking orders from girls at her posh school and, for a fee, going to shoplift the goods from the shops on the high street. Now it was Cilla's turn for intakes of breath and tutting and murmurs of disbelief. When the head teacher and local bobby had opened Jennifer's locker, they had found a compact warehouse of bright polyester V-necks and jaunty tank tops. There were coins and pound notes and a record of who wanted what and when and how much she was charging and which shops had the least watchful assistants and which had doorbells that tinkled arrivals and departures. There were sketchy diagrams of shelves where the most expensive perfumes were kept; notes of the shops with wide bay windows to reach into and filch scarves and brooches. Crib notes on how to get assistants to go into the back, a plan for six months hence and a rotation of visits to avoid suspicion. She'd thought it through.

She was to be expelled from school. Nell said they'd had visits from police in uniform, *to the house*, where statements had been taken and Jennifer had been made to sit and listen to those men with iron in their voices who could make you cry by staring at you with their grey eyes. Jennifer might have to go away to school said Nell – a school that transformed its pupils into nicer people through cross-country runs and prayer. She seemed to think this was a better option than having her complete her schooling at the secondary modern where Lizzie was a pupil and where they shoved each other's overcoats down the lavatory for a laugh.

*

Sheila came home on the night that fireworks were dazzling blue in the November sky. She walked in – a ghost in her own house, quiet and fragile as glass. Lizzie orbited her mother like her own small, devoted planet. Sheila moved from room to room taking in all her territory again, breathing as steadily and relaxed as a nun, touching furniture as if she was anointing it.

'So,' she said to Lizzie. 'What have I missed?'

Tightrope

KAVITA BHANOT

It was a sight Kamala had never seen, in all those years that she had lived in her old home in Handsworth. The small porch outside the front door was full of shoes: sandals, high heels, children's trainers, men's shoes, chappals. There were layers of them balanced on the plastic white rack, overflowing from it, infesting the lino floor. Kamala slipped out of her own sandals and turned to take Sunita's shoes. But her daughter refused to take them off. She had a hole in her sock, she said. It didn't matter, Kamala told her, but, at eleven, Sunita was already particular about these things. Grumbling that she didn't know why she had to take her shoes off anyway, she peeled off both her socks, rolled them into balls, tucked them into her trainers and handed the shoes to Kamala.

The front door was open and they could hear his voice, a heavy raw voice, giving a sermon in Punjabi. Wrapping her chunni round her head, and then the extra red one she had brought with her around Sunita's, Kamala followed the voice.

She hardly recognised the sitting room. Almost all the furniture had been taken out and the carpet was covered with white sheets. But still, the room was too small for all the people, mostly women, packed into it. From the doorway Kamala saw a sea of colours; red, green, blue, pink head-shaped chunnis and handkerchiefs rippled here and there, along with the odd turban. At the front, in contrast, everything was white. The only settee in the room had been covered with a white sheet, and he sat on this. He also wore a white kurta pyjama; there was a white towel in his lap. His face, outlined by black hair and a black beard, seemed to float amid all this whiteness.

The first thing that Kamala thought was that his face seemed very familiar to her. And then she noticed with surprise that he was only a boy. She had known this, but somehow, over these months, he had grown in her head, had become too big, too threatening, to be just a boy. And then there was the weight of his voice, which was misleading. It hardly matched the youthful skin that peeked through the beard and glasses, or the youthful bones of his narrow shoulders, slim hips and cornered elbows poking through the flow of his kurta.

Kamala had been alarmed when Mata had told her that she had taken in a lodger, a boy whom she had found on the Soho Road. She knew that her mother felt lonely sometimes, but she couldn't, she tried to explain to her, bring a stranger into her house just like that. He could be anyone. He could rob her, could hurt her, could kill her in her bed at night.

But her mata was like a child who had found a new toy and refused to let go. 'He's a very nice boy,' she said. 'His parents are Radha Soami. He doesn't eat or drink. He calls me Mata-ji.'

When, a few months later, Mata told her that the boy was a Baba-ji, that he had a direct link with God and was doing satsangs in the house, Kamala had to phone her brother. 'He's making a fool of her, Ravi,' she told him. 'He obviously won't be paying her any rent. She's letting him take advantage of her. Maybe her mind is going a bit now she's getting old.'

Mata had always been a bit simple. Their father would often look at her and shake his head. 'Your mata is so innocent; she doesn't know anything about the world. I'm here to protect her now, but what will happen to her when I'm gone?'

And they would get angry at him for saying things like that. 'Be quiet, Daddy-ji,' Kamala would say. 'As if you're going anywhere.'

How could she imagine him not existing? When he'd died, the terrible thought had come into her head that it would have been better if it had been Mata instead. It was not that she loved her mata less – but perhaps, if she was honest, she did love her less. Loved her less, respected her less, needed her less. Maybe it was because she knew this, because they both knew that they had abandoned her, that Kamala and Ravi threw their energy into the new project: to save their mother from the lodger-guru-boy.

Sitting in the shop in Plumstead, between customers, and sometimes while she had customers, Kamala made phone call after phone call to her brother, weaving analysis of her mother's behaviour, with customer small talk. 'I've heard that she's opened up her house, any time of the day there's at least ten people there. Yes, you get a battery with that, no I'm not talking to you. Hold on one sec, is that the right change, love? I'll see you later, no, not you.'

She called her mata every day and, as if she enjoyed all this new attention from her daughter, her mata listened, sometimes for hours, making noises of agreement, or letting Kamala go over the same arguments again and again, wasting her time, because, as Kamala soon realised, she had no intention of throwing the boy out.

Kamala reported all these conversations back to Ravi, calling him at his office, so she didn't have to speak to his wife, who didn't like Ravi having much to do with his family.

'Why don't you just go there and sort it out?' he asked her.

'Why don't you come here and sort it out yourself?' she snapped. 'You're the son. You should be looking after her. But you've fucked off to Canada, without a thought that Mata's alone here.' Afterwards, she regretted talking to Ravi like that. But how could she explain her situation to him, that she wasn't free? She lived just three hours away in London, but she didn't have the time to go to Birmingham. There was the shop, and Sunita's school. And the family. It became such a big thing when she said that she wanted to go home that she had stopped even bringing the subject up. It had been bad enough when they had seen the phone bill: £353. Almost ten times the usual amount, Prakash told her. The whole family got involved. It was as if she had stolen the money by using the phone so freely. 'It's my money too,' she said. 'I work all these hours, without getting a penny.'

And then, one day, a customer told her about a man in Handsworth, who was performing miracles and healing people. He had healed her sister, who had been paralysed for years. When

Kamala asked his name, she discovered that it was the same boy – his fame had spread even as far as Plumstead. Confusion and pride mixed with the indignation she had been feeling for so many months.

As they stood in the doorway of her mata's sitting room, Kamala and Sunita caused a disturbance. Those who recognised her, nodded and waved, including Anu, a school friend Kamala hadn't seen for almost ten years. Others turned to look. Kamala, embarrassed, bent to sit in the doorway, but her mata had already seen her. Full of excitement, she waved Kamala to come over to where she was at the front. Kamala put up a hand to indicate that she was fine where she was, but her mata kept insisting. With a sigh, Kamala dipped a foot into the gathering. It was difficult to keep her balance as she made her way through the room. She created ripples as she went along, people shifting this way and that to make space for her and Sunita behind her. They created the biggest splash at the front, next to her mata, as they went to sit. There was not enough space, but space had to be made for them. Everyone around Mata moved back, or made themselves small – hugging their feet closer to themselves – until they could both sit.

Mata put a hand on Sunita's face. 'You've come now,' she mouthed to Kamala, adopting an expression of mock anger, but Kamala could see that she was happy. She squeezed her mata's hand, gave a half-nod, showed an 'I'll explain later' palm, and turned her attention towards the boy.

He was telling a story about Guru Nanak and Mardana, the conversation between them as Mardana was dying. Kamala tried to follow it, but within minutes her mind was wandering, thinking about that morning, thinking about the difficulty with which she had managed to come that day.

It had been almost two years since she had last come home to Birmingham. She had planned a trip a year earlier, but Bobby, the boy who helped in the shop, had gone to India unexpectedly, to look for a wife, so she had to cover his shifts, had to stay on to look after the shop full time. And then she had planned another visit, five months earlier, during Sunita's Easter holidays. They had been packed and ready to go, when the Taneja family, distant relatives from Jalandhar, had turned up unannounced. 'Well, she can't go now,' Mata-ji had said. 'Who will make the food?' Remembering this, Kamala found herself clenching her fists.

And now, during Sunita's summer holiday, when the family had again agreed that she could go home, she had almost lost the chance at the last minute. Her body grew stiff as she remembered what had happened that morning. So grateful they were letting her go, she had spent hours cleaning the house, making paranthe for everyone's breakfast, and then dhal and sabzi and rotis for their lunch. It had been almost eleven o'clock when she finished. By the time she had got dressed and got Sunita ready, she had been sure they would miss the coach.

They had been at the front door when they heard her mother-in-law's cries. She was ill, she moaned, and there was no one to look after her. She was pretending, of course, but Kamala looked at Prakash's sad, pleading face and was too angry to argue. 'Forget it, I won't go,' she said.

Kamala remembered how relieved Prakash had looked at that moment; he'd been happy to accept her sacrifice. She'd dragged her bag upstairs and started to unpack, throwing the contents, one by one, onto the bed.

Prakash stood in the doorway, watching her, his pathetic face melted in confusion. She had worked so hard to teach him; lecturing, nagging, crying, screaming, telling him to look beyond the surface, not to always give in to his mother, to be more sensitive, to think of his own family too – his wife and daughter, to stand up for his wife, to be a man. And still he was always torn, often pushing her aside to give priority to his mother.

He stepped forward. 'Don't come near me,' she said through gritted teeth. She was breathing heavily, tears falling. Kamala hardly knew what happened next. It was only when she regained consciousness that she realised she had had another fit. She lay on the floor in the bedroom, her head in Prakash's lap. He stroked her wet hair – she was soaked with sweat and tears. Sunita stood in the corner of the room watching.

He repacked her bag himself, and they followed him down the stairs. Kamala saw him wince as he shut the front door with a bang, slicing his mother's cries. In the car, she didn't say a word. It was pointless, she knew, making the journey to Dadoo's on Plumstead High Street, where the coach stopped to pick up passengers; they had missed the bus. But she didn't have the energy to fight him and she wanted to let him do this, even as a gesture, a sign, to prove that she was something to him, too. The bus, they were told by the man behind the counter in Dadoo's, had been late. It had left just ten minutes before. Kamala pressed her lips, said nothing. She had resigned herself to the fact that she would not be going.

They all got back into the car and Prakash started to drive. It was some minutes before Kamala realised that he was not going back towards the house, that he was trying to overtake the coach, to reach the next stop on Eastham High Street before the coach did. The whole journey, even after he had put them on the coach, she didn't say a word to him. That expression of relief on his face when she had said she wouldn't go replayed over and over again in her head, was still replaying even now as she sat listening to Baba-ji.

'You are too much in the world,' the boy was saying, as Kamala returned her attention to him. 'Sitting here, it is just your body that is present, but your thoughts are back at home. You're thinking of the fight you had with your mother-in-law, or with your husband or wife, it is replaying in your mind, making you angry. All your energy is going into that. How can you sit with a clear mind, to remember God?'

Kamala looked at the boy. Was he reading her mind? He was right – she could never switch off. That was why she didn't go to gurdwaras and mandirs. There was no point. How could she turn her attention to God if she was always too full of these things? Before she could forget one thing, there would be another incident to put fire inside her. She had got better after all these years; she had learned to hold her tongue, to let things go, to make herself numb. She didn't let herself get excited any more, had trained herself not to expect, not to think of herself, to try to keep those around her happy. But sometimes she slipped.

'Stop fidgeting,' she whispered to Sunita, who was crossing and uncrossing her legs.

She wondered if she had been selfish, leaving like that, coming to Birmingham. They were paying Bobby extra money to replace her at the shop for the week. It would be expensive. Sunita put her head on Kamala's lap and, without thinking of the people sitting around her, stretched out her legs and closed her eyes. Kamala tried to gather up Sunita's legs, but a lady sitting next to her put out a hand to stop her. She placed Sunita's feet into her own lap. As Sunita slept, Kamala combed her fingers through her daughter's hair. If things were easier with Sunita at least, if the girl understood her, helped her, it would be some support, some happiness. But the girl argued and fought with her about everything. She was so stubborn. Sometimes it seemed to Kamala that she didn't care if her mother was ill or tired. She didn't care at all about her mother.

'You keep getting frustrated by the same things,' the boy was saying, 'but you don't do anything to change your situation either. You tell yourself that you're unhappy, but the truth is, you love to be unhappy. You cling to your misery. It's the only thing you have that is yours alone. You don't want to lose it. Otherwise you wouldn't carry on in the same way; you would do something to change your life. But instead you waste your life in these cycles of pettiness and small thinking. You will think about the bigger things later, you tell yourself. Saying later, later, you get old. And still you don't change.'

Kamala shook her head. The boy was young, he knew nothing of problems. She couldn't change anything. She would have to carry on like this her whole life. She had thought this way before marriage; that she wouldn't suffer in her life, she wouldn't let anyone treat her badly. Her life had been so simple, so beautiful at that time. There had been rules and restrictions then too, Daddy-ji's, but they had been easy to follow, perhaps because she loved him so much, perhaps because they seemed just and fair – she understood that he loved her and wanted the best for her. She had walked as if on a tightrope, step by step, careful not to veer too much to the left or right, trying to stay balanced. She had walked with her back straight, her shoulders back, proud that her father was proud of her, proud that she was not doing anything that would make his head fall in shame.

She would have been happy to continue like that for her whole life. But, after marriage, it became complicated. No matter how much she tried to stay balanced on the rope, she kept falling off, sometimes she couldn't even see the rope, and there was nobody to guide her. No matter how hard she tried, they always saw something wrong in the way she was, the things she did. It seemed to be a lost cause, trying to be loved.

'Don't think that we're heartless,' said the boy. 'We know your pain. The illnesses of your body. The pressures. Life is not easy. But you have to stay pure and untouched, like a lotus in the muck. It's difficult alone. You need the help of a holy master, to hold your hand along the way. To pull you out when you sink into the depths. But we are with you. We will help you.'

The boy seemed to be looking directly at her; he seemed to be talking just to her. Kamala felt her eyes fill with tears.

In the last ten years, she had had appendicitis, gall stones, thyroid problems, kidney infections, dizzy spells, migraines. And then there were the fits, which no doctor had been able to diagnose. Kamala had been more and more certain, in recent years, that it was Prakash's mother, doing something to her. But when she told Prakash, he said he didn't believe that such things were possible.

Before marriage, Kamala had not known what it was like to be ill. Her body had been so healthy, she had hardly been aware of it. As long as something worked smoothly, it was invisible. It was only when it broke down that you appreciated it, or even noticed it. A woman was like that. Nobody noticed all that she did, until she stopped. When she became depressed, or ill, or died. Then it became obvious, how she held everything together, how much she did, quietly, without a word.

The satsang ended. The room was silent. The boy used his towel to wipe the sweat off his forehead. 'So, how is everyone?' he said eventually, looking at them all. 'Gurpreet, how is the baby? And Munim Bhai, how is business?'

Munim Bhai laughed nervously. 'It's going well, Baba-ji, with your blessings.'

The boy's eyes travelled round the room. Slow and measured, taking their time, as if he was gazing into every person, one by one. He looked at Kamala. And, in that look, it seemed as if he knew everything about her, her past, her present, her future. 'You've come at last, Kamala-ji,' he said.

Kamala found herself pressing her hands together. 'Yes, Baba-ji.'

'Good. We've been waiting for you. And how long are you with us for?'

'Baba-ji, one week.'

'That's not long enough,' he said. 'You will have to stay longer.'

Kamala said nothing. He looked away, around the room again. 'So,' he said. 'Are there any questions you would like to ask?'

'Sing for us,' Mata-ji called out.

'That is not a question.'

'*Can* you sing something for us?'

A titter spread through the followers. Even the Baba-ji smiled. 'Are there no spiritual issues you want to raise?' he said. 'Is anyone finding difficulty with meditating?' Nobody spoke. 'They don't like to talk about such serious things,' he said, almost to himself. Then he smiled again, to show that he was not angry. 'So, what shall we sing, Mata-ji?'

'You know every corner of my heart, Baba-ji,' said Mata. 'Why do you ask what I want to hear? Whatever you sing will make me happy. What about that one you sang last week, "When you are near me, my heart goes dhak dhak"?'

The Baba-ji nodded to a young man sitting at the front, who pulled out his harmonium from behind the settee, settled himself behind it and started opening and closing the fan. He looked familiar to Kamala. After a moment she realised it was Harminder from number 13. He had been about seven years old when she had left Handsworth. She had played with him when he was a baby, had carried him up and down the street, had brought him home and pretended that he was hers. He was a handsome youth now. He played a few notes, then waited, looked up at the Baba-ji. Baba-ji cleared his throat and began to sing. The faces around Kamala were arranged in expressions of bliss. It was a popular film song but, by changing a few words, the Baba-ji turned it into a religious hymn.

As the chorus began, the harmonium joining in, Munim Bhai, Hari, Mrs Moonga and some of the other ladies started to clap and sing along. Mata-ji reached out to squeeze Kamala's hand, her eyes were shining. What magic, Kamala wondered, had this boy performed on all these people? To show their appreciation of his singing, a few people sent their children to the front with five pound notes, ten pound notes, which the children placed before Baba-ji.

*

More than two hours must have passed by the time Baba-ji stopped singing. Amid the chatter, everyone began to stand. Kamala tried to wake Sunita, but she was deep in sleep, dead to the world. Kamala left her lying on the floor and gave a hand to help her mata up.

'Hai,' said Mata, as she tried to balance, a hand on her thigh. 'Your mother is getting old.' When she was standing, she gave Kamala a hug. 'Why have you come after so long, girl?' she said. 'I waited so long for you.'

'You know how much work there always is to do,' said Kamala. 'It's difficult to get out.'

Mata wrapped an arm around her waist. 'Haan haan, I know how busy you keep.' She pulled Sunita up from the floor. 'You're not going to meet your nani?' she said, shaking her. Sunita looked bewildered and, still half asleep, almost fell. Mata kept her propped up with her arm.

One by one, everyone came to greet Kamala: Mata-ji's friends, her own old friends, and she felt almost like a celebrity. It had been many years since she had seen them. Weddings, birthdays, funerals had gone by and she hadn't been to anything, hadn't been allowed. She had heard her mother-in-law say once, in the first year of her marriage, that they shouldn't spoil her by letting her go anywhere, any time. They had to train her to adjust to life with her new family. After that, Kamala hardly asked to go anywhere, saving the arguments for the things that mattered.

Kamala had thought she might have offended her old friends and neighbours by staying away, but she saw now that no one minded. They all understood. Once you were married, you belonged to another family. Your life was not your own.

Anu came towards Kamala. She had put on weight since their schooldays and Kamala might not have recognised her had it not been for the big smile that still dimpled her face – it was a smile which had once kept a long line of admirers behind her. 'How are you, Kamu? How thin you have become,' said Anu. 'They're not looking after you in your in-laws' house?'

Kamala laughed. 'I've been doing dieting,' she said. 'You know it's fashionable to be thin these days. I'm also doing fashion.'

'I must be old-fashioned then, an old model, Mumtaz style,' said Anu with a loud laugh. 'Have you met Baba-ji yet?'

She hadn't, Kamala told her.

'He's God,' said Anu. 'The doctors said they didn't know what was wrong with him.' She nodded towards a boy, about seven or eight years old, who had paused to pull up his trousers. He wiped his nose with his hand and continued running after another, younger boy.

'Acha, so he's yours.'

She nodded. 'He would get fever, he fell ill every week, the doctors kept giving him medicines, but they made no difference. Since I brought him to Baba-ji, he's been fine. Go and speak to him.'

'Go,' said Mata-ji, coming up behind her. 'Go and get prashad from Baba-ji.' She pushed her towards the queue that had formed in front of him.

The Baba-ji sat on the covered-in-white settee, dipping his hands into the steel bowl next to him, giving sugar crystals and almonds to each person who kneeled before him, listening to everyone, a line between his eyebrows, as they told him their problems. He put his hand on Hari's forehead, splashed jal from a bottle he was keeping beside him into Geeta's face.

Watching him, Kamala felt as if a string was pulling her towards him. As the line got shorter and she came closer and closer, she felt herself grow warmer, her heartbeat faster. It seemed, she thought again, as if she had met him before, as if she knew him. As she rearranged the chunni on Sunita's head, wrapping the ends round and round her neck so it didn't keep slipping off, Sunita asked her, 'Mum, who is that man?' Kamala wasn't sure why she said it; it wasn't what she believed, of course. But the words just came out of her mouth. 'He's God,' she said.

It was their turn. She kneeled before him with her palms out and Sunita copied her. He dipped his hand into the bowl, pouring the prashad from one of his curled palms to another, looking all the while into her eyes, saying nothing for a few moments, simply looking at them both.

'We know,' he said, looking at Kamala. 'We know everything.'

Kamala felt the tears coming into her eyes again.

'We know what your body suffers. We know what your mother-in-law is doing to you. God has heard your prayers. Your bad times are coming to an end now – you've come to us.' He put prashad into her open palms, placed a hand on her head in blessing and at the same time pressed the tip of his thumb to the centre of her forehead. She closed her eyes, focusing only on that point. Then he took the towel from his lap and placed it round her shoulders. 'Keep this,' he said. 'Use it. Whenever, wherever you have pain. You are here for some days, no?'

Kamala nodded.

'We will talk,' he said. 'We will sit down and talk at ease.' He gave prashad to Sunita too, called her closer to him, put an arm around her. 'You must look after your mother,' he said.

Kamala was crying freely now and through her tears she saw it, why Baba-ji looked so familiar to her – he looked just like her father had looked at that age, in the photographs she had seen. She was certain, suddenly, that God had sent her father back into their lives, in the form of this boy. And she knew that she would be okay – that Baba-ji would give her the strength in life to do anything.

For Crying Out Loud

JOEL LANE

It wasn't exactly a lovers' lane, but then they weren't exactly a couple. Just two young office workers on a date in early summer. They'd been for a drink at the Kerryman in Digbeth and listened to a local singer. That and the warm evening had put them in a tender mood. Ian drove randomly around the back streets, looking for a quiet place to park, as night fell. Lisa watched the sunset burn through the gaps between workshops and scrap yards. Eventually they stopped under a railway bridge. The car engine shuddered and fell silent. He ran a hand through her auburn hair. They kissed slowly, dusk blurring their faces. Then she froze.

'Can you hear that?' she asked.

Ian shook his head and lowered his mouth to hers. Lisa didn't move. Tears were glittering on her cheeks. 'Oh, my God,' she whispered.

He touched her arm and felt a shudder pass through her, as if a train had gone by overhead. 'Don't,' she said.

Though he drew back, she carried on repeating the word and only stopped when he took hold of her and pulled her against him. Lisa was crying so hard she couldn't breathe. Then she looked up at him, a blind darkness in her eyes. 'Drive on,' she said.

A minute later, he stopped in a narrow street, next to a mound of stripped cars. Evening was draining the colour from the buildings. 'What was the matter?'

'Just a voice. I don't know.' Lisa's eyes were closed. 'Like someone being choked to death. But if you didn't hear it, then . . .' Her hand reached up in front of her face. He slipped his fingers between hers and felt her begin to shake again. It worried him, how cold her hand was. The street lamps had come on. In one of the factories near by, a machine snarled into life.

Suddenly Mike felt lost. Towards the city centre, the Grand Union Canal seemed to fall apart. The line of factories ended in a cluster of derelict buildings with no clear identity, the canal surface was broken up with rubbish, and even the bridges were less well made. Clouds of midges shivered above the dull water. It was like a kind of still estuary. He couldn't remember how you got back to street level. At least these ruins were more comforting than the recently boarded-up shops on the Coventry Road.

The sound of traffic was getting louder. Above the next bridge, the sunlight flared from the windows of a new office block. There it was: the worn staircase leading up to Fazeley Street. He was tempted to stay on the towpath until trees and silence came back on the far side, but there wasn't time and he was afraid of getting lost. As he neared the steps, a cloud shifted: sunlight was reflected from the canal, the nearby buildings, like the district was on fire.

That was when he heard the cry. It made him stop, turn around. Where was it coming from? It was so close the voice could have been his own, but with another few steps it faded. He walked back down the stone stairs. There it was again – but how could it go on like that? How could anyone scream that way and not die? Mike stood there, looking around, as the cry tore through him. Was it a child? An animal? Nothing was moving, but he could feel a tremor in the ground like the beating of wings.

And then he was running up the stairs, out onto the roadway, a car swerving to avoid him, its horn breaking his trance. The pavement glowed with sunlight, but he was so cold he had to cup his hands around his mouth and blow into them. He walked rapidly onward, not daring to stop in case another voice touched him. It took him a long time to reach Digbeth High Street and the bus stop. The sight of St Martin's, the one old building in a cradle of redevelopment, calmed him down. *The long way round*, he thought.

Where did that come from? On the bus he remembered: a moment from his childhood. At the back of the Bull Ring market, an old couple laden with shopping, the woman saying, *We seem to be going the long way round*, the man replying, *For cryin' out loud, woman, shut yer face. I know it's the longest bleedin' way of soddin' round, don' I?*

Lisa had walked from Tyseley to the Swan Centre, though there seemed to be less of it every time she went and the new Tesco hadn't opened yet. Unwilling to use the subway even in daylight, she crossed over the Coventry Road on the narrow walkway, trying not to look down at the stream of traffic. On the far side, traffic cones guided her past a long ditch to the pavement. She was only yards from the entrance to the shopping centre when the cry wrapped itself around her head. She stopped, both hands moving in front of her face, then fell to her knees.

There was no clue. No flowers tied to the lamp-post or police notice stuck to the wall. When had it happened? The voice was old, hoarse with despair. Lisa bit her lips. A passer-by shot her a look of disgust. Then she felt a hand touch her shoulder. 'Are you okay?'

She turned her head. A young man, rather pale. She nodded and stood up, keen to get away. This was a place she'd walked through before. It had to mean she was going insane.

Then he said: 'Did you hear it, too?'

They sat in the Old Bill and Bull, drinking cider and trying to talk about the voices. It wasn't easy. Neither of them liked the g-word for a start. Lisa called them *cries*, Mike called them *echoes*. They agreed that it had something to do with death – probably violent death. Neither of them had experienced anything like it until this summer, when it had happened a few times to both of them. Lisa told him about her date in Digbeth. 'He never called me again. I don't know if he was scared or just frustrated.' They swapped phone numbers and agreed to keep in touch. Afterwards, Mike wasn't sure if it helped that there was someone else. He wasn't good at sharing.

The next weekend, they met in an Irish pub in Highgate. Lisa said she'd been trying to reconstruct the events behind the cries – who had died there and why. She'd looked online, but there was nothing by way of local news that could help. Mike said he was more bothered about where the voices came from, the boundary between worlds. Were they just involuntary sounds or did they have a message? Unable to answer any of these questions, they drank Black Bush and listened to the forlorn jukebox. It turned out they had something else in common: a fondness for 'Fields of Athenry', which was so popular among Irish Brummies that he'd even heard its chorus dubbed over rapid beats at a Fox Hollies disco night.

'That song, you know what it's about?' Lisa said. 'How the English caused the famine by selling all the wheat grown in Ireland, so farm workers had nothing but potatoes to live on. A blight on one crop meant that thousands died. And the English government refused to help in case it created a *nation of mendicants*.'

Mike frowned. 'I thought it was about how loneliness is the same whether you're in an open field or on a prison ship.' Lisa gave him a look that was half pity and half curiosity. 'Folk songs should have mystery,' he said, feeling awkward.

'That's all very well, Mike, but some things are real.' As if to underline the point, she gripped his hand. The jukebox moved on to 'Donegal Danny'. He stared into her dark eyes, but didn't try to kiss her. He didn't want her to think he was doing that because he was drunk, or because she was. And, somehow, the voices held them apart as well as binding them together.

The undertow of loneliness was more powerful than fear, however, and a week later they slept together for the first time. There was a desire in both of them that the events in Lisa's narrow bed couldn't satisfy. 'Not everyone's good at everything,' she reassured him.

Perhaps this was the start of love, this hunger for something beyond reality. Perhaps it had to do with the voices, another of which pulled him into its cave of pain on the bridge over Moor Street station. Or perhaps he needed to spend more time online.

Taking advantage of the bright evenings, they went for some local walks in places not too likely to hold echoes of violence. Neither of them wanted that as an element of their dates. They visited the Lickey Hills, the Ackers, Sandwell Valley. Mike always found Lisa particularly attractive in such surroundings, but they were never intimate out of doors. There was always the sense of being witnessed.

It was Lisa who started the group. She said it was important for 'listeners' to share experiences and ideas, try to identify a common purpose. Mike was initially against it: 'These are mysteries of life and death, it's not a fucking Facebook group.' The way she politicised things was starting to get under his skin. But when Lisa told him three local people had got in touch with her online, he couldn't pass up the chance of meeting them. Perhaps the group could achieve some mystical breakthrough that he couldn't imagine on his own.

They met at the Briar Rose in town, the kind of place where you could talk about whatever you liked because no one else was listening. The other three were older than Mike and Lisa. There was Trevor, a former mental patient who'd assumed the cries to be a new symptom. And Jane, a bitter civil servant who thought the voices were warning of the coming breakdown of society. And Eamonn, a white-haired Irishman who said very little. They all seemed to hear something terrible in the voices, something that drained the energy from them. Mike was depressed by the lack of any collective vision. When Lisa said she hoped the group would serve as a focus for 'the listener community', he laughed harshly and knocked back the last of his pint.

Afterwards, Lisa asked him what he'd been laughing at. Too drunk to hold back, he snapped: 'Everything's a *community* these days, isn't it? The this community, the that community, every website, every Yahoo group, every bunch of people with a hang-up or a shoe size in common is a community. It's all just a way of disguising the fact that there's no community, not any more.' He expected Lisa to argue, but she just quietly said goodnight.

Despite the alcohol, he had trouble getting to sleep. Why hadn't he been more tactful? It was hard to say what you meant when you didn't know. For some reason he thought of the Asian boy who'd been waiting in a bus shelter late at night when he was walking home, a year before. The bus wasn't running due to local roadworks. Mike had told him that and they'd walked into Yardley together. He'd been drunk that night too, keen to get home and sleep. The boy had asked him if he was married, then said, 'I don't bother with girls.' The next day, Mike had realised the point of that comment. It had saddened him, any failed communication saddened him. Eventually he drifted into sleep. His phone rang during the night, but when he woke up it was silent.

Early the next week, they took a day off to visit the Wren's Nest in Dudley – a nature reserve wrapped around the college where Lisa had studied. Mike had never seen a place like it: miles of woodland, mostly ash, on slopes that plunged steeply below the footpaths. Here and there, limestone rock faces showed through the hillsides. It had been one of the most important fossil sites of Victorian times. Wood-framed steps made it possible to climb through the breathtaking curtains of ash, beech and oak leaves, the giant trees hung with creepers. Along the footpath, twisted charcoal pillars marked where local kids had started fires.

Mike thought he could make out the faint cries of creatures that had died here, hunted by birds of prey. Like the human voices, they didn't sound far away but rather inside his head. He would have asked Lisa if she could hear them, but she kept talking about something that had happened in London that weekend: the police had shot a young black man, then a protest in Tottenham had turned into a riot. 'They dragged him out of a cab and blew his head off. They told the press he'd shot at them, but eyewitnesses said he was unarmed.' He didn't want to listen, not out here in this vision made real, on this dizzying overgrown slope. This was a place of eternity.

That evening, the bus taking them back to Birmingham terminated at the north-west edge of the city. The driver said there'd been trouble on the streets. They waited for the number 11, which wouldn't have to go through town, but even that seemed to be cancelled. The only pubs in sight had closed early. Stopping to eat in Dudley had been a mistake, real ale or no real ale. They both lived in East Birmingham – too far to walk, and the centre might be dangerous. Mike wondered how things could have changed so fast. He didn't know the number of any cab firm out here. Eventually they found a curry house that was open and asked the waiter for a number. He let them wait in the restaurant. The cab took nearly an hour to come.

They went back to Mike's flat in Yardley. Lisa didn't want to go home alone, even by cab. She listened to the local news on his radio while he hastily tidied the bedroom. When she came to bed, her face was pale. 'All hell broke loose tonight,' she said. 'People have been killed. I don't understand it.' She was trembling. They embraced for a while, but didn't try to make love. It was already past midnight and they had work in the morning.

Mike stared at the front page of the *Birmingham Mail*. The face of Tariq Jahan was taut with grief. He'd tried to resuscitate his own son after looters had run him and two of his friends down in Winson Green. They'd been trying to protect local businesses. The next day Tariq had called for peace, for no violence in response to the killings. His haunted face and stumbling voice had reached across the country, and the riots and looting had ended. When he talked about 'community', he meant real people in a real place, people who could die.

There'd been violence all over the city that night. Shops were boarded up in the city centre and the local high streets. He wondered how many of them would reopen. The Prime Minister had said the cause of the rioting was benefits. Even Mike could see how stupid that was. But he couldn't see much point in what Lisa was doing now, going to a meeting held by some political group 'against austerity'. People needed to look inside themselves.

As night fell, he went out for a short walk. The off-licence near the Swan Centre was open late these days. It was cheaper than drinking in pubs. He paused on the bridge over the Grand Union Canal and looked up towards the city centre. The pill-coated bubble of Selfridges was coloured blue after dark. Recently, one of the echoes had caught him as he stood here, sung him its lullaby of eternal pain. But tonight, the only sound was the traffic in the distance.

Snow was drifting across the roadway like fine particles of ash. Mike's hands felt like knots of wood, despite his gloves. At least winter meant things would stop changing for a while. He'd been walking for hours, stopping at every pub he saw, trying different brands of gin and white rum. One of them was the pub where he and Lisa had first held hands, but he was past caring. At least they were still in touch. But their relationship was like a pub they'd both been banned from: it hadn't burned down, but neither of them could go there.

He remembered the sunlight filtered through a veil of leaves, making highlights in her auburn hair. The end of August. His memory was gentler when he was drunk than when he was sober. That wasn't the only reason for drinking, but it was one.

The next pub was the last on his way home: the tiny Irish one at the top of the Warwick Road. No more pubs for two miles after that – whether that was due to past Quakers or present Muslims, he wasn't sure. It occurred to him that Birmingham's original population was still in the background, but the city took its modern identity from exiles – whether they came from Ireland, Jamaica or Pakistan, they never went back.

He was just in time for last orders. They didn't have Black Bush, but Jameson's was an acceptable substitute. He gulped the drink and ordered another, mentally showing the bank manager his arse. Something in the corner of the pub caught his eye: an old man's face, fringed with white hair. Had they met before? The old man smiled and Mike remembered: it was Eamonn. The Listeners had met one more time after the riots. Nobody had said as much, but they'd all realised that the voices had gone away.

Eamonn reached out a hand as Mike approached him. 'How are you keeping?' the old man asked.

'Not too bad. Are you well?'

'Can't say I am. But it's okay. Nice to see you.'

'Likewise.' They sipped their whiskies. The jukebox had faded; it was drinking-up time, though a pub out here wouldn't be as clock-obsessed as the city centre ones.

'Eamonn, did you ever, you know . . . hear one of those voices again, the cries?'

The white head shook slowly.

'Me neither. But why?' Mike realised his voice had risen, though no one reacted.

The old man drained his glass, his eyes closed. He beckoned Mike to lean over, then said very softly: 'I don't know. But I think . . . they called. That was all. They called, and nobody answered.'

Ruby Cufflinks
FIONA JOSEPH

Marcus woke early on the day of his lover's funeral. It took him long moments to realise the old lady barring his way into the church existed only in the turmoil of his subconscious. For a minute he lay still, breathing slowly to reset his thudding pulse rate back to normal. Next to him, Claudette slumbered undisturbed, giving off a ferocious heat; the sleep of the righteous.

He slid his hand under the pillow to retrieve the mobile he kept inside the cover. Squinting from the sudden glare, he tapped in the password – 0904 (the day and month of her birthday) – and scrolled to the inbox, simply to see her name again. Sharon, Sharon, Sharon.

The phone told him it was 4.40 a.m. Just over five hours until the service. Since she'd died, Marcus had been training himself not to think about her too often. For instance, he only allowed himself to look at the phone three times a day. If he could get it down to twice a day that would constitute progress. But first he had to bury her.

When he was a child, his nana had had plenty of advice about burying the dead. *If you cahn make plenty eyewater fi funeral,* she used to say, *then start a-bawl early mornin'*. But then she was a wit. He remembered her telling gullible strangers that churches in Jamaica had no windows (*because you'd cook*) and how her blood was green when she first came to Englan'; it was only years of living in the damp climate of Nechells in Birminam that had turned it red.

How Nana would've cackled like crazy to hear the man from the BBC pronounce Nechells to rhyme with Seychelles. Nana's passing all those years ago had been slow and expected, in the natural order of things. When she'd finally slipped out of life, Marcus had turned sixteen, already tall and a proper college boy, going places. He'd helped carry her coffin down the aisle, mastering the slow-step rhythm of the pall bearer, bringing dignity to the woman inside the box. Afterwards, his father had told him – the only time ever – that he was proud of him.

When the display on the phone finally ticked over to 6 a.m. Marcus eased himself out of bed and went into the bathroom. The shower was the only place he could cry freely, although out of necessity, his crying must be done in silence. Marcus was glad; Lord knew what guttural roar might emerge from his chest without that fragile restraint in place. He let the spray assault his face first so any tears were sluiced away at source.

He towelled himself dry and lotioned his legs to stop his skin turning ashy, aware how shaky and weak his thigh muscles seemed. He buzzed his scalp with the shaver. Its electronic caress was comforting, momentarily obliterating all thought. But his morning routine always triggered a memory. Sharon couldn't get over how soft his skin had felt the first time he'd undressed for her. 'My God, it's really beautiful. You feel like silk.' And, as if in awe, she'd continued to explore him, experimentally, in different places – his stomach, the inside of his wrist – until she kneeled down and put him inside her mouth.

Marcus had been at the office, trying to fight late morning brain-fuzz by sipping at a lukewarm cappuccino, when he heard the news.

Frank was swearing at the printer, screwing up a mangled sheet of A4 before tossing it in the bin. 'Oh yeah,' he said casually, as he perched on Marcus's desk, 'shame about Sharon Williams. Got killed in that pile-up yesterday.' And Marcus's first thought had been, Now there's a coincidence. I know a Sharon Williams.

But when Frank carried on, 'You must have met her, works at McKenzies down the road,' Marcus felt a strange tilting sensation, as if the world had been knocked a couple of degrees off its axis.

He excused himself to go to the men's, walking carefully,

hardly trusting the carpet beneath him. At the toilet door he almost collided with the cleaner. She pointed at the yellow caution sign and gave him a sharp look, daring him to walk on the still wet floor. Marcus had known then that the stench of industrial-grade bleach would remind him of this moment for ever. He went into a cubicle and vomited into the sparkling clean toilet bowl.

'I fixed you some breakfast,' Claudette said, bringing a tray into the bedroom. Marcus eyed its contents: a dollop of scrambled eggs, spiced with harissa, a slice of corn bread and a tumbler of cloudy pineapple juice. Everything he ate at the moment seemed to get stuck in his throat, taking three hard swallows to get it down. Claudette, he knew, suspected he was ill. She'd been making noises about him seeing a doctor for days now. Her internet searches (could he be bothered to check) were for stress symptoms, or – on a gloomy day – testicular cancer.

He sensed her watching as he shuffled his hips into his trousers, slack now around his waist. They would need to be belted to stay up through the service. He took the shirt off its hanger. As far as his wife was concerned he was going to the funeral of an old grammar school friend.

'You can't wear that,' Claudette said. 'It needs cufflinks.'

'I know. I've got some.'

'Where from? I never bought you any.'

'I got some last Christmas.' He went to the drawer. 'Secret Santa at work. Don't you remember?'

On his thirty-third birthday, two months ago, Sharon had presented him with a box. Inside was a pair of silver cufflinks, hexagon-shaped, set with polished red stones. They looked expensive. Hand-crafted. He hadn't known what to say.

'Oh, I know it's a cliché,' she'd said, lightly. 'Only lovers buy cufflinks, never wives.' She'd looked at him with a frank expression. 'They're ruby stones. Put them under your pillow and they'll ward off bad dreams.'

'But I don't have bad dreams,' he'd replied, laughing.

'Don't laugh,' she'd said. 'When you give rubies as a gift, you're also giving friendship and love.'

'Friendship, eh? Just what I wanted for my birthday.'

And she'd punched him in the arm, before kissing him long and deep.

The drive to the church took him along the Aston Expressway, past the Matalan superstore on the roundabout, and through the tired back streets of Hockley. At some point he must have lost concentration because he ended up on Vyse Street in the Jewellery Quarter. It was hardly a surprise. His affair with Sharon had begun just here, in the Rose Villa Tavern. They'd come for an after-hours business supper that somehow drifted into personal terrain over shared plates of chorizo stew and lentil dhal. At ten o'clock she'd shuffled her papers into her bag and joked, 'Same time next week?' They'd left together, passing the green and gold Chamberlain clock tower, which looked down on them like a strict disciplinarian from Victorian times.

Marcus pulled into fourth as he drove down the long street and headed for Newtown. Images sped through his mind: their noses bumping together in the back of his BMW; using his coat to cover her against the biting cold; steamed up windows. Once, scarily, on their way to his car, they'd been surrounded by a gang. Older than kids, early twenties maybe, Marcus had guessed, but with a teenage swagger in their walk. They'd looked ludicrous to him, with their low-hung trousers and gangsta attitude, deserving of every stop and search they got. One of them deliberately bumped into Marcus and told him, 'Watch it.'

He had let it pass, but now he'd like to meet them again. He'd show them. Every one of them.

Ten in the morning seemed early for a funeral. The church was to his right: a squat, functional building, redeemed only by its amber stained-glass panels and the pink rose bushes that grew inside the wire fence. He eased his car along the road, made narrow by vehicles parked with bovine indifference, and pulled into a cul-de-sac. He leaned back in his seat and let his mind drift.

He'd expected to be the first, but a group was already huddled together. Mostly women in their thirties and forties, they formed a circle, dressed in black suits, with shirts of quiet pastel or peacock brilliance: her work colleagues. He'd gone for a drink with them once, in the Rose Villa, passing himself off as Sharon's cousin. 'Kissing cousins,' she had breathed in his ear as she squeezed his thigh under the table. The deceit had turned her on that night and given the sex between them a hungrier edge.

A woman with a gap between her teeth smiled, as if trying to place him, but failing. 'How did you know Sharon?' she asked.

'She was my cousin,' Marcus replied, twisting the ruby cufflinks around. *Liar*, his inner voice silently screamed. Only now could he admit to nursing a quiet dread that he'd be forbidden to enter the service.

Up ahead an elderly woman negotiated the steps into the church, grabbing at the handrail as she walked sideways. Her bulky coat and fur hat gave her gravitas in spite of her spindly legs, thin as a six-year-old's. She was the woman from the dream he had last night – it was as if he'd dreamed her into life. As Marcus joined the flow of people making their way towards the church entrance, he pictured her waiting in the vestibule, ready to say to him, 'You're not welcome.' In the dream she'd been looking down on him, her finger jabbing his chest and disappearing into his ribcage and that's when he'd woken up.

Then he was inside. Amazingly, he'd made it into the church with no affronted busybody stopping him, nor a gang of broad-shouldered heavies ready to pick him up and chuck him out, like in the soaps. Up at the front, the coffin was surrounded by white lilies. Marcus imagined their cloying scent competing with the body sprays, perfumes and hair oils worn by the squash of bodies occupying the front pews. He had no legitimate place there.

He felt a sudden wallop between his shoulder blades. Marcus turned to see a familiar face. Jesus, it was Taylor – his father's sometime drinking partner. As if reading Marcus's mind, Taylor answered the unasked question: 'Sharon mi sister husband niece.' The man found a space at the end of a pew at the back and made its displeased occupants shuffle along so there was also room for Marcus.

'Who are they?' Marcus asked, nodding in the direction of the tutting women.

'Dem the professional mourners. You watch dem plates pile high at the reception,' Taylor said, chuckling to himself.

Marcus gave a weak smile. He could smell the brandy on Taylor's breath. The man lurched forward in Marcus's face.

'What's up wid you, man? Sleep and you not on speakin' terms, huh?'

The service began. As the minister spoke in soothing, gentle tones of grief and loss, the scene in front began to blur. Marcus's hands sought roughness, but everything around him was smooth – the polished oak of the pew, the brushed cotton of his shirt, the ribbon strip in the service book. He wanted a pin, something to draw blood, to distract him. He tipped his head backwards, urging himself to control the tears. Even blinking would be dangerous. He knew that sitting next to Taylor meant it would soon get back to the family and Claudette if he broke down.

His mind raced to find distractions. He thought of school, a science lesson, crunchy apples, random thoughts of innocent times, until he became aware of people standing up around him. The organ thundered into life and shattered the tranquillity. Someone pushed him to his feet and made the elongated sibilant sounds of teeth sucking. Taylor thrust a hymn book into his hands and pointed at the required number. *Love divine, all loves excelling.* Marcus remembered it from his boyhood, but when he came to sing no sound came out. It was if a child's heel was jammed inside his throat.

He blinked at last, he had to, and water sprang from his eyes, splashing his suit jacket. With his left hand he palmed away the tears. He was aware of Taylor watching him, watching and wondering.

'And now,' the minister said, 'we move to the more personal aspects of the service. I invite you to share your thoughts before we hear some music chosen by Sharon's family and friends.'

A young man shuffled forward. Marcus wondered who he was and what part this gruff-looking, ear-ringed man had played in Sharon's life. A brother perhaps. He and Sharon had never really talked about their families; there'd been no time in the beginning, and later his instinct warned him not to. Marcus fixed his eyes on the young man now facing him. His baggy clothes and weary demeanour carried echoes of the sad city outside as he stumbled through an anecdote about his sister.

It seemed that everyone wanted a piece of Sharon's death, to be able to say, *I knew her, isn't it tragic?* People came to the lectern to testify to her dynamic and loving nature. Marcus recognised the boss who'd tried to grope her once; her so-called best friend, who was forever borrowing money. Sharon Ava Williams. Dearest sister. Esteemed colleague. Loyal friend.

He could give his own testimony, Marcus suddenly realised. If he didn't speak now, where was the proof that he and Sharon even existed, apart from a few texts on his mobile? Why not stand up now and have his say? Sharon. *My* Sharon. Friend. Lover. Music began to play - some cheesy pop ballad she would have hated. Marcus felt how he was the only one who really knew her. Who decreed that he should forfeit the privilege of speaking up for her? Whose protocol? Nothing was stopping him apart from his own diffidence. A surge of adrenaline went through him as he made to stand. This would be his own eulogy, his own special tribute. But he found he couldn't move. Something, no *someone*, was holding him in his place. Taylor, drunken Taylor, had his hand clamped to Marcus's shoulder.

'Hush, man. Hush. Let the girl res' in peace.'

Marcus slumped in the pew, aware of having fought a great battle and come off worse. But he was still living and that was a start. He took off the ruby cufflinks, held them to his lips in quiet prayer, then pressed them into Taylor's hand. It was time to go back home.

Seagulls in Sparkhill
POLLY WRIGHT

Amy Winehouse was sitting in my therapy group. Black hair up in a beehive, false eyelashes, white face like a china doll and lippy. And stiletto heels so spiky I couldn't believe they hadn't taken them off her.

As usual it was hot in the Activities Room. Although it was the middle of winter we'd all stripped off to our T-shirts, but little Miss Amy Winehouse's arms were folded and she was jiggling her legs up and down as if she was cold.

Sam was going on about her relationship with her father and nobody was saying anything, except Doreen, our support worker, who asked questions with her head on one side, like: 'How does that make you feel?'

The Amy Winehouse girl kept looking for something in the corner of the room. There's only a sink and a draining board, but she craned her neck and shifted around to look through the gaps between our heads. Suddenly she looked straight at me and said, 'Is there a baby in the sink?'

I knew there wasn't, but I went over and had a look just the same. 'No,' I said.

'No?' shouted Sam, from across the room. 'What d'you mean by that?'

Doreen intervened quickly. 'Of course you can build your life up again, Sam. You didn't mean it, did you, Jasmine?'

'Are you sure?' whispered Amy Winehouse, when I sat back down.

'Yes,' I shouted. Of course there wasn't a baby in the sink.

'*Yes?*' There was uproar. Everyone was looking at me in horror. Doreen stood up. 'Now, Jaz. You must stop being negative.'

I hated it when Doreen called me Jaz, as if she was my friend. 'Oh, fuck off,' I said and went off for a fag break.

When I came back the girl had gone.

I asked where Amy Winehouse was.

Sam said, 'She died, Jaz.'

'I know that!' I stopped. Everyone was looking at me. 'I *know* Amy Winehouse died.'

Doreen tilted her head so much her ear was almost level with her shoulder. 'Would you like to have another chat with Dr Khutan about your meds, Jaz?'

The next time I saw Amy she was sitting by the Christmas tree in reception, wearing a sticky-out dress with faint strands of tinsel in the white fabric. All she needed was a wand and she'd have been the Christmas fairy. I was waiting for Mary O'Shea, my social worker. That awful loop of Christmas carols was playing, reminding me of my first stint in the Centre, a year ago.

Tell you the truth, I was a bit worried about my state of mind. I mean, if I was still having *visions* I'd better tell Dr Khutan. So, I went over to the girl and opened my mouth to ask her name, but she got in first. 'Are the presents for the children?'

I said, 'What children?'

'Sure, doesn't the hospital like to be doing its good deeds at Christmas time by giving presents to the little children?'

Her accent was the same as Mary O'Shea's. I'm not a great follower of Amy Winehouse, but I didn't think she was from Ireland.

'No kids come into this place,' I said.

'Not to see their mas when they're poorly?'

'Not this type of poorly, no.'

She pointed at the wrapped gifts around the tree. 'Who are the presents for, if not for the children?'

'They're probably not presents at all,' I said. 'Just empty boxes.'

'That is cruel, so it is. What sort of place is this?' The mascara came off the big thick lashes and made black channels down her white face.

I put my arm round her bony shoulders. 'Don't you know, love?'

She was wearing a heavy perfume. It reminded me of the really old-fashioned stuff which our neighbour wears.

And then I saw Mary through the glass doors, stuffing her car keys into her bag and holding papers in her mouth as she approached the Centre. She looked a mess. Her coat was buttoned up wrong and her grey hair was all over the place. Her glasses swung on a chain and she put them on top of her head to hug me when she came in.

'Hello, dallin.' She's been known to call judges that, apparently. 'Not good news, dallin, I'm afraid.'

Only later, when I was on my own in my bedroom, unable to sleep, did I remember the look on Amy's face when she saw Mary. It was as if she'd seen a ghost.

The next time I saw Amy was a few weeks later, in the middle of the night.

I hated nights at the Centre. Sometimes I was kept awake by people pacing around or crying in the next-door rooms, but what really got me was the silence. Because then nothing distracted me from thinking about Salama. Who was looking after her? It wouldn't be Sandeep, he'd have no idea what to do. It would be Amarjot, my mother-in-law. Shouting at her all the time, and worse. Sending her to nursery in dirty clothes.

But this night it was different. I could hear the sound of water running and it took me a long time to realise it wasn't next door but in *my* bathroom. I stood by the door, listening hard, before I pushed it open.

There was blood in the basin.

I hugged myself to stop the shaking. How was I going to clean it up? They weren't stupid at the Centre. They didn't leave bleach and cleaning fluids where we could access them. But whose blood was it? Had I tried to kill myself? If so, with what? Where were the razors, the knives?

Then I saw the shadow of a woman behind the door.

I screamed.

'It's only me, so it is.' Amy. Fully dressed with a towel wrapped round her head.

'There's blood in the basin,' I whispered.

'No, no. Sure there isn't, dallin. Don't you have hair dye in this godforsaken country?' She took the towel off and put my hand on her damp hair.

But this was even worse! The red was all over my hands. I pushed her off so hard she fell back into my bedroom. All that mattered was getting my hands clean. I scrubbed them with a nailbrush until the skin was off and I could see the baby pink coming through.

I was so absorbed I forgot about Amy, but a rattle of metal made me look round. She was standing with a mop and a bucketful of goodies: Jif, Dettol, bleach, Harpic, air freshener, J-cloths, wipes and scrubbing brushes. She squirted a bit of Jif onto the sink. 'What a lovely smell,' she said. 'Lemon, so it is.'

'Where did you get all that from?' Nobody ever gets into the cleaning cupboard. There are keys and double locks and it's alarmed up.

'Now that's my secret. I'll have a go at the basin and the floor.'

'Can I help?' It didn't seem right that she should be cleaning my bathroom.

'You could get me a nice cup of something.'

When I got back from the machine with two drinks, she was sitting in front of my mirror, towel drying her hair, which was now wine red.

'Can I have a lend of your rollers?' she asked.

'Rollers?'

'How else do you get that bounce in your lovely dark hair?'

'It's natural. But my hair's nothing special. Everyone has this sort of hair where I come from.'

'Where's that?'

'India.'

She never seemed to have heard of the place. 'Is it hot there?'

'Of course. Why?'

'I'm wondering if that's where you got your tan.'

Now I had Amy Winehouse down as a lot of things – but never

a racist. She was Jewish herself, wasn't she? I stared hard at her in the mirror but she was concentrating on holding up clumps of wet hair and backcombing it.

'This'll have to do,' she said, when she caught my eye.

'Are you here because of the drink?' I said.

She dropped the comb. 'What have you heard? Someone's told you about Da, haven't they?'

'Why? Is he an alcoholic too?'

'*I'm* not an alcoholic. *I* wouldn't touch the stuff. Not after I've seen what it can do.'

'Then why are you here? In the Azalea Centre?'

She returned to backcombing her hair. This time she picked up fewer strands at a time and dug at the roots so hard I thought she might cut her hair to pieces.

When she'd finished, she turned away from the mirror and faced me. Her hair stuck out all over her head as if she'd had a fright.

'I told you before. I'm looking for somebody.'

'Who?'

'Who's a nosy parker poo? As my mum would say.'

'Fair enough,' I said, and we both laughed.

She reached up and touched my hair. Like Salama used to. 'I know your hair's lovely an' all – but don't you ever think of cutting it?' she said.

'Good Indian girls don't cut their hair.'

She laughed. 'What about bad ones? I'm a bad Irish girl. That's why they won't let me into heaven.'

She's off again, I thought.

'What meds are you on, love?' I asked. 'They can help you, you know, with your – drink problem.'

Then she did a peculiar thing. It reminded me of the dog my in-laws had bought to guard the shop in Leicester. I loved that dog. Before I had Salama I used to curl up with him by the gas fire when everyone else was out. Sometimes he would suddenly hear something, sit up and bark when, to my ears, there was no sound. That's what Amy did now. Her eyes were alert and her whole face tensed in the effort to hear something.

'What is it?' I whispered.

'Can't you hear crying?'

We both sat very still. All I could hear was the distant flush of a loo, somewhere in the building.

'How can they do that to little chillun?' she said and I could see she was crying herself.

'Do what, Amy?'

She came out of her trance. 'Amy? My name's Philomena. Philomena Connell from Doohoma in County Mayo.'

Philomena Connell from Doohoma in County Mayo, I repeated in my head. So you're not a dead singer I didn't even like. Thank God for that. 'So you're not Amy Winehouse?' I said.

'No. Who in heaven's name is she?'

'Never mind.' I squeezed her hand. It was freezing cold but it was real. So was that old lady perfume which tickled my nose and made me sneeze.

'Are you sickening for a cold?' she asked. She had a quaint way of putting things, which I liked. 'Let's have those drinks before they go cold.'

She put both hands round the polystyrene cup as if it was her favourite mug and I watched her face change as she drank the hot chocolate.

'Why, that's grand, so it is. It's a piece of heaven.'

'Well, if they won't let you into heaven, you might as well drink it.'

She laughed and this time her laugh was screamy and a bit mad, which made me fear that someone might hear her and think it was me.

'Sshh,' I said. 'People are trying to sleep.'

'Sorry,' she whispered and settled back on my bed with her back against the wall. 'Who's this?' she asked, pointing at the photo of Salama on my bedside table.

I didn't answer.

'She's your daughter, isn't she?'

'Who's being nosy now?' I said.

'She's so pretty,' she said. 'Like you. Have you lost her?'

I said nothing.

'I lost *my* child.'

'Did he die?'

'I think so.'

'You don't *know*?'

In *denial*, I thought. She's blanking the bad memories out. People are always doing that in our therapy group. 'Was he a boy?'

'I think so.'

'You *think* so?' She looked so mournful I changed the subject. I said, 'Philomena. That's a pretty name.'

Her face brightened. 'After my auntie. She was a lovely lady. But I never asked *your* name.'

'Jasmine. But mostly I get called Jaz.'

'Why?'

'That's what they do here. It's like a nickname.'

'So, if I lived here, would they call me Phiz?'

I smiled. 'I suppose so. But you *do* live here, don't you?'

'No,' she said. 'I'm from somewhere else.'

We're all from somewhere else in here, darling, I thought.

'I know,' she said. As if I'd said it aloud. 'But I'm only here for one night.'

She kicked off her stilettos and I saw her big toe poking out from her orange tights. Her toenail was cracked and yellow and needed cutting.

'You know that woman I saw you hug? In reception?'

'Mary O'Shea you mean?'

'O'Shea is it now?' Philomena widened her eyes.

'O'Shea's her married name. Though she split up with her husband a long time back,' I said. 'Mary O'Saint we call her.'

'*Saint*. Why would you call her that now?'

'She helps people when they have their kids taken off them. She's the social worker for lots of the women in the centre.'

'Does she get them back?' The look on her face was spooking me out.

'Who?'

'The children.'

'Sometimes,' I said, getting up to stand by the radiator.

'She always said she wanted to help people.'

'Who?' I asked.

'Mary, of course. But she didn't help me.'

Now she was doing my head in. I wanted her out of my room so I could think clearly.

'Okay, I'll go,' she said, again as if I'd spoken out loud. 'Can you show me the way to ward eight?'

I opened the door and pointed to the light at the end of the corridor. You could hear Sam kicking off and a nurse trying to calm her down.

'You can't miss it,' I said.

'Are you sure?' Philomena faltered. 'It wasn't like that before.'

'Before what?' But I shut the door before she could answer.

The sleeping pills didn't work after all that, so I lay on my bed and went over everything that had happened. What did she mean when she said she'd only been here for 'one night' – when I'd first seen her before Christmas? And – if she was on the wards, why hadn't Sam mentioned her? Sam was always on about new people coming in and disturbing her peace, as if she was quiet all the time. And what did Philomena mean about Mary not helping her? Was Mary her social worker, too?

But then an Irish voice came in my head – *phizzzzz, phzzzz* – like they put in cartoons to show you someone's snoring. I fell asleep and, for the first time since I was admitted, I slept right through until morning.

The next time I saw Philomena was a few weeks later. She was rooting in the dustbins like a bag lady.

I was having a smoke with Sam after our therapy group when I spotted her. She was standing on tiptoes, propping a green dustbin lid open and peering inside. After she'd looked in one dustbin she moved on to another. At one point she got hold of a broomstick and was pushing stuff around inside the bin.

I said to Sam, 'What's that new girl on the wards doing poking around in dustbins?'

'What new girl?' said Sam.

'Over there. Scavenging in dustbins.'

Sam stared at me as if I was the only mad person in the Azalea and said, 'There's no girl looking in the dustbins, Jaz.'

In the group that day I had told everyone that I wasn't having visions any more. But now I looked at Philomena with her mascara running in the rain and her hair all bedraggled and I couldn't believe she wasn't real. I started to tremble and was about to go back inside when Mary opened the back door.

'There you are,' she said. 'Doreen said I'd find you here. I was thinking of having a wee puff myself, so will we go and chat in the smokers' shelter?'

So we stood in the Perspex cubicle, which looked straight out onto the dustbins and Philomena. We lit our cigarettes and smoked for a moment until Mary said, 'Well, I'll be damned.'

I thought for definite that she could see Philomena too, so I said, 'It's disgusting, isn't it? Going in the dustbins like that.'

But Mary didn't seem to hear me. 'I never realised they'd kept it.'

'What? Kept what?' I grabbed her arm.

'The arch over the old front door. Don't tell me you haven't noticed it either?'

I hadn't. I generally had other things on my mind than looking at the architecture when I stood out here. So I read the words out loud: '*Birmingham Women's Hospital*'.

Mary explained. 'They knocked it down a few years ago and built the Azalea Centre on the site.'

'Oh,' I said. I was watching Philomena fish out a packed bin liner with the broom handle.

'Jaysus, it doesn't bear thinking about,' Mary muttered.

I turned to her quickly. 'What? Stirring up rubbish?'

'What used to go on here. Young girls used to be brought here after back-street abortions. Especially young girls from Ireland.' Mary took a deep drag on her cigarette. She turned to me and said, 'Look, Jasmine dallin, it's stopped raining. Will we go and sit in the park?'

Once I'd been in the Azalea for a while, Sparkhill Park came to represent the whole outside world. The people walking through it looked much the same as inside: fat, thin, young, old, beautiful and ugly. Dressed in hoodies and T-shirts, hijabs and turbans, jeans and burkas, skirts and shalwar kameez. But they were doing things you don't see inside the Azalea: running, playing football, pushing kids in buggies, walking dogs. And mostly they had places to go on the edges of the park: the children's centre; the swimming pool; the library. Or they were cutting through on their way back home from the mosques and gurdwaras and shops on the Stratford Road. When it was sunny and I was feeling okay, I'd walk so I could eavesdrop on people's conversations and imagine what sort of lives they were living and what sort of homes they were going back to.

Sometimes, and not only when the weather was bad, the park frightened me. The dogs fouled the football pitch; abandoned polystyrene cartons were bowled along the path by the wind. The mud at the edge of the grass was packed with cigarette butts and roaches and used condoms. Sometimes the rubbish was so bad, I would have to run back to the safety of the Centre, tucked behind high trees in the far corner of the park.

That day it was lonely. Only one man in a hoodie was making his way along the path, his hands deep in his pockets for warmth. The trees were black with rain, and the air smelled sour.

On the football pitch a team of fat birds were nodding their heads up and down, in search of food.

'What are all those pigeons doing?' I asked Mary.

'They're not pigeons, you townie,' replied Mary. 'They're seagulls.'

'Seagulls in Sparkhill?'

'Yeah. Seagulls travel. Anywhere they can scavenge. I know seagulls. I was brought up by the sea.'

'Where was that?'

'A little place called Doohoma in County Mayo.'

I turned and stared at her. In my head I heard *Philomena Connell from Doohoma in County Mayo*. Loud as anything.

'What was your name before you were married?'

'Connell.'

Connell? I thought. They must be related.

'Why d'you ask?' asked Mary.

'Did you meet your husband over here? Is that why you didn't go back to Ireland?'

'Partly. I was happier in Birmingham, believe it or not.'

I thought of all the times Amma had told me how much she missed her village in India. 'But don't you miss Ireland?'

'Who's little Miss Nosy Parker Poo, as my old ma would say?' Mary said, her accent thickening.

'Miss Nosy Parker Poo?' I repeated.

Mary took out a new cigarette packet and wound the red strip round her little finger so the cellophane fell off. She's smoking a lot, I thought.

'Someone else said that to me the other day,' I said.

'Oh well,' she said, cupping her hands over her lighter. 'Common parental phrase in the fifties.'

'This person was young.'

Mary took off her anorak so we wouldn't get wet when we sat down on a bench. She had an old fleece on underneath, filthy and stained with food. I couldn't bring myself to sit on it. I preferred to have a wet backside.

'Look, dallin – we'd better get on.' She opened her briefcase and got out a file with *Jasmine Bhatti* typed on a white label on the top corner. She didn't open the file, or look at me when she said, 'Your in-laws are really pushing to adopt Salama.'

I watched a young mother and her daughter leaving the children's centre. She stopped by the gate to button up her little girl's coat. Why didn't she do that before she left the building? I thought. 'But they can't do that – can they?'

'They say she needs to be with her father. It's a point the judge will consider.'

'Sandeep can't look after himself, let alone a kid. It's my mother-in-law who does everything.' I started to cry. 'Salama hates Amarjot. She smacks her, and sometimes she puts her in dirty clothes.'

'Mmm.' Mary opened the file. 'And your parents are great with her, which should go in your favour.'

It had started to rain again and the little girl was getting wet. Her mother was fighting with her to get her arms in the coat.

'Can't Salama come to live with me and Amma and Baba? Dr Khutan thinks I'm getting better.'

'I know, dallin.' Mary sighed. 'But you've been sectioned twice in the past.'

'I never hurt her!'

'Well, dallin – that's not quite true.'

'I was only washing her. She was dirty.'

Mary said gently, 'It was what you washed her with which was the problem, dallin.'

The little girl started to scream.

I wanted to say to the mother, *You should have rolled the sleeves up first to make it easier.*

'We can't deny what happened in the past. What we have to show is that things have changed. If we can get positive reports from Dr Khutan, we might get contact at your parents' house.' Mary's mobile went off. She looked to see who it was, pressed 'ignore', then started to put her file back in her briefcase.

'Look, dallin, I've got to go.' She put her arm round me and rubbed her face against my hair. Her smoky smell comforted me but I couldn't stop crying.

I watched Mary walk back across the park to the Centre's car park, shifting her weight from side to side. I thought I saw Philomena standing in the trees and calling to her, but Mary didn't notice. Just headed for the car.

I didn't see Philomena again for ages, but some nights I heard her. Whenever I was having more than the usual trouble with getting to sleep, an Irish voice would come into my head and whisper *phzzzzz* until I dropped off.

The next time I actually saw her was on a warm day in April. I was watching a rerun of *Strictly* with Sam when Doreen came in to tell me that Mary was here. She said we could go into the Activities Room because the art group had gone out on a trip.

The Activities Room was one of the nicer rooms in the Azalea, with paintings on the wall and yellow plastic boxes full of squidgy tubes of paint. The sun was pouring in, so I was surprised when Mary said, 'It's fekkin freezing in here. Could we go somewhere else?'

Doreen's okay with patients swearing because she says it's all part of our illness – but she puckered up her mouth when Mary did it.

'Sorry, Mrs O'Shea,' she said. 'There's nowhere else.'

'Are you having an Irish menopause, Mary?' I said. 'The type that makes you get cold flushes, not hot?'

I expected Mary to give her hearty smoker's laugh, but she didn't. She got a cardigan out of her bag and put it on pointedly. 'Let's get on,' she said.

'Can I get you a cup of tea, Mrs O'Shea?' Doreen's head edged towards her shoulder.

'No thank you, Doreen,' Mary said briskly and nodded for her to leave us.

As soon as Doreen had gone, she said, 'If we play our cards right, Jasmine my love, I think we can swing very good contact rights for you.'

It was at that point that I saw a figure crouching in the corner of the room with her back to us. She was wearing one of those overalls which gape at the back that they put you in for an operation.

Mary bent down to pick up her briefcase and said, 'Salama's social worker has expressed concern about some of the things your mother-in-law is saying to Salama about you.'

The figure in the overall turned round.

It was Philomena. She walked up to where we were sitting and touched Mary's face. 'It's been a long time, big sister,' she said.

Mary paused for a second before delving into her briefcase. 'Now, where was I? What was I looking for? Oh, yes, Miss Johnson's report.'

Philomena looked at me. 'He *is* in the sink, isn't he?'

I didn't reply.

'My baby boy. He *is* in the sink, isn't he?' Philomena's eyes were huge.

'I printed off the fekkin thing before I came here.' Mary pulled out a wad of papers, two highlighters, some old pens and a box of paper clips.

Philomena went over to the sink in the corner and climbed up on the draining board. She curled up in the foetal position and cradled her middle like she was having period pains. 'This was where the operating table was,' she said. Her voice was thick, as if she was drugged. 'And they sluiced him away, down the drain. Come here, Jasmine.'

I crept over to the draining board.

Philomena called over her shoulder in Mary's direction. 'Don't feel guilty any more, sis. You've done well. And Jaz . . .' she said, her voice becoming very small, 'you won't lose Salama. While you're both alive, you still have . . . hope.'

I looked down at the draining board. There was nothing there but a rivulet of red paint sitting in one of the metal channels and a strong whiff of scent.

And silence.

I said, 'Oh Phiz.' In my head.

'What's that smell?' Mary's voice sounded dreamy. 'Palma violets. My sister Philomena and I each bought a bottle in Murphy's chemist in Dublin. Before I got on the boat and left her on her own.'

I gripped the side of the draining board. I started to shake as if the cold from the metal was moving from my hands into my whole body.

'Till she came to me in Birmingham and I didn't help her,' said Mary, a sob in her voice.

My teeth started chattering. I had never felt so cold.

'You're helping me, Mary,' I whispered, but I don't know if she heard me.

Mary blew her nose and said, 'Let's get on.' I heard the shuffling of papers and swearing until: 'Found it! Let me see. Yes. Here you are: *Mrs Bhatti frequently tells Salama that her mother isn't ill, but is possessed by evil spirits. I am concerned that this may be adversely affecting the child, who is having difficulty sleeping*.' Mary broke off. 'What are you doing, Jaz – come and sit down. I know it's upsetting about Salama, but this is good news for your contact rights!'

I staggered back to the table and slumped in the chair.

'With these reports, you could be seeing Salama much more often. We might even get guardianship for your parents eventually. Jasmine. Are you all right?' She leaned forward and took my hands. 'Jaysus, you're cold. Did you hear me, dallin? Things are looking up.'

I smiled at her faintly. I nearly believed her.

First thing I did when I got discharged was to cut my hair. Amma hated it, but everyone else said it made me look younger and healthier. Salama loved it. We had a whole week of playing hairdressers when she came to stay with us for half-term.

Mary rang me after she'd gone back. She knows that the more perfect it is with Salama, the more depressed I feel afterwards.

'Ice creams in order? Will we go to Sparkhill Park?'

It was a very hot day and we bought the ice creams from the van by the children's centre and sat on our favourite bench to eat them. We watched the seagulls skitter around by the goal posts.

Mary said, 'Ice creams and seagulls. All we need is the sea and we could be in Doohoma.'

She was staring at the trees which hid the Azalea Centre.

Is Philomena waving at her? I thought.

She said, 'My sister died in that place, you know. After a botched abortion.'

I squeezed her hand. 'I thought something like that might have happened.'

'It was a back-street job. I recommended the man.'

'It wasn't your fault, Mary,' I said.

'No,' she said. 'I think I believe that now.'

'What was your sister's name?' I asked, although I already knew.

Phizzzz I heard in my head. *I thought you'd gone for good*, I said, silently.

'I've got contact rights,' the voice said. And then, 'Nice hair!'

The Nacelle
JAMES B. GOODWIN

Jim stands inside the nacelle. It's hot from the inspection lamp which hangs from one of the formers. Arthur's gone to the bogs and taken the *Mirror* with him so there's ten or fifteen minutes to kill. He could climb out from underneath into the cooler air of the workshop but he prefers the isolation of the metal pod. He feels distanced from the noise in the hangar, the scream of air-braces, the riveters that clatter like machine guns, the blokes.

The nacelle is three feet wide at the open end and Jim can see a section of the shop floor as if from the mouth of a cave, a narrow V running away to the far wall, workbenches with vices, a drilling machine, air-lines and power cables hanging down from the steel girders somewhere up in the roof, blokes working, an aileron, an undercarriage door, a section of tail rib. The tea-woman passes in and out of his field of vision collecting enamel mugs.

The hangar is a quarter of a mile long, a couple of hundred feet wide. It's the central one of three. It's where sub-assemblies are made: sections of tail, fuselage, flaps, and nacelles like the one Jim's working on. It will cover the inboard engine on the underside of a Shackleton wing.

He can see Arthur on his way back, the *Mirror* stuffed under his armpit. He feels the weight of the dolly, getting ready to start riveting up again. He's been working with him a couple of months now. Ever since he made his mistake.

It still haunts him – that day – just after his transfer to Sub-Assembly.

He was eighteen, time to be grown up. No more asking for help: you're a man now; on your own. But he hadn't looked at the blueprint properly, thought it was third-angle projection and he'd riveted the stiffeners on the wrong side. A couple of dozen before he realised. He'd felt stupid, making a basic error like that, thought he'd be in a bit of trouble – but what followed still made him feel humiliated, even after all these weeks. In front of everyone, the gaffer shoving the assembly in his face: 'A fucking abortion, a five-year-old could do better. Why didn't you check with Inspection? Too fucking easy were they, a smart arse like you. And what are they now? They're all fucking scrap, you useless twat. What the fuck do you think Inspection are there for? A fucking abortion. You're nothing but a fucking abortion yourself, you stupid ham-fisted prat.' Then being marched to the superintendent's office, a couple of foremen looking on as he got it all over again.

Then Vern, the shop steward, arrived. He was shown the scrapped work. 'Over twenty of them. Didn't check with Inspection,' the superintendent said.

Jim wanted to tell them how busy Inspection had been, how he'd wanted to get on with the job, earn his money, make a good impression. He'd felt cold, shivering slightly even though his face was burning. He wanted to explain how it happened, but couldn't speak.

'We're sacking him,' the superintendent said to Vern.

'No, you're not,' Vern said. 'He's only a kid. You can give him an official warning, but you're not sacking him.'

'Three days' suspension,' said the superintendent. 'That's the least I'll consider.'

'Do yourself a favour,' Vern said. 'An official warning or you'll have trouble on your hands. Where do you think you are, the nineteenth century?'

It was Vern's defence that brought him to the verge of tears. Terrified he was going to cry, he was glad to escape when Vern told him to wait outside the office.

He remembered getting back to the section, blushing, fighting back tears, seeing blokes glancing, turning back to their work, not saying anything.

'He's working with you, Arthur,' Vern said, pointing at a man in his mid-forties, five-six tall, his dark hair slicked down with Brylcreem. 'Keep an eye on him, will you, make sure he doesn't fuck anything else up.'

Arthur worked at the other end of the gang to Jim. Jim had seen him but didn't know him, hadn't even spoken to him. He was leaning against the bench looking at drawings, fag in one hand, mug of tea in the other. Arthur glanced at Jim, said nothing, turned back to the drawing spread out along the bench, ten feet long, biggest blueprint Jim had ever seen, a complete side view of an engine nacelle. Next to it, drawings showing other views and cross-sections, spec sheets detailing construction. Jim stood to one side, looking down, not knowing what to do. He waited for Arthur to tell him.

In the hangar air-braces screamed, riveters clattered. Somebody was singing 'Hound Dog', bits of Elvis slicking in amid the clamour. Lights high up in the roof changed from blue to yellow: time to change the rivets.

'Where's your toolbox?' Arthur said.

'At the end of the gang,' Jim said.

'No fucking good there, is it? You might as well bring it down here, stick it next to mine.'

Jim felt him watching him as he carried it back along the gangway. He slid it in place next to Arthur's

Hours later, another mug of tea, another fag, and Arthur's still looking at the blueprint. Fred the gaffer walked past, staring. Jim tried to look busy, frightened he's going to get told off again. Finally Fred walked over, looked at Jim, said to Arthur, 'Where the fuck do you think you are, Arthur, on your daddy's yacht? Get off your arse, get some fucking work done.'

Jim blushed, stood close, looked over Arthur's shoulder at the drawing. Arthur studied the blueprint for a moment, straightened up, took a sip of tea, a pull on his fag, turned and said, 'If you don't like it, Fred, you could always do the job yourself. If you've got the fucking brains, that is.' Jim thought Arthur would be in trouble, talking to the gaffer like that. But Fred just grunted and walked away muttering to himself. Arthur turned to Jim. 'Gaffers, eh! What a bunch of useless cunts.'

Later, Arthur took Jim to the end of the gang where all the

components were stacked; formers, stringers, aluminium skins curved to fit the tapering shape, inspection doors and frames, cotton bags of smaller components, Dzus fasteners, anchor nuts, screws, bolts, stiffeners and information tags. Next to the racks, a jig to build the nacelles on. It sat on a couple of trestles, a series of thick plywood formers reducing in size showing the final shape of the engine cover. Arthur read out the part numbers from the spec sheets and Jim checked the tags. Then he showed Jim how to locate the formers on the jig and the first stringers were fixed with clamps. They stood back to see if it looked like the drawing. It did.

It was the first time Jim had worked a two-hander. He stood inside the skeletal structure and Arthur explained how to dolly the rivets down. 'When we're skinning up, you'll be on the inside. I won't be able to see you and with all this racket going on I won't be able to hear you either. I'll put in a rivet, you push it back with the dolly so I know you're in place. Make sure you are. If you're not we'll fuck it up, okay?'

Jim nodded.

'Okay, let's give it a try.'

Without the skin on they could see what each other was doing. Jim held the dolly, a steel bar with a small flat anvil on the end. He held it tight to stop his hands shaking. 'Ready?' Arthur said. Jim nodded. Rivet in, dolly push-back, rivet gun push-back, a short blast from the gun, rivet mushrooms under the dolly. Another rivet. Then another. Soon they had a rhythm going.

'You always done this?' Jim asked. He felt calmer, realised the headache he'd had was now just a dullness behind his right eye.

'Worked at Fisher's before the war. Fisher and Ludlow when I was about the same age you are now. Served my time there, coach builder, back in the days when half the body was made of wood. Pretty good with the old spoke-shave.'

'You haven't always been an aircraft fitter then?' Jim said.

'Been here about four years.' He said years like *yurs*, strong Brummie accent. 'Used to work at Longbridge on the track, on the Mini line. What a fuck-up that was. Had a special lever to get the doors on.' He laughed. 'You could hear the welds crack as I levered 'em into place. Rust boxes in twelve months. Piecework, you've got to make your money somehow, ain't you? What did you do before this?'

'Worked on Details for a few months, Boys Details in the next hangar. The girlfriend's old man fixed it up for me; some union bloke he knows up at the club got me in. Funny name, isn't it, Boys Details, as if we were all ten-year-olds. It's where you get trained up, you know, learn the basics. Then when I was eighteen they moved me here. Worked at a sign-maker's before that. Different sorts of stuff: sign-writing, illuminated signs made out of Perspex, a bit of engraving, brass plates for solicitors, that sort of thing.'

'Like it?'

'It was okay.'

'Why the move?'

'Good money here.'

'That it?'

'What else do you come to work for?'

'You're at work a long time. Might as well be something you like.'

'You seem to like it. You're good at it as well.'

'Not bad, I suppose. It's a good job for me. But you're what, eighteen? You're going to be stuck here for the rest of your life? Must be something else you want to do.'

'Maybe.'

'My son's around the same age as you. He's training to be a chartered accountant. You want to hear him play the piano, just like that Jerry Lee Lewis, boogie-woogie, y'know. Plays down the pub at weekends. He was in a group for a while, mates of his, rock and roll. They've gone to London now, try their luck. He didn't go. Pity. Wanted to finish his training, he said.' They gun down another row of rivets. 'Do you play anything?'

'No.'

'No, nor me. Be good though, wouldn't it?'

'It would, yeah.'

'You don't want to put up with it, you know.'

'Put up with what?'

'Anything you don't like.'

Their faces were inches apart, the formers curving over Jim's head, the stringers running laterally between them. Jim was holding the steel dolly, his mop of hair flopping; Arthur, with short back and sides, holding the rivet gun aloft, the compressed air hissing. He gave a short blast of the trigger. 'They only do it when they think they can get away with it. Everybody makes mistakes. See those wing ribs over there?' He pointed at a hefty row stacked against the wall. 'I did 'em. Supposed to be quarter inch countersunk. I put in snap-heads. Must have misread the drawing. By the time anyone noticed it was too late. They've been there eighteen months now. Nobody knows what to do with 'em. Gaffer comes down at the time, stands in front of 'em, grim look on his face, turns to me, chin out, lips tight, playing the hard bastard, says, *How the fuck did you manage to do this?* Spits it out, know what I mean? I turns to him, spits it out back. *Fucking easy*, I say. *Want me to fucking show you?* He's taken aback. It's not the reply he's expecting. I suppose he thinks I'll apologise or something. *No need to be like that, Arthur*, he says. Cunt.'

A week to get the first skeletal structure complete. Some of the stringers need trimming. Arthur shows him what needs to be done and leaves Jim to get on with it. As the stringers are put in place, Jim can see how they form the gently curving shape of the nacelle.

When they try to fit the aluminium skins they can't get them to sit right. Arthur decides they're the wrong contour. He explains to the gaffer. The gaffer listens, nods his head, says something and walks away.

'I'm getting the tinnies down,' Arthur says. 'Roll 'em to the right shape.'

'I'd have tried to fit them,' Jim says.

'So would I when I was your age.'

'What were you doing at my age?' Jim says.

'In the army. Got conscripted. Said I was an apprentice and needed to finish my time. Tried the reserved occupation story, working in a factory helping the war effort. They weren't having any. *You can finish your apprenticeship when this is all over*, they said. *You're just what we're looking for, a short-arsed Brummie, we've got just the job for you*. They sent me out to the desert with a bleeding great gun. Royal Artillery, chasing all over the place looking for Rommel.'

'Christ! Were you?'

'No, course not. Didn't have a clue what we were doing. We'd no sooner get to one place, set up the gun, get new orders, pack up and head for another bit of sand. Gaffers, see, they're all the same, don't know what the fuck they're doing half the time.'

The tinsmiths arrive. They have a rolling mill with them, a cast-iron frame with a couple of rounded steel wheels running against each other like a small clothes mangle. They take the skins and roll them back and forth between the rollers. They offer the skins up against the nacelle frame, make adjustments to the pressure on the mill and reroll until the skins sit tight.

While the tinsmiths are rolling the skins, Jim and Arthur take a look at the stiffeners, the next components to be fitted.

'These don't seem the right shape either,' Jim says. He's standing inside the nacelle frame, holding the stiffener against the former. 'Look, the curve here ought to follow the curve of the formers. If we fix them like this, when we fit the skin we'll distort it, won't we?'

'Looks like it. What do you suggest?'

'Buggered if I know,' Jim says.

Arthur climbs inside the frame and shows Jim how the contour needs reshaping. He puts on pencil marks. 'Here and here,' he says, 'the curve needs to be tighter.' He takes Jim to the far end of the hangar. They stop in front of what looks like a small press. 'It's a shrinking press,' Arthur says. Jim's never seen one before. Arthur shows him how the hand lever works the jaws. 'A bit like the way you make a paper fan, see? It crimps the metal on the inside edge, changes the curve on the outside edge.' He lets Jim have a go. He's too soft on the lever, then too hard, the curve too sharp. But he soon gets the hang of it, eye and hand and brain working to get the right pressure to correct the contour.

Over the following days and weeks, Arthur shows Jim how to cut and fit the inspection doors, how to trim the panels with Gilbows and file them to fit without binding. He shows Jim how to avoid 'pants' when skinning up the frame, fixing the panels with skin pegs and gradually removing them from the centre outwards as the rivets are put in place, binding the metal skin tightly to the formers and stringers. When they have the first one complete, Jim stands back and looks at the ten-foot-long curving metal pod, inspection doors fixed in place by Dzus fasteners and anchor nuts, rivets flush, aluminium as tight as an apple skin. Arthur notices him and turns away.

They're on the second, fixing the stringers, the rivet gun rattling away when Arthur says between blasts, 'When I was in the army I did a bit of painting and drawing. Y'know, sketches of the blokes I was with, the guns and tents set up in the desert. They were in an exhibition just after the war. You were a sign-writer. Ever done any art?'

'Only at school. Although I made this model theatre once for a niece of mine, a stage and little sets, curtains that drew across.'

'Did you?' Arthur puts in a line of rivets and they gun them down in rapid succession. 'Interested in the theatre, were you?'

'In a way. I went once to ask about being a set designer,' Jim says. 'There was this group of actors there, y'know, on stage, standing around or sitting on chairs. Nothing special, just ordinary, like me and you. This woman, dead friendly she was, showed me around, showed me the machinery that works the stage, all the different sorts of lights they use. I never realised it was so complicated. But she said I'd need to go to art school.'

'So why didn't you?' Arthur says. There's a snag with one of the rivets, the holes don't line up properly. Arthur wiggles a skin peg in place and pulls them into line. He puts in the next rivet and they gun it down. As Arthur removes the peg, Fred appears.

'Too much talking, not enough working,' he says. 'Pull your fucking fingers out, will you?' He looks at Jim: 'Are you slowing him down?'

Jim blushes, feels an uncontrollable surge of temper. 'No I'm not,' he says. He spits it out, shaking with anger. 'Where'd you get that fucking idea from? We're getting faster, not slower. The first one took us nearly a month. We'll do this one in a couple of weeks.'

Fred looks to Arthur, then back to Jim. 'Yeah, well, just make sure you fucking do.' He saunters off to another part of the gang. Arthur slots another rivet in place and they gun it down.

'So why didn't you?' Arthur says.

'What did he say that for, the bastard?'

'It's what gaffers are like. They can't help themselves. So, anyway, why didn't you?'

'Why didn't I what?' Jim says.

'Why didn't you go to art school?'

'Art school?' he says. For a moment he can't answer, doesn't know what Arthur's talking about. Then realisation dawns on him. Arthur grins. Jim says, 'Oh that. When I went to the theatre? Yeah, I sometimes think about that, what it must be like, doing something, y'know, different.'

'Fancy doing it?' They gun down another rivet.

'You know what you were saying about being in the desert with that gun, that's what I'd like, something like that.'

'What, the army?'

'No, just to go somewhere different, see what it feels like. You see all these places on telly – Lisbon, New York, Los Angeles. Be great to go. Only been to London twice. Where were you in the desert, which country?'

'Libya, Tunisia, Egypt.'

'Egypt? See the pyramids?'

'No. Went to Alexandria, though. That's the place you should go and see. I thought I'd go back after the war. Never did.'

'What stopped you?'

'One thing and another. I had the missus back here for a start.'

'I know what you mean. Saving up to get married, me and Helen. That's how I got the job here. Her old man knows some union bloke up at his social club. He worked me in. Thought he was doing me a favour, I suppose. That's why I felt such a twat when I thought I was going to get the sack. Christ, I don't know what I'd have said to him after all the trouble he went to.'

'You're engaged to be married?'

'Sort of, y'know, unofficial like. You want to see her. Helen. She's a cracker.'

'Where d'you meet her?'

'At the dance. She was with this other bird, Shirley, who was going out with my mate Roy. We all used to go to the Majestic, on Saturday nights, me, Roy, Bill and Pete. We'd have about six pints in the Silver Sword, join in the free-and-easy for a bit, then bugger off up the dance. It was a right laugh.'

'What does she do?'

'Works in this dress shop, that big one in town that sells

wedding dresses, evening dresses, that sort of stuff. *High class*, she always says, *none of that cheap tack*.'

'Still see your mates?'

'Not much these days. Go up Helen's most nights. Roy's getting spliced soon, silly sod. Shirley's got a bun in the oven.'

Arthur gives him a hard look. 'Why don't you go?'

'Go where?'

'Anywhere you fancy. Lisbon, Paris, London. London's only two hours away.'

Jim laughs nervously. 'Oh, yeah?'

'What's stopping you?'

They stop work for a moment, air-braces and riveters clattering all around them.

'I know,' Jim says. 'Pack a case and you're off, free as a bird, eh? Frightening, isn't it?'

'The thought of going?'

'No, the thought of not going. Drifting into, I don't know . . . settling down? A wife and house and a mortgage. That's what frightens me, being settled down. And, I don't know, missing out on things.' He looks at Arthur. 'Fuck me, Arthur, stick another rivet in, will you?'

Arthur puts in another rivet and they gun it down.

'You only get one crack at it,' Arthur says. 'Make the most of it while you can. I was like you once. Just before the war I was going out with this bird when I got my call-up papers. You only got a feel up in them days. Getting your hands on French letters was a right fucking palaver, so most of the birds wouldn't risk it. It must have been the war, I suppose. She must have thought she might not see me again because the night before I left for overseas she let me have it. I couldn't believe it, in her old man's garden shed. Then I didn't see her again for nearly three years, running about the desert all over the place. Shit scared some of the time, but absolutely brilliant. I never wanted it to end. We went to Benghazi. Beautiful place. I did loads of drawing there. They started calling me Art because of the drawings. Some of the lads took them home when we left. I thought I might try my hand at it properly when I got back, go to art school, travel a bit. She was a stranger when I met her again. She'd sent me letters all through the war, but I'd forgotten what she even looked like. She'd saved all sorts of stuff for us to set up home. I didn't see how I could get out of it, marrying her, I mean. I felt I owed her something, her waiting about all that time. So I finished my apprenticeship at Fisher's then went to the Austin.' Jim catches Arthur's eye. Arthur squeezes the trigger of the rivet gun, a short machine-gun blast. It's getting quieter in the hangar, men packing their tools away. 'Still, I've got a nice wife, and a house, a mortgage I've nearly paid off, and a son who's training to be a chartered accountant. Good, eh?'

They stop work and begin tidying up for the weekend too; coil up the air-lines and put the rivet guns and air-braces back into the cupboards at the end of the gang. They put all the hand tools: files, hacksaws, Gilbows, hammers, screwdrivers, pliers, grips and clamps into toolboxes and brush down the benches, sweeping the swarf and detritus into the gangway for the labourers to clear up. The air-lines shut down, the last air-braces and riveters stop and a calm silence settles over the hangar. Men talk quietly to each other, what they're doing at the weekend. The foremen stand at the ends of the gangs in twos and threes, hands in the pockets of their white cowgowns, making sure no one leaves their workplace until the hooter goes. *Two pints of gold top, please,* someone shouts. The foremen ignore the piss-take. Arthur with his mac on, knapsack slung over his shoulder, elbowing his way to the front to get a good start on the run to the bus.

'So long, Arthur,' Jim says.

He doesn't respond.

'So long, Arthur,' he says a bit louder.

Arthur turns. 'So long, Jim,' he says. 'Take care.'

The hooter goes and the mass of bodies makes a dash along the gangway, heading for the waiting buses to take them home. Jim walks slowly, jostled by blokes hurrying past. Then he stops and turns and makes his way back through the oncoming stream of men, thinning now, back to the section. He stands by the engineers' vice, his vice, a section of the bench he has made his own. He leans across and pulls his toolbox towards him. It leaves a big space next to Arthur's box. He grasps the handle and holds it by his side. It's heavy and pulls at his shoulder. He glances around to make sure he hasn't forgotten anything. He looks down the section to the nacelles, one up on trestles half finished, the other next to it, complete and waiting to be taken away for final assembly. He stands for a moment, his shoulder hanging. Then he lifts the toolbox and slides it back to where it came from, next to Arthur's. He looks at it, then turns to rejoin the stragglers leaving the silent hangar. As he passes the finished nacelle he runs his hand over the apple-tight skin.

Special Evidence

GEORGINA BRUCE

It was a bad scene, not the worst I've encountered, but bad enough. Drowned, he was. Bobbing at the edge of the water, skin white and beginning to bloat up. No one spoke as they heaved him out of the canal. Even the birds stopped singing, for a moment, when the officers spread his sodden body over the towpath. The silence felt like a halo of pressure around my head, squeezing my brain, just enough to give me a headache. But then the radio crackled and someone choked out a morbid laugh, and it was as if someone had turned up the volume of the world again.

The drowned man's name was Greg Odell. When I heard it, I thought about the crocodiles that live on the banks of the Nile. How their scales are jewelled with diamond drops of water. How the white sun refracts into the entire spectrum of colour across their backs. How they glint, like teeth, in the grass. I remembered the picture in a children's encyclopaedia. All afternoon, I had gazed alternately at the picture and then through the window at the rain. My mouth filled with the taste of sweet rice pudding, sugary milk coating my tongue and teeth. The *tink* of the spoon in the bowl.

It's been a long time since I've tasted rice pudding. My mother had a sweet tooth; she often cooked those kinds of things. It's better not to remember. Nothing good comes from thinking about the past. That day, at the canal side, I knew this was special evidence and I berated myself that I could not think what it all reminded me of.

Greg Odell had been a lawyer before he wound up in the canal. He had a wife and a couple of kids, lived in one of those big Victorian places in Edgbaston. Probably had a lot of enemies, I shouldn't wonder. Probably everyone hated him, smug bastard, with his posh house and his pretty wife and spoiled kids. And no one likes lawyers, do they? Especially not coppers. But it didn't look suspicious, not on the surface anyway. Nicky Newlove, my partner, thought it was a straightforward accident. We asked around, but it was all shrugged shoulders and raised eyebrows and the sort of haggard expressions you can only really imagine seeing on the faces of those who have sold their souls to the law.

'No one knows anything,' Newlove said. 'Because there's fuck all to know.' She had her feet up on her desk, so I could see the soles of her shoes. Mud and leaves wedged into the grooves, from where we'd been walking up and down the side of the canal. I clean my shoes every day, but you can't expect other people to be as fastidious.

'I don't believe in accidents, Newlove. You know that.' Something didn't sit right about the whole thing, but Newlove was immune to hunches and intuitions. She was a straight down the line, no nonsense, by the book copper. It takes all sorts to make a world, as I often have cause to remind myself. 'Let's go for a smoke,' I said.

That was one thing Newlove and I had in common: we were both serious smokers. Me, I started when I was nine years old. My mother smoked, and she'd accidentally left her cigarettes and lighter on the dresser in my room.

She wanted you to start smoking.

I remember picking them up. Benson and Hedges. The packet was gold and shiny, tight with cigarettes. You could smell them through the cardboard. When I lit my first, there was a dry crackle and smoke filled my lungs. I knew how to do it – I had been watching her all those years, after all. I didn't even cough.

You coughed like a dog. You threw up, out of the window. Crows pecked at your vomit.

I was a natural. Took to it like a duck to water. Thirty-five years later, I'm on two packs a day. Never even tried to stop.

Newlove was a different story. Every other week, it was

something else. Hypnosis, patches, glass of water every time she felt a craving – disaster – we kept having to stop interviews so she could go to the loo. She tried everything. The problem was that she loved it too much. And, I had to admit, it suited her. The O of her mouth when she blew the smoke into the rain made me wonder what it would be like to kiss her. Perhaps to put my mouth over hers and suck the smoke from her lungs into mine. But you don't go there with your partner, not unless you're looking for trouble. Besides, I wasn't Newlove's type. She had some smooth-faced girlfriend in Operations; she was the one who was always telling her to quit smoking.

'I don't get it,' I said. 'So, this guy's walking home from work, in his business suit and everything, and he just so happens to fall into the canal and drown? Just like that?'

'Why not? He'd been drinking, lost his footing.'

I guessed it was plausible, but it didn't ring true. So I said, 'Have you ever made rice pudding, Newlove?'

'I've bought it, from a shop.'

'No, then.'

Put the milk, sugar, rice and butter in the bottom of a glass bowl. Add full cream milk. Tap your cigarette ash onto the surface. Stir everything together.

Nutmeg. Cinnamon. Not cigarette ash.

Whatever.

'It's easy to make,' Newlove said. 'I mean, I've never done it, but all you need is . . .'

'All right. You don't have to give me the recipe. You're not exactly Delia Smith now, are you?'

Newlove took another drag of her cigarette and blew the smoke towards me. Her eyes narrowed with pleasure. 'Fuck. I really must stop smoking. Have you talked to his wife yet?'

'You go. Get statements from the colleagues, too. Find out who saw him leave the pub.'

'Forensics said it all looked kosher. No sign of a struggle. I don't think there's anything suspicious here.'

'Come on, Newlove! Of course it's suspicious. It's rather too much of a coincidence, don't you think?'

'Sorry? What are you talking about now?'

I ignored her tone and said, 'There are more miles of canal in

Birmingham than there are in Venice. Did you know that?' Because she hadn't grown up here, she was unaware of some of the city's common geographical features.

'You've mentioned it before, yes, but I fail to see how it's relevant.'

'Well, perhaps it isn't. Perhaps not. But it doesn't hurt to be in possession of all the facts. And out of all those miles and miles of canal, Odell just happens to wash up on our patch? Coincidence, you say?'

She gave me a strange look, then. Or rather, she looked at me as though I were strange. I really would have liked to explain myself better, but I didn't know how. I couldn't say what it was about Odell's death that particularly bothered me. He was drunk, he slipped. It was a bad bit of the canal, maybe.

His wife had told Newlove that Odell often walked that way home, which was plausible. It was derelict and uninviting, but a short cut. Some said that the canals were full of dead bodies, dogs, snakes – but clearly that didn't bother Odell. His colleagues described him as sensible. Everything about Odell was unremarkable, even boring, barely worthy of notice. Yet he stood out to me, startlingly vivid, and I knew that he was a part of the story. Perhaps even the key.

You know them when you see them.

I walked home by the canal. There was the usual haul, nothing special. I found a couple of shoes, one men's size ten brogue, the other a size five trainer with a hole in the bottom. A child's blue hooded cardigan, hanging from a twig. A thin rain jacket, twisted and stuffed into a gap in a tree trunk. A pair of brown corduroy trousers, lying on the towpath like a pair of drunken legs. I shoved them all into my rucksack, to be taken away for further investigation. It was a mystery to me how these things came to be there. A cardigan, I could understand. You took it off because you were too hot and it slipped from your hand or from around your waist. But trousers? How do you lose a pair of trousers? How do you lose a shoe? Surely you would notice if you were walking along and suddenly you only had one shoe. I had found other things at the canal. Other, special things. Suit jackets, ties, a black stiletto.

High heels with sharp points. Useful punishers for bad children.

When I got home, I went straight down the gully into the back. All the stuff from the canal went into the Evidence Shed at the bottom of the garden. I tried to keep it organised, but the only real system was that the older the evidence, the deeper in the pile it was buried. I slung this latest stuff on top. The special things, the stiletto and other important items, were in bags on the shelf. I thought about getting all the special evidence together and going through it again, but really I just wanted a couple of beers. Besides, it stank to high heaven in the Evidence Shed. Stank of canals.

In the house it was much better. Smelled of the Summer Breeze air freshener I'd plugged into all the wall sockets. That Summer Breeze fragrance is better than nature. It hit me in the back of the throat when I walked through the door. Everyone likes a fresh-smelling house, don't they? That made me think about Greg Odell. He had mints in his trouser pocket when they pulled him out of the canal. Those really strong ones, blow your mouth off. What did he want those for?

Doesn't matter how much you wash, you can't wash off a bad smell like that.

Now Greg Odell, he had been drinking all afternoon, but that was no secret. His wife told us he'd been celebrating with his work friends, some big case they'd won. So it wasn't his boozing he was trying to cover up. Something else. And, suddenly, I knew what it must be.

'So, he's a secret smoker. So what?' Newlove tapped her fingers against the desk. 'It's hardly a crime. Hardly a motive for murder, either.'

'Murder? Who said anything about murder?' I leaned forward, over the desk.

'I thought . . . oh never mind,' said Newlove. 'Can we just close the case, please? Nothing but nothing is going on here.'

'You are so wrong, Newlove, that I hardly know how to begin telling you just how wrong you are.'

'Fine by me.' She stood up, patted her pockets for her cigarettes. 'I'll just be wrong and ignorant to boot, then, shall I? Excuse me.'

Damn it. I followed her outside, noting that great stride she had. No one messed with Newlove. Except maybe me, on a bad day. She kept walking all the way to the car park, then stopped and leaned against the bonnet of her Ford.

'I'm never going to hear the end of this, am I?' She lit a cigarette and blew the smoke towards me. She really was a fine-looking woman, even when she was looking at me like she wanted to stab me in the face.

'The point is, why was he lying? And who was he lying to?'

'The point is, why does it matter? He fell in the fucking canal! Haven't we got any real work to do? By which I mean, actual crimes.'

'Okay! Fine. Close the file.' I snatched the cigarette from between Newlove's fingers and took a drag. She glared at me. I grinned.

Why don't you tell her about the crocodiles?

'Oh shut up,' I said, out loud.

Newlove shook her head. 'I worry about you, mate. I honestly do.'

My mother's room was more or less exactly as she'd left it. Not that she had left it. She had died, though, and that's what I mean by that. Sometimes, after I'd had a few drinks, I'd go and stand in there and look through her stuff. I did that now, looking for anything that would lead me to Greg Odell. The file might be closed, but I wasn't convinced. Something had gone down that day, the day he died, and I couldn't let it go.

I found the children's encyclopaedia, all seven volumes of it. The red leatherette binding was intact, but the gold lettering had eroded, so I couldn't tell which volume contained which alphabetical references. I had to open the books to the flyleaf to see their titles. I started by looking under 'C' for crocodiles. There was a picture of a crocodile, but not the picture I remembered. There was a guy standing over the crocodile, holding its jaws apart. Next to the picture was a drawing of the crocodile's mouth full of teeth. I read through the entry. Nothing. But at the side of the page was a box of text entitled 'Crocodile Tears'. Oh yes, I thought to myself. They get your sympathy then bite your head off.

I picked up all seven volumes to take downstairs with me. Before I left the room, I gave it a good spray with air freshener.

The next day was a Saturday, so officially I was off duty. But I like to think that a good copper is never really off duty. I took the bus into town, and walked the canal towpath to Edgbaston, coming out on

Gillott Road. That had been Greg Odell's usual route home. I looked for a place where he might have fallen. Even though the towpath is pretty rough here and there, there's a clearly defined kerb that runs all the way along. You'd have to be fairly drunk to fall over that. Mind you, his work colleagues said he'd been downing shots and pints like nobody's business. Of course, no one tried to stop him, take him home or anything like that. Lawyers, eh? Scumbags.

His house was one of those mansion type of places, three floors, the columns either side of the front porch, two cars in the driveway - both Beamers. If I'm honest, it made me feel a bit self-conscious about my Saturday clothes. I had a shirt and tie on, but I was wearing jeans and trainers on my bottom half. I'd given myself a good dose of Summer Breeze before I left the house, so at least I smelled nice. Mrs Odell opened the door after the fourth ring. She frowned at me, looking me up and down as if she couldn't possibly imagine what someone like me was doing ringing *her* doorbell. Her face was thin and drawn; she looked like she'd been up half the night crying. Could have been. She was wearing one of those silky kimono dressing gowns. Very nice. I made a mental note of it, in case it became relevant later.

'I'd like to ask you a few questions about your husband,' I said, flashing my ID.

'Now?' Incredulous.

'I'm here now, so yes. Now would be a good time.'

She shook her head, but opened the door wide so that I could enter. I followed her down a long hallway into a large, bright kitchen. The cabinets were glossy blue and there were black and white tiles on the floor. Like something you'd see in an art gallery.

'I thought the police file was closed? They said there were no suspicious circumstances, nothing to worry about?' Mrs Odell poured herself a coffee from a percolator, then turned and looked at me. 'Coffee?'

'Milk and three, thanks. No, there are just a few loose ends to tidy up. Mrs Odell, did you know your husband smoked?'

She put the coffee in front of me and sat down heavily at the kitchen table. She looked worn out. No make-up. I suddenly realised that I had never seen my mother without make-up. She had always had a perfectly painted mask. I mean face.

Ha ha.

'He smoked socially,' said Mrs Odell. 'Like me. We'd have the occasional cigarette with a drink. Why is this important?'

'Good question, Mrs Odell. At this stage, I'm not sure. So you knew all about his smoking? He wouldn't hide it from you?'

'Of course not.' She pulled her hands through her hair, rubbed them over her face.

'The children? Would he hide it from them?'

'No, no. Quentin is eighteen; they smoke cigars together sometimes. And Poppy – well, she never liked his smoking, but she never made a big deal out of it. And Greg wasn't a liar.'

Little liar. Clean your mouth out with soap.

'Mind if I take a look around?'

Mrs Odell shrugged. I bet that felt nice, shrugging in that silky kimono. 'If you must.'

I went into the living room. They had a piano and a chaise longue. I guessed that was all Mrs Odell's doing, the fancy interior decoration bit. Looked like something out of one of those magazines Mother used to read. Apart from that, it wasn't special. There was nothing in there that interested me. The dead man's study, though, that was more promising. He brought a lot of work home with him, by the looks of it. I had a quick rummage through his desk, saw nothing of importance. Picked up his photographs – him and his wife and kids, all smiling into the camera. Well, you would smile, wouldn't you? Living this life. Nothing, again nothing. Some instinct made me push the door to, so I could see behind it. Hanging from the back of the door was another photograph, this one black and white. There were two adults wearing formal clothes, and a child standing between them. A boy. Must have been four or five, in his Sunday best. His father had his hand in the boy's hair.

If you don't smile for the camera I'm going to pull the hair right off your head.

I picked the photo from the door and went back to the kitchen. Mrs Odell was dressed now, in a simple jumper and jeans. How elegant she was. How poised. I put the photograph on the kitchen table.

'Who are these people?' I asked.

She picked up the photograph. A flicker of a smile crossed her face. 'That's Greg, when he was a little boy. And his parents.'

'They're still alive?'

'His father is,' she said. 'In fact, he was coming to stay with us that day, the weekend . . . He didn't come, though. I rang him, of course, as soon as we heard.'

I'd found the killer. But I didn't feel good about it. I felt like my stomach had turned into a stone.

On the Monday, Newlove told me she had put in for a new partner. She said she couldn't handle all my 'strange obsessions' and she even suggested I go and see a counsellor.

'You think I'm crazy?' I asked her.

'I don't know. I'm not a doctor, am I?' She blew a smoke ring and we both watched it wobble upwards.

'Let me explain again,' I said. 'He killed himself because he couldn't face his father. He was a cruel man. You can tell, from how he's standing in the photo. Odell had to hide everything from him – his drinking, his smoking, everything. He couldn't take it in the end. Couldn't face the thought of seeing his own father. So he fell into the canal. Accidentally on purpose, if you know what I mean.'

It made sense to me. All those years, the fearful years of childhood. You can't ever leave them behind, not even a man like Greg Odell with all his money and success. He was carrying those years around like bricks in his pockets – they were sure to sink him in the end.

Newlove shook her head. 'Even if that were all true, which seems pretty unlikely to me, no one has committed an actual crime, have they? Except maybe you. Mrs Odell has made a formal complaint. She thinks you think you're fucking Columbo or something. And you've wasted all that time and energy to try to prove something that is totally fucking irrelevant and unimportant.'

'I'm sorry,' I said. 'You're right, obviously you are. This case has got to me, that's all.'

'It's not a case! It's all in your damn head.' Newlove stamped her cigarette out on the ground. I'd never seen her so cross.

It's all in your silly little head.

I took the rest of the day off and went home. Locked myself in the

Evidence Shed and went through all of the special evidence. I took it out and lined it up on the shelf. Then I decided I needed to see it in a different context, so I brought the pile of things into the house and took it through to the front room. We hardly ever used the front room – that was for special occasions and guests. All the best furniture was in there and you had to keep it nice, everything polished, expensive air freshener too, scented candles and all that. I put the evidence on the table. It all looked really dirty in that nice, clean room. I put the encyclopaedia on the table too, all seven volumes, stacked high.

The crocodiles.

The crocodiles. I found them under 'N' for Nile. Funny how the picture had faded, in my memory. Now, on the page, they were bright and vivid as new.

What are you looking at?

Look, Mummy! Crocodiles.

Eat your pudding. Stop whining.

I brought the spoon to my mouth. I hated rice pudding. The maggoty-white rice swimming in sickly sweet curdled milk. I pretended to put the spoon in my mouth, but instead put it back into the bowl. She saw.

Upstairs. Now.

I sat in the window of my bedroom, with the encyclopaedia and the bowl of rice pudding. Not the dessert bowl, but the big glass dish she had made it in. And she sat beside me, her long legs in her high-heeled black shoes, flexing her ankles, digging the points into the carpet. She lit another cigarette, took a few puffs and flicked the ash onto the milk skin that had formed across the top of the pudding.

Eat your rice pudding. It's your favourite.

It took a while before I fully understood the message I'd been given by Greg Odell.

But one Sunday evening, not too long afterwards, I drank half a bottle of good single malt, then packed the special evidence into a sports bag. Slung it over my shoulder and walked to the canal, the quiet bit where Greg Odell had been dragged up. It was gloomy down there; I half expected mist to rise up from the water, like some old Sherlock Holmes film.

I filled my pockets with stones, gravel, bits of brick left lying on the towpath. Didn't feel heavy enough to sink me, but the weight was starting to drag my jeans down. It got harder to move. I stuffed a load of bricks in my bag and hefted it over my shoulder. That would do it.

Get on with it, then.

I stayed on the towpath for a few minutes, thinking. After a while, I threw the bag in and watched it sink below the brackish water. There was an old bike abandoned in the hedge behind me and I wrestled that in as well. Knew then that I wasn't going to do myself in. I'm not the type, am I? Haven't got the poetic bent or whatever. But it felt good to say goodbye to all that stuff. I didn't know if I should say a few words, say a prayer or something. It was the last of my mother, after all. Well, not quite the last of her, perhaps. It was all just crap really, but you know. Anyway, I didn't say anything because I would have felt like an idiot, talking to myself.

I stood for a while, looking in the canal, and it was getting dark; just the reflection of the moon let me know where the water's edge was. Then I saw something in there. Just a flash. Green and white, it was. A sparkle as it dived beneath the water, the glitter of diamonds pouring off its scaly back.

The Champagne Bell

CHARLES WILKINSON

Today Donna Joyliff is early for lunch at a restaurant whose prices she cannot afford. She finds herself hating the prospect of a solitary wait at the bar or, even worse, being alone at a table, propitiating the waiter who is so anxious to take her order by asking for the small glass of white wine she never intended to have.

Sunny days used to go past without her when she was stuck in an office, face deep in a filing cabinet or hunched over a computer, her back to the weather. Now the unfamiliar freedom of being outside at an hour when she would normally be making her way down to the basement canteen has quickened her pace – although retirement is bringing a taste of what seems almost like poverty: noticing the price of small things and walking rapidly past the places where she'd once shopped with abandon, knowing what cruelty it would be to stop and look longingly at the displays.

Yet when she approaches the steps that lead up to the Mailbox, she is uncomfortably aware of the soap-shiny, featureless faces of the mannequins in the shop window, their heads a little too small for their slender Armani-clad bodies. As she moves closer, she can see that the material they are made out of is pearl-grey but almost translucent. Some wear small black hats, but others have a light-bulb baldness.

Then she is past them, without having paused to look at the prices, and moving up the first of the escalators, past aluminium vats filled with neat evergreen shrubs clipped to resemble obelisks, their lines almost as geometrically exact as the narrow pillars, the rectangles of the windows. There is no one above her on the escalator and no one below. On the first floor, the shops have no customers, though in one an assistant shifts uneasily, as if to separate himself from the almost identically dressed mannequins in business blue with a white, shell-like smoothness in their eyes. Their mouths are sealed.

The shrubs are all precisely the same height and their leaves are a matt green. They are memorials to a lost vitality, their bases chained to the railings as though someone fears they will quit the building in search of a proper climate, a place where they will grow with honourable, asymmetrical profusion.

Then Donna remembers her husband, Martin, who is probably still sitting in their ragged back garden where she left him that morning.

When she awoke two hours earlier, Donna looked out at the surface of a day no less bright than many others, the sun bringing out a soft pink in the red brick of the house opposite, the orange roof tiles glimmering behind dark foliage. She knew that in the office where she had once worked, the screen would be turning red: numbers bleeding across the globe; sharp falls in Asia; billions wiped from exchanges in London, New York and Tokyo. Soon there would be closures: share prices shrivelling before disappearing from the financial pages. A flight to gold and the Swiss franc, the radio said.

Martin was outside doing nothing. Since the sale of the umbrella shop she had never seen him read a paper or watch the news. They seemed to have just enough money to survive, but he had always been guarded about his finances, perhaps ashamed to reveal how he had allowed every breeze of the market to blow away his once not insubstantial inheritance. There had been times when she suspected that it was her salary keeping them afloat, but now and then he would reveal a sudden windfall, a policy that had finally matured or a legacy from a forgotten cousin. But it was hard to be sure that there was anything much left. She made two cups of coffee and went into the garden.

'Is it today that you're going into town?' he said. He was

breaking his croissant into pieces and trying to attract the attention of an unusually rotund sparrow. It was now three years since the receivers had been called in. Martin had never grazed on the sunny uplands of professional competence.

'Yes, today. Do you really have to give the birds our croissants from that very expensive patisserie? You'll be serving them cappuccinos and skinny lattes next.'

'But they deserve the best. Only the very best for the Joyliff birds,' he rallied. She thought how he had just about enough happiness left to get him through the day. 'Who did you say you were meeting?'

'Penny.'

'Penny!' Martin tore the remains of the croissant into tiny pieces, which he flung into a confusion of lupins and weeds. 'I really don't know why you have to go on seeing her.'

'I've told you. She's a friend. Just because you hated your brother it doesn't mean I can't be civil to his wife. I only see her twice a year.'

How many years had it been since red-faced Ralph had wrapped his Daimler round a tree on the way back from a Rugby Club dinner? More than ten? She thought of the veins on his cheeks, always so close to the surface of the skin, and that bluish-pink and white sheen he had – like a prime cut straight from the butcher's block. Somehow it had seemed appropriate that he died like he did. A claret-and-crushed-steel death, rich with blood to match the bright red bonnet that had concertinaed into the windscreen. Martin had refused to go the funeral, but Donna had attended, sent a wreath of white flowers for Penny's sake.

The fat sparrow secured the largest section of the croissant. Martin smiled and tried to concentrate on two blue tits that were rocking on one of the bird feeders.

On the CCTV cameras there is only Donna on the escalators, ascending in the almost silence. Her hair is a silver helmet, a simple style, inexpensive to maintain and suitable for the professional woman she was once was. Few can remember her head of pale gold, the hair she had as a child. She is wearing a dark blue skirt, one that she used to wear at the office. There is no one in the art gallery, just a few pictures waiting at the edge of emptiness. Donna is not aware that the watch she was wearing is no longer on her wrist.

On level 7 she is pleased to see that there are a few people in the cheaper cafés, although the waterfront restaurants contain only waiters, idling at the bar or inspecting the tables. Outside, looking down at the canal and the narrow boats moored beneath the converted warehouses, she notices a metal-grey in the green of the water, a hint of winter in the sunlight. In the distance is a tower built in the Italian style, a Birmingham campanile.

They are to meet at Café Lussac, where they have lunched twice a year for almost a decade – a regular rendezvous that began after Ralph's death. As she arrives, Donna sees that there are no customers and not a sign of a waiter. A black grand piano on a raised deck stands in a corner to the right of the door. Its lid is closed. Behind the bar is a large silver bell attached to the wall. She knows it is the task of the barman to ring it when champagne is ordered. Somewhere behind all of this, she thinks, the prices of commodities, insurance firms, telecommunications and pharmaceutical companies are falling; in the forest fire of figures, there is hardly a trace of green.

As she takes a seat by the window, she realises that in fact there is one other person in the room. A woman is seated at a single table. Her hair has been conservatively permed; she wears a cardigan the colour of prune mousse and blue-framed glasses. Her skin is alarmingly pale and rough, as if it has been pasted on to her bone structure like stucco. She is sitting upright and looking straight ahead, her jaw heavy and firm. There is something slightly familiar about her: a resemblance, perhaps, to an actress in some long-discontinued situation comedy.

A waiter carrying a basket of bread emerges from the back of the restaurant. Donna glances down to check the time and sees her bare wrist, the skin paler than on her forearm and left hand. She has been meaning to change the worn strap for some time. The watch must have slipped off, possibly on the bus journey, which is when she last remembers looking at it. A wash of sadness starts near the base of her back and flows up her spine until it seems to solidify, pressing down heavily on her skull and shoulders.

At last she sees Penny walking rapidly past the outside of

the restaurant, then entering. For a moment, taking in the silence and the emptiness, she looks puzzled, much older. She spots Donna and smiles, breaking the years off her face. But there is something different about her that Donna cannot place. It is not the countrywoman's clothes she has been affecting since she started seeing a divorced farmer; rather it's that her friend, she suddenly realises, is unencumbered by the House of Fraser bags that normally have to be safely stowed away before they can eat. Donna forces herself not to think about the lost watch. She rises and kisses Penny lightly on both cheeks: soft hair brushing against her, the scent of a familiar perfume.

It is only after they have ordered that Penny notices the woman in the corner. She glances sideways, checks what she has seen, then leans forward as if about to speak, a smile playing on her lips, her eyes narrowing confidentially. Then, appearing to change her mind, she sits upright and swallows, as if consigning the words she was about to deliver into the custody of her digestive tract.

'You were going to say?'

'No. I really shouldn't,' she replies, looking down but still smiling. Her whitebait arrives, but once she has taken a mouthful she puts down her fork and glances sideways. A second waiter is discussing the wine list with the woman in the corner. Penny rests both forearms on the table and tilts forward as far as she can: 'Do you know who that is?' she whispers.

'No.'

'Father Francis. Well, I suppose I should say the woman who was Father Francis. I believe she's known as Alison now.'

'Did she . . .?'

'Oh yes, all the way. In Morocco, I believe.'

'But she's not a priest any longer.'

'No, she runs a tea shop in Lichfield. Quite a good one, as a matter of fact. I'm told you sometimes see her at evensong.'

Donna looks at the woman in the corner, whom she now knows to be Alison, formerly Father Francis. It occurs to her that it is possible that she attended a service, a wedding or christening at which Father Francis officiated. There is certainly something about the face hidden beneath the make-up that she recognises. But the woman in the corner, whose eyes once looked upwards as the host was raised, now stares in the direction of the clouds, soft blue mounds building behind the warehouses. On her side plate, the bread, which has been baked to the colour of rust, is unbroken.

And Donna's watch, with its worn snakeskin strap, which may have fallen down the side of a seat on the bus that is now on its way to Druid's Heath – or could, perhaps, have slithered to the ground when she bought a paper in a newsagent's not far from St Martin's Church – is ticking through the hours without her. Although she will retrace her steps and make enquiries, she will not find it.

But now Penny has persuaded her to look at the sweet menu. And, at the moment that she opts for the profiteroles, Martin, who has already had his cheese sandwich for lunch, walks into the garden. There are no birds, not a solitary sparrow clinging to the side of the feeder, no fluttering in the hedges. What had started as a fine day is an undifferentiated white-grey sky.

He remembers Donna mentioning there has been another crisis on the stock market, that the bears are closing their short positions on silver. Martin still has a few shares left in a company whose name he cannot remember. He is finding it hard to cling to those little moments of happiness that have sustained him. He can no longer recall the way the light fell through the cloud last week, shining for a moment with such composure on the leaves – and, so attentive to the sparrows, heightening every detail of colour: chestnut and dark brown, flecked with black, the cream on the underbelly. He will not ring up to find out what he already knows: that he should have sold months ago; his shares are probably worth nothing.

He considers putting out more food for the birds, but the remains of half a croissant and a stale crust are already on the table. The number of garden birds, he has been told, is diminishing. He knows this to be true. Once he used to count twenty sparrows, all lined up on the garden wall; now on most mornings there are only three or four. Nevertheless, it is odd that there should be such a deep silence in the garden, not a flurry of wings or the faintest chattering in the bushes.

When he steps back into the house, the door slams with a sound that reverberates in his head not so much as a pain but as a moment of blackness. For a second, he is aware of a figure behind him and then something is pushing him to the floor. The kitchen has become a basement wine bar in central London. There are no windows, the walls are panelled in stained oak and there is sawdust on the floor. A list of wines is chalked on a blackboard. Martin knows where he is, although he finds it strange since he has been reliably informed that the place closed ten years ago. Still, it seems exactly as it was: the beer barrels that act as tables, the bottles with candles in, the wooden snugs and alcoves where private business may be discussed, the champagne bell just to the left of the till on the rear wall. Ralph, resplendent in pinstripes, is standing at the bar. As he lifts a pewter pot to his lips, the light ripples across its cold sea-grey surface and then winks for a second on his gold signet ring. A semicircle of men in dark suits, the bubbles rising in their flutes, lean forward to listen to him, before rocking backwards with raucous laughter, their open mouths tilted to the ceiling; the barman replenishes Ralph's pot with champagne.

Martin finds himself at the edge of the group. If only he could recollect which triumph was being celebrated, he might find something to say. The champagne bell is being rung: the gunfire of corks, flutes overflowing with foam. And Ralph's face is something straight from the slaughterhouse, ready to be turned into rare beef and tallow. Martin's glass is warm, but he can feel the acid rising in his stomach; he only wants water to drink. Now it is Ralph's turn to laugh. His scalp, visible through his thinning hair, flushes a shade deeper, pink to mulberry. Every capillary on his cheeks competes to reach bursting point and Martin can see the tiny red veins stitched into his nose. His mouth is wide open: the yellow teeth, the blue steak of tongue ready to be sliced.

Then the champagne bell is rung again and again, as if the markets will soar for ever. Martin can feel his brother's gaze on him, the pale blue eyes protruding like the stumps of icicles. The champagne bell rings and rings, again and again and again, a gleeful carnage of sound that becomes the pain inside him.

Outside, rain falls, breaking the silence in the garden: a patter in the branches punctuated by deeper notes when the fattest droplets fall on the leaves. A gust of wind sighs in the treetops before swooping to catch a sheet of water which it sends rattling across the tin roof of the potting shed. Uninterested in the nuts in the feeder, the wet loaf, the seeds swimming in puddles on the paving stones, the birds are staying deep in the hedges. Three and a half miles away, a hooded figure sees a watch lying in a bus shelter. He picks it up and puts in his pocket, snug against the BlackBerry that he will use in a few hours. In another place, prices drip digits, move inexorably down; red bleeds on the screen.

Penny, late for another appointment, has already bustled out of Café Lussac, leaving Donna to linger over her coffee and mints. Behind the bar, the waiter is peering into the till, then shuffling notes. The man who is now a woman called Alison has paid and departed. Soon she will be in New Street Station waiting for her train to Lichfield.

Those in the city for whom the champagne bell has never rung sleep late, but now they are rising from mattresses in high-rise inner-city flats; from beds in sooty brick terraces and stone-clad former council houses on the northern fringes of the sprawl. Some are texting their friends, checking the messages in their inboxes, connecting with the social network that confirms they are alive. A few are moving through the streets, past boarded-up shops, third-floor balconies with towels hung from them, patches of threadbare grass. Their eyes on the pavement, their faces tucked into their hoods, they seem more purposeful today, proceeding at a steady slouch. Small children on bicycles cease their restless wheeling and look at them curiously.

Donna has walked out of Café Lussac, past the orange awnings and the empty tables. There is rain in the left hand of the sky, but to her right there are blue scrawls mixed in with the shifting wisps of whiteness, wool tattered with greying tails.

There is nobody in the restaurants and even the cafés are empty now. The windows in the apartment blocks on the other side of the canal are the shade of negatives on a roll of film.

As she approaches a shrub in the shape of an obelisk, some impulse causes her to stop and look more closely. The leaves, she notices, are exactly the same size and the plant is growing in a bed of stones. She takes a leaf between her thumb and forefinger; it feels as lifeless as wax. Donna quickens her pace until she is under cover. The atrium is darker here, although there are rows of tall lamps with a lilac glow. The lights in the restaurants are dim, as if they are already waiting for night. Donna walks past them.

Those who have not heard the champagne bell rung do not favour bright colours. Their hoodies are black, dark blue, grey or concrete white. You would hardly notice their trousers, though a few wear navy tracksuit bottoms marked with thin white lines. It is afternoon, and the space that is not here is thick with their messaging, their spider texts scuttling across the screens much smaller than the ones that have turned red. You cannot read what is being written. A few youths are making their way towards the city centre; in the suburbs, others are gathering; their clothing matches the clouds: white, soft grey, rain black and blue.

Donna has stepped on to the escalator. She imagines the line of her descent through the heart of the building like a share price falling sharply across the page of a company report. Green obelisks are chained to the railings. The very idea of them has been borrowed from a different age: a memory of formal gardens and a burned-out chateau. She sees again the headless mannequins in the shops; their necks neatly guillotined, their faces blurred with the mere suggestion of eye sockets and noses – as if stockings have been pulled hurriedly over them. There is no one above her on the escalator and no one below.

The boy who has Donna's watch takes a metal bar out of the bag he is carrying and shows it to a friend. Wall Street has opened down and there has been no late rally on the London Stock Exchange. Martin is lying next to his empty wallet on the kitchen floor. He is no longer in a wine bar near Blackfriars and the sound of the champagne bell is starting to fade. Blood has trickled from his left ear and dribbled onto the floor, a red line across the graph of the kitchen tiles.

Now Donna is standing at the top of the steps outside the Mailbox, a spot that will be occupied in five hours by a wall of helmeted men, visored and holding transparent Saxon shields. The roar of traffic on the Queensway has yet to merge with the sound of police sirens. She walks quickly into the underpass, shivers as a cold wind wraps itself round her ankles, disturbs the hair that was once pale gold. She has forgotten her coat and her skirt is too thin.

In the car park to her left, two figures wearing beanies and black masks are standing behind a BMW. The one nearer to her is slightly built, but something about the way he has positioned himself - feet planted apart, neck hunched into his shoulders - makes it impossible to sense the boy submerged in him. His companion is larger, with a stomach that lolls over his jeans. As she looks away, she sees that someone has strung what looks like a row of giant fairy lights across a couple of pillars: a festival of dusty unlit bulbs of orange, red and green - the remnants, perhaps, of some forgotten initiative to brighten the city. Their awkward, defiant loveliness reminds her of Alison eating alone.

She wonders what it must be like to be a man.

The Call
SIBYL RUTH

Julie had been in the room for two and half hours. She stared out of the window, which looked onto the window of another office.

It had been a quiet shift. One of the regulars wanting to talk about her new cat. A woman who had been referred by her GP for counselling. And somebody wanting information leaflets. Julie had put the contact details for the last two into the file. Neither of them lived anywhere near Oakford Road.

The Project was not like she had expected. Julie had thought the phone would ring all the time. Women asking, 'Help, what can I do?' Immediately after the event. Instead there were long stretches when nobody rang at all. And men got in touch wanting support – more of them than Julie had thought possible.

She turned over a page of the newspaper to check the listings. And came face to face with a smiling photo of Bridget, who was on TV again tonight. Julie tried to decide whether the image was digitally altered or if her old housemate had gone for cosmetic surgery. Maybe it was just an old picture.

With some people you wondered what had happened to them. You might make fruitless searches online. In Bridget's case, there was no need. It was no great surprise that she'd made a name for herself. The woman had always been single-minded.

Julie reminded herself that she too had been successful in her own way. And would be still if it wasn't for partners who got offered the job they'd always dreamed of. (Just not in London.) Who went on and on until you found yourself agreeing to go with them. Julie had taken a post with a small firm in the Black Country. She told herself it was not a backwards move, but a sideways one. After three months the small firm had amalgamated with a larger one, leaving her without a position of any kind.

Sometimes Julie thought she should have seen it coming. But however good you were, however experienced, there was always a risk you'd get shafted.

Volunteering at the helpline was a way to fill time. And Julie was good at it. She knew how to sound empathetic, so people would talk. She understood the need for boundaries.

The phone was ringing. Before she took the call Julie checked her watch. Only a quarter of an hour to the end of her shift.

'Survival Project. Can I help you?'

She filled in the record sheet automatically. Subject of call. Duration. Ethnicity of caller (if known). Then Julie replayed parts of the conversation. Everything she had said.

Hello?

Yes. I'm listening.

You sound very upset . . .

That's when the girl had begun speaking, so fast the actual words hadn't been easy to catch. Julie had done her best to follow.

So there was a group of you at first?

Not exactly a friend. Just a guy you knew . . .

And (this would have been last thing): *It's very common for people to blame themselves.*

Somebody was standing over her. It was Naz, the manager.

'We thought you'd gone.'

Julie pushed her chair back. 'I was about to . . .'

'Are you all right?'

'It was this girl . . . Woman. She put the phone down.'

Naz reminded Julie that sometimes people would ring several times before they could pluck up courage to talk.

'No, this one talked. Said she was a student. And she was telling me about what happened. But then she hung up.'

'Maybe there's something you want to discuss?'

Julie hesitated. Chris was away, so there was no hurry to get back. Then she remembered how people used to come to her with difficult cases. And now, with Naz, it was the other way round.

She began clearing her things off the desk, and Bridget's picture grinned up at her.

'I'm okay, thanks.'

In London, if Julie didn't feel like going home she walked by the Thames. This city had no proper river.

She'd cross one or other of the bridges. But here the only bridges were over the ring road.

She'd have sat on a bench in one of the squares. There were no beautiful Georgian squares in the middle of Birmingham.

So many reasons not to come back. But Chris kept saying the city had changed. Julie agreed to move because sometimes it was politic to concede. Then, when Chris got keen on a house in the vicinity of Oakford Road, Julie had felt able to put her foot down. Out of the question, she'd said. It was a rough area. And Chris, who didn't really know about Birmingham, had believed her.

Julie was still replaying the phone call as she waited in Corporation Street. The lit-up display at the stop promised a bus would appear soon.

It was all my fault. That's what the girl had said. If only she'd managed to get a name, a few more details. Anything to give her a sense of who the girl was, where she might be.

For years Julie had believed the incident with Paul was her fault. She had made mistakes, behaved like a complete idiot. Although it couldn't ever have happened without Bridget.

At some point the sign over her head had been rewritten. The bus must have gone into reverse because now it wasn't due for ten minutes. It was raining and more people had joined the queue. Meanwhile a stream of buses was scooping up passengers from the nearby shelter, where nobody had to wait.

Julie took another look at the newspaper. She had folded it with Bridget's picture on top.

She was prepared to bet that Bridget never stood in bus queues. Bridget would take taxis. On the train, Bridget would go first class, taking full advantage of the complimentary tea and coffee.

That man who was too big for his suit – ahead of her in the

line – was staring back at her again. He'd been doing this off and on, even though Julie was sure she didn't know him.

At times she has wondered if Paul could still be in Birmingham. They might have gone to the same film screening, bought drinks in the same crowded bar. Or even sat at nearby tables, without the least suspicion. For twenty years Julie has had her hair cut short. Paul could have put on weight or shaved his moustache off. He could have gone grey or bald.

The staring man gave her the creeps. Plus, everybody had begun squashing together because of the rain and Julie hated it when people got too close. She went and stood out on the pavement, then – after getting jostled by passers-by – to the relative space of the next shelter.

Another empty bus pulled up in front of her, opening its doors with a hiss. Julie stepped back, right into some bloke who said, 'Do you mind?'

So, to get away from him – and everybody else – she got on.

She had meant to press the bell after just a couple of stops. But instead she went on sitting there and didn't get out until the university. She thought of it as 'the University', even though in recent years the city had acquired several more of them. But this one was still the biggest.

Over the road young people were streaming in and out of the massive gates. Maybe the girl who'd rung her was among them.

Walking on further, Julie realised the main street was different. There were still a few pubs, but the butcher's and the baker's had disappeared. Now it was all mini-marts and garish takeaways. *Chicken.Com. Tasty Pastry.* Only everything was the same underneath. You only had to glance above the shop fronts, up at the grimy brickwork.

Of course she had been along here in the car. Avoiding this area completely was out of the question. But as a driver you only see what's in front of your nose.

Oakford Road was really very close. Having come this far she might as well pay the place a visit.

Julie was not sure why she'd gone to live there.

She'd hardly known Bridget during the first year – apart from lending her pens and letting her borrow the occasional essay. So she had been surprised when the woman suggested a house share. Flattered, too. Because even then Bridget was the sort of person everyone talked about.

Only once they'd moved in had Bridget's strategy become clear. She had invited Julie for the same reason she asked Dan, the shy biochemist, to take the third bedroom. Bridget reckoned neither of them would be any trouble.

As Julie turned off the main road there was a gust of wind. She tightened her grip on the newspaper.

Bridget had never anticipated that she and Dan might become allies. Who would challenge Bridget about not washing up, not cleaning, never having her cheque book when there was a bill to be paid.

Only it was impossible to make her do stuff she didn't want to do – Bridget just switched tactics. She was in the house less and less. Often she'd only drop by for as long as it took to scoop up an armful of clothes.

Mostly that was a relief. Except – this being long before mobiles – blokes would keep calling round to see her.

Having turned another corner, Julie went back to read the sign. Yes, it was Oakford Road. It was as if she'd hung onto the knowledge, stashing it away.

At number 12, a man was letting himself in. Julie could glimpse a rug, the edge of a coffee table. All the houses had doors which opened straight into the living room.

Why did it never occur to her to blame the architects, the builders, who put up these terraces? So little had changed: landlords were still hungry for profit, eager to pack in tenants. When Julie had answered the door to Paul that night, he immediately stepped inside.

'I've come for Bridget.'

'She isn't here at the moment.'

'Okay, I'll wait.'

Paul laid his motorbike helmet down on the chair. He wasn't wearing a leather jacket or a denim one, but some hairy ethnic garment. Julie reckoned he looked a bit odd. But there was no accounting for Bridget's tastes. She felt sorry for the men sometimes.

'Would you like a coffee? While you're waiting.'

He followed her into the kitchen, and – because Julie was in the middle of making toast – she gave him a piece of that as well.

They'd sat in the front room. Dan must have been at the library.

Julie wasn't in the mood for small talk. Fortunately the silence – apart from the crunch of toast – didn't seem to bother Paul. All the same she got up and pressed play on the tape machine, without even checking the cassette. (It was Bob Marley.)

After a couple of tracks she said, 'I don't think Bridget's going to show up.'

Paul said it was cool. He added, 'How about a smoke? In exchange for the toast.'

'That's kind – but there's no need.'

Only he'd already got a Golden Virginia tin out of the weird jacket and was starting to roll a joint.

After a minute he handed it across.

'Thanks.'

The cardboard was damp where his lips had been. Julie took a quick drag, then attempted to pass it back.

'No,' he said. 'That's good stuff. You have to inhale properly.'

He came and sat next to her on the sofa.

'That's better. Yes.'

And Bob Marley played on: *Movement of Jah people.*

'You know,' said Paul after the joint was finished. 'Perhaps no one's told you. But you're a lot more attractive than Bridget.'

She tried inching away, but the sofa was too saggy. It was a useless sofa.

'Bridge the Fridge is what some people call her . . . Frigid Bridget.'

Julie did laugh at that. All the same she was puzzled. Surely Paul must like Bridget – or else he wouldn't have come to see her.

'Why . . .?'

Except she never finished the question. That's when he'd slid an arm round her, pulling her close.

Julie stopped. The house was there all right. But which one was it? Not 104, because the door was at the wrong side. It would either be 102 or 106. Julie tried peering into one window, then the other. That didn't help. They'd got nets up at 102, and 106 had a bunch of gaudy artificial flowers blocking the view. How could she have forgotten the house number, when she remembered so many other things?

*

At first she quite liked kissing Paul.

There was a feeling of triumph – she was getting one up on Bridget. And it was a new experience. Julie was positive she'd never kissed anyone with a moustache. Not properly.

It was only when he started tugging at her jeans that it stopped being fun.

'I don't want that.'

Paul told her she was gorgeous. Sexy.

'You can't . . . No.'

Julie got the idea that Bridget could pick that moment to walk in. How would she react to seeing her with Paul? She might think it was funny. She might lose her temper. It was conceivable she might want to join in. Or Dan could be outside, fumbling for his key. Julie could picture him backing off, shutting the door softly, as he wondered what was wrong with the women he lived with.

Living here was already bad enough. To be found like this would be the absolute end. And no, she wasn't going to suggest to some dodgy mate of Bridget's that they go upstairs.

Julie tried shifting Paul, who had moved his weight onto her. He was quite tall, but she should have been able to do it. Except the dope was making her floppy, not as strong as usual.

Number 102 looked more likely to be the house, though that could be because the exterior was shabby, with peeling paint. Whereas the owners of 106 had got themselves shiny new uPVC windows.

Number 102 had a low wall. Julie sat down on it.

It was possible the girl on the phone lived on one of these streets.

What would she be doing now? Did she intend to talk to anybody apart from Julie? Someone from the Students' Union maybe – like the women's officer. Did they even have women's officers any more? Julie hoped they did.

'Just relax.' That's what he'd said.

Paul wasn't rough. It didn't hurt when he began to move inside her. What upset Julie was feeling that she had not made herself clear. She hadn't used the right words or behaved in the right way. Because if she had done, then Paul would have got the message.

So relaxation was out. But she did lie motionless. That meant it would be over sooner. Her guess was that Paul wasn't planning to stick around for long.

This turned out to be correct.

Julie was still trying to do up her buttons while he was retrieving his bike helmet, saying how he had to be getting along.

Somebody had come out of 102 with a crate of rubbish. A woman with purple hair and a tattooed neck was glaring at Julie – in her smart jacket – as if she was a suspicious character.

'Can I help you?'

Julie scrambled to her feet. Was it possible to say that this house, or the one two doors down, was where she'd got raped?

'I've been trying to work out where I am.'

'You're lost?'

'Yes. I was looking for . . . for Bampton Street.'

Julie stared at the crate while the woman gave her directions. There was a pizza box on top. *Fresh and delicious. A taste you can't deny.* She must head towards the main road. It was the second on her right.

'Thank you so much.'

She walked off, but ignored the woman's directions, which had been wrong. Bampton Street was on the left.

Julie was almost back by the university. Her breathing was ragged, so she forced herself to slow down, look at the display in the nearest shop. It sold office supplies, but the window was full of row upon row of masks. These had the faces of celebrities, oddly flattened, with holes for eyes. Scary, but also sad.

As she waited for a bus into town, Julie realised she'd still got that newspaper. Taking one last glance at Bridget, she put her gently in the bin.

Beneath the Surface

NATALIE WHITE

I look up and down the towpath but Ashley is nowhere to be seen. He's late, but I'm not worried. He said he might be. I've walked past the trees that weep into murky green water, the green of rotting tree bark. The path is narrow, the water wide; an invitation. A shopping trolley breaks the surface; it is always here. Empty lager cans float in circles of oil adding rainbow colours into the quiet darkness. The dying roars of an infrequent train or a sleepy canal boat scarcely disturb the peace. Only elderly loners or meandering students come stumbling upon a part of the city no one sees. Drunks group under bridges and greet me as though they've never seen me before, but I know every path, every bridge, every tunnel. I know the honeysuckle's hiding place behind brambles and ivy walls. I inhale deeply, breathe out laughter. Saliva builds in my mouth like rising water in the locks.

So far so good. It can take me up to two hours to leave my flat. I haven't used the oven or done any washing; it's been warm enough to turn off the heating. Only eleven sockets. I once lived in a nightmare house with an excess of forty. Now I walk around the flat and don't check, only a quick glance. Twenty minutes today. I couldn't be late. I brought my trainers; I can run fast when I need to. It's hard not to break into a run. But the meeting must be controlled.

Dad warned me about posting my picture. Things on the net last for ever, he said. Do I believe in forever? He said he would love me for ever. The photo of him gazing at me from my mantelpiece is silent. My photo is a few years old. The light is poor, but you can see my long hair and the contours of my face. You can see the shadow of a smile, light eyes, maybe green or blue or hazel. It was taken at my stepsister's wedding. My stepsister is wearing a silky, clinging white dress which gleams in the sun as though it is slimy, like a toad's back.

'I don't want to be in this photo on my own.'

'But you're with us.'

I tried to argue, but she cut me short.

'Don't be stupid. What's the difference? You've always been on your own.' She is next to her new husband. He's too young for her and won't let go of her waist. My dad always stood with his arm around me in photos, never my mum. If I concentrate really hard, I can still feel the warmth of his leather jacket on my skin.

I have only uploaded a photo for others to see I am telling the truth: I am young, white and slim, with long curly hair. My only lie: my address. The cafés where I search could just as easily be the room in my flat where the self-help books prop up the lampshade. I should throw it away. It's just another socket.

Sometimes I look at Ashley's photo in bed after I've checked the switches and re-closed the blinds to make sure I can't see outside. He has shadowed eyes and slightly receding long hair and a nose piercing - good looking enough to meet a girl in any club. When I asked why he didn't, he wrote that he was too old, sick of small talk and empty flirtation. I asked him what it was we were doing. He said 'connecting'. I sent a question back to avoid the issue. What did he most like about me? Your maturity, he replied. You make me feel younger.

I'm lucky. It can take months to find a good match.

I can picture how he'll approach Brindley Place in his leather jacket, his stride measured, his face purposeful. When he sees me being sprayed lightly by the fountain, his face breaks into a smile and he hurries over. Excited, not desperate; immediately he takes my hand in his. His first words?

'Lily; my flower!'

No, ridiculous. But what could he say that would be nothing and everything? I can get over this part. I make my daydreams mute. Whatever he says I see myself laugh. I take his proffered hand in mine, leading him to a little café on the side of the canal. We have to walk down the steps and I am so giddy with his touch I nearly fall. He pulls my hand closer and grips my waist. We sit outside in the sunshine sharing scoops of ice-cream sundae from the same spoon and I feel other couples glancing our way. We talk until the café closes and instead of leading him down the canal path, I take him to my flat. It's not safe; Dad would kill me, but Dad isn't here. I turn the photo with his silent eyes to face the wall but I don't check the switches. Ashley only sees me and the bedroom and my clothes and my nudity . . .

That's when my daydreams stop.

Ashley is twenty-three minutes late. I walk back the way I have come. He said he would join the canal where the three bridges diverge, the spaghetti junction of the waterways. But there are six geese barring my way. They look at me and flap their wings. I don't know what to do. A group of lads on the bridge in front is watching. I take one step forward; the geese hiss, the boys cheer. Two steps forward, the geese move forward too; they surround me, ready to attack. But this is my territory. I reach into the top of my rucksack and pull out my weapon. Some girls carry deodorant to spray in men's eyes or alarms like a female cat's screech. When you're meeting strangers it's important to come prepared. I run at them, lurch the hammer at their spiteful faces. At first, the geese shriek, then they split and head for the water. I am free. The lads' silence shows their fear, but if I were a man they'd still be cheering. Perhaps somewhere Ashley is watching and the whole performance has scared him away, too. A little girl wails as she points my way. Her family has just emerged from the Sea Life Centre. Her mother shakes her head. I have to smother the urge to go over and ask whether she'd be angry if a goose attacked her daughter and her husband smashed it with his fist?

And then there he is, my knight in shining leather. But suddenly I know there will be no romance. He's flung his jacket over his left shoulder; he's trying to be trendy all in black, but he looks like a criminal. He's taller than I imagined with his metal-heeled cowboy boots. His long, lank hair is loose and swishing in his face like a horse's tail. He grins at me and I want to ask him why he's so confident. He's meeting a friend from cyberspace yet there's no hint of insecurity. He speeds up and tosses his hair out of his eyes. Have I such misplaced arrogance? My knee-high lace-up boots are pulled tight over dark leggings. I have on my favourite pink top. It was a present from Dad, to say sorry. He left it wrapped in pink paper. My curls gleam in the sun and Ashley's smile suggests he's pleased. I can't help staring at the way he chews his gum, as though it's been lost and he's pleased to have found it. His teeth are nicotine-stained, weirdly patterned, like Dad's. I nearly forget how to greet him. Do I use his name? Should I say, Hi, how are you, all right? Why be so bothered about a conversation when we've had so many?

I've always wanted to be able to tell everything to someone . . . you know what I mean? I don't want surface friendship. I'm looking for more, to be honest.

So am I, Ashley. Since Dad . . . The thought of us fills my mind with butterflies. So many beautiful colours!

Did you lose your dad? What happened?

Nothing, don't worry. Dad's fine. It's nothing. Tell me more about what you're looking for.

Easy to type anything. The letters are all there. You're talking to yourself, indulging your fantasies. You might as well masturbate to the sound of your own voice. Perhaps men always are.

'Sorry I'm late. Lily!' Ashley smiles; his teeth are so yellow. He doesn't wait for me to greet him, but takes my hand in his. It's moist. He asks me where I want to go.

'That way.' I take my hand back to point away from the cafés, the staring boys, the wailing children. There will be bridges and honeysuckle. Miles of quiet.

He raises an eyebrow. 'You just want to walk?'

My turn to smile. 'I don't want to be disturbed.'

We have talked about our hatred of people, our love of nature, but still he's very trusting. Once upon a time I was, too. I believed Dad when he said he'd stay. He promised. He was standing behind me in the bathroom; I didn't hear him follow me in. He must have watched me wash and wash and wash my hands so clean the skin started to bleed.

Ashley leads but doesn't pull. Dad used to hold my hand

firmly, his stride gentle; somehow it always felt like I was the one taking him for a walk. In the summer, when it was still light in the evenings and Mum was no longer around, I would pester him while he was doing his paperwork. He always gave in.

'On the understanding that you *never* walk here on your own. If you ever did . . . if anything were to happen, you run. You don't talk to any strange men.'

I liked to tease him. 'Why? I'll be fine! You're a man!'

'Exactly. So I know what we're like. It's not *you* I'm worried about.'

A few weeks before Dad left me, he told me about men. They only think about one thing. He said if he hadn't had such a rough time with Mum, then me to look after, he would be out every weekend. My friends at school thought it was weird how Dad was always so honest with me. When he broke my trust, it got easier to break his.

'Are you okay?' It takes time for me to realise it's Ashley, not Dad, who's talking. He's turned to face me, bothered by the silence.

My head's as noisy as ever. 'I'm fine. Why?'

'You wanted to chat but you've not said a word.'

'I was waiting for you.'

Ashley smiles again; he smiles too much. The canal's bright sunshine highlights lines around his mouth; opened and scrunched paper. 'Ladies first.'

I hide my laughter in a cough. Now I understand why he insisted on walking next to the water; the frail female space I inhabit might drown me. It will be another half an hour before he feels the seclusion. We are still within shouting distance of the last few pubs at the water's edge; people still cross the bridges. I can 'chat' for half an hour. I smile flirtatiously. 'How much time did you spend looking before you met me?'

Hesitantly at first, he tells me the story of his loneliness. I keep one ear on his words, pitching in here and there with a question. And I track our progress. I can see the brick wall that balances alone in the dark water. It's as if the bricks built themselves to create a water pathway either side. I'd like to climb up, see if the few passers-by notice. But I can't swim out to it. The dark water is full of death and disease. I daren't even touch it. Ashley doesn't see the wall; his eyes are fixed on the path while he tells me about an ex-girlfriend who nearly drove him to suicide. I don't ask why we feel the need to give new people the stories of our old people. And he does not know the importance of this tunnel that separates city and no-man's land. It leads to a little ledge on which pretty pebbles laze in the sun's rays. I speed up.

Dad created the beach. I must have been about seven. It was when Mum left; when I was the only one he still loved. He found a piece of light blue glass on the path and went to throw it in the water. It was so pretty I started to cry and asked to keep it. We climbed up the path beneath the bridge and put it on the ledge. There were remnants of a fire below and some empty cans of cider. Dad called it the tramp's treasure trove. Sometimes the trove grew bigger than the ashes of the fire below, then for weeks it lay abandoned and almost forgotten. It's still there. But when Dad left, things stopped being shiny. I found small animals torn apart by magpies, old abandoned shoes. I didn't add anything for nearly a year until I saw a documentary on the Jewish faith's mourning traditions. Jews put stones on graves to show the dead have not been forgotten. Now I bring pebbles. I always knock the mound down before it becomes visible from the path.

Ashley is no longer talking but he takes my hand in his and squeezes it to show he feels lighter. He thinks he's now justified why it is he's allowed to shop for company. Or sex. Or both. It's the only way he can test women objectively and it is only a dating site; he cannot be let down. He's already at the lowest point.

'What about you? Why are you on the site?'

'I'm shy.' I can feel Ashley's eyes on me and I avoid them to prove it. 'I've had some bad experiences too. I like the anonymity and, as you said, the lack of expectation. I never expect to meet anyone –'

'– but you keep searching in the hope that you will?' Ashley searches my eyes, believing he is the exception.

His blue gaze is tempting but there's that feeling again, creeping inside. When I walked in on Dad, when I heard – when I saw him . . . that feeling of desire overwhelming me . . . I know it was wrong; I know it enough now to pretend it didn't happen. Yet Dad started it, didn't he? But I'm here now, with Ashley, not

Dad. We must get to the beach. Everything is under control. I try a giggle, then blush and look away. Flirting's not my strong point but I'm getting better. I prise my hand from his and begin to run. I don't look behind because I can hear him following. The path is narrow; I can fend him off for a mile or so just by putting my arms out and flying away. A little girl again.

There is just one more bridge; a painting by Monet. The ivy falls and drapes over it like a veil blurring the vision. The shimmering water reflects the bridge's image upside down, merging the two into one. I hear Ashley calling me to stop.

'On the way back!' I shout.

Whenever I'm alone here I stop and breathe in the rotten aroma of stagnant water.

I dread entering the treasure trove. Perhaps a tramp will be here. Perhaps the trove will have been disturbed. I slow down and see the smoking ashes; no one is around. I climb the slope and see the treasure as I left it. I start to talk before Ashley's finished climbing. 'I don't show this to many people. But I thought you might like it. It's silly, of course, but you said you're into geology.'

He squats down and turns stones over, earnestly searching through. After a few moments he looks up at me, grinning. 'Lily, these are garden pebbles!'

I shrug. 'We can pretend, can't we?' I'm good at pretending, apparently. When he left, Dad said I was messed up – that the whole kiss incident was my pretence. 'Let's pretend they're precious stones . . . Come on!' I start popping one after another into the pockets of his jacket he's put on now the wind's picked up. He laughs and copies me.

'So, what are we going to do with our treasure?' Ashley is looking at me again. Dad's look before our kiss. I'm backed into a corner under the contours of the bridge.

'Up there.' I nod towards the bridge. 'Let's sit up there and watch the world breathe.'

He heads for the bridge. Maybe sitting down will help me forget. Or remember. I linger beneath for a little while longer. Dad didn't like Birmingham; it was only his job that kept him here. And the canals. Our canals. You wouldn't know we were in the second city, he'd say, not out here with nothing but roads of water.

Now I see Ashley sitting with his legs dangling dangerously over the side of the bridge. He's looking into the water, waiting for me. Once I'm next to him I breathe in his sweet aftershave. The height of the bridge and the perfume make me dizzy. Ashley puts his arm round me and I nuzzle into him, feeling safe and warm. Perhaps it's all going to be okay. He moves his arm, takes my hand and follows the contours of its lines with his thumb. He sighs.

'I'm old enough to be your father, Lily.'

All I feel is sorry. Sorry for him sitting here with me. I wish I could let him kiss me; we could walk back together, go for something to eat. But when he puts his arm round me again all I can think of are the noises Dad was making and the disgust on his face when he caught me standing in the doorway, watching. All I can see is the dark water. Ashley follows my gaze.

'Do you think about what's beneath the surface?' he whispers to the still world, as if it's keeping us from falling.

'Always.' It's the first time I have told him the naked truth. More tumbles out. 'It's how I feel about people. You never really know.'

'Don't you think our conversations helped?'

He looks so earnest I almost trust him. 'Do you?'

'Yes.'

I laugh. For the first time he looks confused. 'You don't know me at all! I could be anyone when I write to you. When I talk to you! And what do I know about you?'

'Lily! Where has this come from?' He takes his arm away. 'You know lots about me. How I feel about things. My past. My hobbies. I'd happily sit and talk with you for ever!'

That's the last fucking thing I need to hear.

'For ever?' My voice sounds small above the water.

Ashley answers by leaning over to me and turning my head to face him. His blue eyes pierce mine before he goes in for the kiss, the saliva glistening on his lips in the sunlight. I try to shut my eyes, to focus on the feeling of his lips on mine; he's brushing them apart with his tongue, trying to get inside me. I try to let him in, but Dad's waiting, warning. It's not *you* I'm worried about. The voice echoes as Ashley's hands gently, so very gently, slide down from my face, travel over and down my pink top.

I take my rucksack off, lean closer into him, letting him touch me. I can feel the heaviness of his breath on my cheek. His eyes are closed. As the echoes fade away, the silence on the bridge is breathtaking. Miles of quiet. Then Ashley's hands brush the surface of my breasts and there's that feeling again. And the voice.

Slowly, I reach into the top of my rucksack. My eyes catch a glint beneath the surface of the water. I stop. And I see his silent eyes stare back at me.

The Sea in Birmingham

MICK SCULLY

Cyril's eyes are extraordinary. Every time I shave him, I say that to myself. A rare blue. So clear. All the secrets of the world there. Not watery. Not glazed. Just clear blue. Sometimes, in the sitting room, he will beckon me over. I have to crouch down because he wants to whisper. 'I was a sailor you know, in the navy.'

'Would that be with Nelson, Cyril?' I ask.

'No.' He chuckles. 'The war.'

'The Great War?'

'They're all great, son.'

Now I can't get him into his room. 'There is a woman in the mirror,' he says. 'She lives there.'

'I don't think so, Cyril.'

'There is, son. A woman – in the mirror.'

Matron Judy comes into the corridor. 'Lucky you, Cyril,' Matron Judy says and, taking Cyril's shoulder, she walks him firmly into the room. 'She'll probably come out tonight and you can have lots of fun.'

Matron Judy positions Cyril in front of his bed and starts to undress him. He tries to protest, raising his hand, but she has his belt. She pushes his hand away and his trousers fall. 'Sit, Cyril.' A small shove and he is sitting on the bed. His neck cranes backwards, towards the mirror.

'Cyril. Cyril love. Look at me.' His head returns. His lip quivers, a sob takes him, and Matron Judy softens. 'Come on, Cyril, there's nobody there, in the mirror or anywhere else. Pass me his pyjamas, Stu.' Her hand glides down the side of Cyril's face. 'It's your imagination, sweetheart.' She strokes his head. 'You're a silly boy, aren't you? What are you?'

Cyril says nothing. Matron Judy wipes away the tears on his cheek. 'You're a silly boy, that's what you are.' I hand her his pyjama trousers.

'Up. Up. Stand. Put your hands on my shoulders. That's it. Now I'm going to get you all nicely tucked up in bed. Then you'll be all right, won't you?' She turns. 'Okay, Stu. I'll see to him.'

Later she catches me in the domestic corridor. 'I thought I told you to get rid of Cyril's fucking mirror.' It's under her arm. 'Here. Put it behind the wardrobe in Muriel's room.'

I take the mirror. Hold it up. Look at it. 'Bloody hell, Jude, there's a woman in here.' Matron Judy kicks me in the arse.

Tomorrow I am going to strangle Cyril. I shall strangle all of them, starting with Matron Judy, who I will do slowly – in the main lounge, before the cinema-sized television screen, in front of which a horseshoe of the D residents sits. Some glance up at it now and then, some never take their eyes off it, some of course hardly ever open their eyes – but no one watches the television. My nan died while watching TV: *Good Morning with Ann and Nick.*

And when Matron Judy is a lifeless heap, lying like an offering before the screen, I will go round the circle of the sleeping. The circle of the faded, the jaded; the circle of the tired, the deranged. The useless. The dreaming. I will go round snapping necks. Briskly.

Symbolism is important in acts of mass murder. It ensures the perpetrator – the murderer, if you must – will be remembered, he or she taken seriously, considered, written about, the subject of films, the inspiration for fiction. The mystery of symbolism is more climactic, more resonant, more important than the killings themselves. The camera closes in on the teddy bear beside the bloodied knife; the author takes the reader beyond the splayed bodies to the votive candle burning in the corner of the room.

*

Cyril hardly ever sleeps in the daytime. Not like the others. Often the snoring is louder than the television. Matron Judy stands in the doorway, smiles. 'Ah, just look at them, Stu. So peaceful. A shame to disturb them. We'll skip teatime.' She turns to Chris. 'Make Cyril a cup of tea, though, will you, love?'

'I was a sailor, you know. Once.'

'I know you were, Cyril, and you'll be going down with the bloody ship if you don't take a nap. Only one sugar, Chris. His weight was up again last week.'

'You are mad. Mad, mad, mad,' Vladimir says. 'Crazy.' He is making Yorkshire pudding. Holding an enamel bowl aloft. The mixture, like Hokusai's *Great Wave*, rolls from the bowl down into the oblong baking tin beneath. It is a joy to watch. The mixture finds its level and Vladimir shakes it smooth. 'I think you should see some doctors. It is easy. Moseley has many good doctors. I think you should take Sertraline.'

I have been describing my murderous plans to Vladimir for weeks now, but it is only recently, as his English has improved, that he understands what I am saying.

'Judy will be the first,' I say. 'I'm going to wire her up to the toaster. She'll come in here, first thing as usual, pop in a slice as usual, flick the switch – as usual – and then pop, she'll light up! She'll glow, her earrings will –'

'What is *glow*?' Vladimir is placing the mixing bowl in the sink, turning the tap.

'Glow?' I think about the word. 'It's, like, red hot. The tip of a cigarette glows. Anything really hot will glow.'

'You will make Judy glow?' There is a lascivious smile on his face that isn't nice. There is a rumour that Vladimir fucks Judy sometimes when dinners are over, up in Edna's room on the top floor. 'I thought you were going to drown her. You said yesterday you would drown her in Joan's bath –'

'Win's bath. I said I would drown her in *Win*'s bath. I'd need to use the hoist.'

It is you. I've been watching you. All the time. Watching. And I'd know you anywhere. What you did to me. How could I forget you? It is you – it is, isn't it? If I'd bitten your bloody tongue off, I'd know. Not much to say for yourself now, have you? Kissing – you call that kissing? I was drowning under you, I was.

'How many times have I told you, Sonia? Don't let Bill out of the summer room in the afternoons.' Matron Judy is standing in front of Cyril, holding his hand. With his other hand Cyril tries to undo his belt.

Sonia tuts. Or clicks. Some noise with her tongue while simultaneously widening her eyes to Matron Judy then casting them away; she always does this when anyone has a go at her. 'I didn't see him go nowhere.' Sonia speaks to the floor.

'Then you weren't looking. He's gone into the small sitting room and arrested Cyril again. Got him on the floor. Frightened him. Look, he's pissed himself.' Matron Judy lifts her and Cyril's clasped hands, forming a bridge to expose the sodden front of Cyril's trousers. 'Look!'

Sonia turns her head slowly, sullenly, tuts again.

Cyril whimpers.

'Don't worry, love, it's all right. Well, you can change him.' Matron Judy gives Cyril's hand to Sonia. 'I don't think he's got any clean trousers at the moment. Put him in a pair of Fred's tracksuit bottoms.'

'He don't like tracksuit bottoms,' Sonia says, taking Cyril's hand.

'It's only for today. You'd better pad him; I know, he doesn't like that either. He drinks too much bloody tea. God knows why Bill always goes for Cyril.'

'He must remind him of some villain he's arrested in the past,' I say.

'He arrests every bloke in the place. But it's only Cyril he gets nasty with.'

Joan comes into the corridor laughing, carrying her knitting.

'Joan!' Matron Judy says. 'What are you doing out of the sitting room, love? You're supposed to be watching the film.'

'Bill, he's arrested Cyril. Sailor boy. Done for him proper. Tell the black girl she let him get away and he arrested Cyril. Good job, too. He should swing for what he's done.'

'Joan, love. That's not very nice. Bill was a copper so many years, he gets mixed up. Old habits die hard. Cyril's never done anything.'

'That's what you think. I'm a witness, I am. I know. He shouldn't be here. Not in Birmingham. Not a sailor. I know –' As Joan raises a finger to point at Matron Judy her knitting falls. The needles stick up like daggers in the carpet. The ball of beige wool rolls along the corridor, the knitting unravels. Joan, surprised, stares at it.

'Stu, get that, will you, and take Joan back to the film, there's a love.'

'It's over,' Joan says. 'It's snooker now.'

Bernie, the night deputy, clocks on at eight o'clock. I've just finished the cocoa run. She's in the office going through the record sheets. She looks at me, asks, 'What you doing here?'

'Apollonia phoned in. Her kid's sick. Judy blagged me into an extra shift.'

Bernie taps the logbook. 'How did Bill get out?'

'Sonia was on her own.'

There's a shout. Then another. A cry really.

'*Cyril!*' We both head down the corridor to his room. He is outside the closed door in his pyjamas, holding the handle.

'There's a woman in there,' he says. 'Hiding. She's in the wardrobe.'

Bernie's good with him. 'Oh dear, Cyril.' She puts her arm around him. 'Her again. I know all about her. She's a real pest she is, but I'll sort her out.' Bernie goes into Cyril's room, shouts, 'Out you. Out. I've had enough of you. Right, there you go, m'lady. And don't come back.'

Cyril is pissing himself. Realising what's happening, he grabs his balls. 'Oh. Oh. Oh.' He starts to cry.

'It's all right, my darlin'.' Bernie takes his hand, kisses it. Kisses his forehead. 'She scared you, that's all. But I've got rid of her now. She won't be back.'

'She's in the wardrobe.'

'Not any more she's not. I promise you, my love, she's gone, and she won't be back. Stu will clean you up. Put you back to bed. All safe and sound, pet.' She kisses him again. 'All safe and sound.'

*

'When I shoot them all, I might let Cyril off. It's the eyes. I could only shoot him if he closed his eyes. Or if I blindfolded him. Bill would blindfold him for me. He'd like that.'

Bernie and I are standing in the open doorway of the conservatory having a cigarette. You can hear the hum of evening traffic from the Moseley Road. Nesma, the night housekeeper, has collected the day's wet cushions from the lounge and put them against the radiators to dry. Next, she starts sorting out the ironing. St Anne's clock strikes the hour: ten o'clock.

'Amazing, aren't they?' says Bernie. 'Greeny-blue.'

'No, just blue. Clear blue. That's what's so rare about them. The clearest blue.'

'Whatever. I bet they broke a few hearts. Anyway, I thought you were going to use poison.'

Nesma laughs.

'I said that to Vladimir and now he never takes his eyes off me in the kitchen. Thinks I'm going to put bromethalin in the cocoa. No, it's definitely going to be a gun. Judy first, *p-bang*, then I've decided Sonia will be next – she won't look me in the eyes; I might have to get Bill to blindfold her too – then the residents. Well, all the D residents anyway.'

Behind us Nesma turns on the radio. Indian music plays very softly.

'How's Cyril now?' Bernie asks.

'All right I think. Clean. Dry. Not entirely convinced you got rid of his visitor.'

'He's still upset about Bill having a go at him. I wish he'd stop picking on Cyril like that.'

From her ironing at the back of the conservatory Nesma joins the conversation: 'Bill will arrest anyone when he gets aggressive.'

'Judy should talk to the doctor about his medication,' Bernie says. 'Something stronger. It's happening too often. He's arrested me a couple of times. Called me an IRA bitch once. Wanted to know where the bomb was.'

'Did you tell him?'

'Told him I'd stick it up his arse if he didn't behave himself.'

'You didn't, did you?'

'Course not.'

'Judy would have.'

'Then she'd have forgotten the first line of the handbook: *Respect for the dignity of every individual resident is the basis of our care.* I just took Bill's hand, called him love and said it was a case of mistaken identity.'

'You're good with them. Bags of patience. Me, I just –' The door opens. It's Betty. In her nightdress. Holding a pair of shoes. 'Hello, what are you doing down here? You should be upstairs.'

'Should I?'

'Yes, you should, young lady.' I take her hand. 'Come –'

'But I've got an appointment with Maureen. I can't go out with my hair like this. Maureen's got me in for an appointment. I'm going somewhere. A dance, I think. At the West End Ballroom probably. In Paradise Street. I like it there.'

I look at Bill sleeping. A shuddering sleep, the snores like small sneezes. On his door is a picture of him in uniform. A peaked cap, so I suppose he was a senior cop of some sort. Taken in central Birmingham. The Rotunda in the background. His leg jerks suddenly. I wonder what he's dreaming about. Chasing some villain? He jerks again. There's a framed photograph of him and his late wife beside the bed, suntanned and smiling on a cruise, the ocean blue behind them.

Betty's asleep now, too. I've put a couple of armchairs at the side of the bed in case she tries to get out again. It's Matron Judy's rule that women do the night checks in pairs – there's always the chance you'll find somebody dead – but she says it's okay for men to do them on their own.

'Cyril, what are you like, mate?'

He's out of bed on his hands and knees, looking underneath it. 'There's a woman under the bed.'

'Come on now, Cyril. It's the middle of the night – well gone ten, anyway – and I want to go home.'

'She's there. Under the bed.'

'She's harmless, Cyril. She'll be as good as gold. You won't even know she's there, mate. That's it. Good chap. In you get now.'

'I've sailed, you know. Years ago. I've been all over.'

'I know you have. I know you have, mate. Now come on.'

'I've seen action.'

*

His palm cups my chin – her chin – pushing back, pushing up. His fingers are splayed over my face. My nose through his fingers like the beak of a bird through a cage. Her face? My face? Am I watching? Or is it me? He is kissing me. Kissing me through his fingers. Kissing – you can't call it kissing. His other hand is up my skirt, in my knickers, at me. Now both hands hold my head. He is pushing his face all over mine. Pushing me under. Mouth. Holding her under. Mouth. All over hers. All over mine. Close my eyes and I won't see what's happening to her. Close my eyes.

Why didn't I bite the bugger's tongue off? Why didn't I bite?

I see you.

I see you there. I'm watching. And I know it's you.

I'm in the office, filling in my timesheet.

Matron Judy and Chris are trying to solve the problem of space. It is Tuesday. Maureen is hairdressing in downstairs bathroom 1 – all day – and the chiropodist is using downstairs bathroom 2 until at least three. The comp volunteers are in this afternoon doing Living History projects with some of C's residents and they need somewhere to go to talk to them. Usually they use the C dining room, but Father James will be in there giving communion to the Catholics, while the Active Hands lady will be using the smaller D dining room for her exercise class.

Maureen pops her head round the office door. 'Stu, have you got a minute?' She is taking Betty back to the big sitting room.

'That looks nice, Betty,' I say.

'Do you think it's all right?' Betty touches her perm.

'Beautiful. If I was forty years older . . .'

Betty laughs.

'You'll have to watch him,' Maureen tells her. She turns to me. 'Cyril's just gone into the visitor's lounge and I've got to bring Bill through for a haircut. He's already going on about not being first. Says he's giving evidence in court this morning.'

'Oh, blimey. Okay. Give me a minute.' I head for the lounge.

Cyril is on his knees beside the coffee table, peering into the dark sheen of its polished surface. I crouch down beside him.

'She's in there. See. She's there.'

I see his reflection staring back at us, his face framed by flowers in a vase on the table. What does he see? I wonder. *She's in there.*

The face of a beautiful woman, floating like John Everett Millais' *Ophelia*, just below the surface of the wood? And I feel like crying. 'Come on, Cyril. She's all right. Don't disturb her.'

He turns to me; old blue eyes, old blue blue eyes, except these eyes aren't old. 'Is she all right?'

'I think so. Come on, mate. They're laying the tables for lunch. Shall we go and watch them? Or shall we look at the aquarium?'

'The fish.'

But the three armchairs in front of the aquarium are all filled by sleeping residents. 'It's so peaceful watching those fish,' Matron Judy always says. 'Makes me want to drop off myself.'

'I can hear music, Cyril. Can you? That's Kathy Kirby, that is. *Secret Love.* Let's go and see who's listening to Kathy Kirby.'

I know who you are, mate. I've got your number.

What you did to me. Kissing in a cage. A bird with a broken beak. What's kissing got to do with it? Banging my head against the floor – and kissing. Uniform means nowt to me. Soldier, sailor, rich man, poor man. Thief, you old bastard – thief. You know what you took from me.

But I've got you now.

I've got you now.

We're all crowded into the kitchen, Matron Judy leaning against the fridge.

'God knows what the comp are going to think now. They'll never let their kids anywhere near the place. Vladimir, cut that coconut sponge up into fingers. Chris, make up some squash, will you, love? And some tea for the police. A few biscuits as well. Stu, go and see what's happening, will you?'

'I can't. She told me to stay here – the policewoman in charge. You know she did. *Stay in the kitchen.* She said it to all of us. They've put Sonia in the lounge.'

'That's so they can question her,' Chris explains. 'They're going to talk to us all.'

I jump up onto the draining board and kneel on the window ledge. Open a window.

'Stu,' Matron Judy squeals. 'You can't get out that way. You've got to stay here.'

I'm leaning out of the window. Half in, half out. 'I'm not going anywhere. I've got to have a fag, that's all.'

'You can't do that. Not in the kitchen.'

'Fuck off, Judy.'

'Leave him, Jude,' Chris says. 'He's upset. He's had a nasty experience.'

'We're all upset, Chris. We've all had a nasty experience. I am still having one.'

Vladimir reaches for my leg. I pull away, tumbling to the ground outside. 'He's escaping,' Vladimir shouts. Matron Judy shrieks.

Chris is at the window. 'Are you okay, Stu?'

'Yeah. I'll just have a fag then I'll climb back in.' Pressed against the kitchen wall, I light a cigarette. Inhale. The smoke burns, the smoke calms. A miracle. And in the smoke I see the shape of Cyril, under a white sheet. Lying as he does in bed sometimes, on his side, one leg drawn up so that a foot rests on the knee of his other leg. Under the sheet he looks like a seahorse, carved in plaster of Paris.

What colour would describe these walls? the police officer wonders. Pea green would probably do it. She is aware of beads of sweat breaking on her back; a trickle running down her spine. They keep these places so warm, she thinks, no wonder the old folk sleep all the time. 'Let's open a window, shall we?' she says to the man before her. 'Let some air in.' She moves past him to do it.

It's a good move. The young man – youngish, he's probably thirty – is visibly disconcerted by the sight of his sketchpad on the table she's been using as a desk. *Prominent silent display*: her old boss Sean Dowd's tip. Just let it sit there. Get on with other things. You'll soon find out if it has any evidential value. *Evidential value*, that's what it's all about at this stage. *Initial questioning*. Almost informal. Just her with each staff member in turn; her colleague WPC Morris sitting quietly beside the door, almost invisible.

The police officer breathes in the cool air: 'That's better.' She turns back to the room, leans against the sill. Another old Dowd technique: speak to the suspect's back. 'Tell me exactly what happened, Mr Hibbs. Stuart. Exactly as you remember it.'

The man's head turns a little as he shuffles round in his chair.

'Just stay where you are, Stuart,' she says. After what the

chef has told her she needs to go in fairly hard with this one.

'I was in the lounge. On my own –'

'On your own?' Cooler now, she returns to her seat.

'Sorry. I was the only *member of staff* in there. Just me and the residents. They were watching television. Well, it was on. Most of them were asleep. Not Cyril, though.'

'This is Mr Turvey?' She places a hand on the sketchbook. Mr Hibbs notices. Blinks. She thinks again of the chef's peculiar smile as he handed her the book: *In here, I think, you will find things you should see.* His hand deliberately brushing hers. Unpleasant. You get some odd characters in places like this.

'That's right. We call them by their first names. To create a family atmosphere.'

'Go on.'

'He wasn't asleep. Then Joan comes into the room –'

'That's – Miss Walters?' She looks down to her notes. So many names . . .

'That's right. She's a B resident, but she sometimes comes into the small lounge. She goes over to Cyril and looks at him, really hard, and she starts to laugh. "It's you," she says. "I knew it was. I'd know you anywhere." Then she called him a bastard. She does swear sometimes, Joan. She said, "I knew you'd surface one day, come bobbing up – and I'd be ready for you." Cyril was upset by this and he started to get up. I called to her to leave him alone. I went over, took his arm and was saying something like, "Come on, Cyril, let's have a little walk," when I saw her behind us. She'd got Brenda's walking stick, the one with an ivory handle, up above her head, and before I can say or do anything she brought it down on Cyril's head. He went straight down. Without a sound. Just crumpled. Joan tried to hit him again. "There, you bastard," she was saying. "Down you go. I knew I'd get you one day."'

The police officer waits. Lets her finger tap the sketchpad. 'And that was it?'

'Yes. Then I went for help.'

He is watching her finger on the sketchpad. Now still; now tapping. She tries to forget the chef's smile, his sticky hand. 'What was Mr Turvey like?'

Hibbs smiles. 'Oh, Cyril was a lovely man. Gentle. Quiet.

Easily scared of stuff. A bit troubled. He had beautiful blue eyes.'

There's a pause. The police officer opens the sketchpad, turns two or three pages until she finds what she's looking for. 'Yes, you seem to have been quite taken by Mr Turvey's eyes, Stuart. You have drawn them several times.' She watches him swallow. 'On this page, just the eyes, drawn twice. Labelled *Cyril's Eyes*, and then –' She flicks on through the sketchbook. '– here they are again, but this time with wings. And here, curiously, in what looks like a goldfish bowl.'

'Surreal –'

'They certainly are.'

She looks at him and he looks back. He's sweating. Forehead. Nose. He swallows again. Indicators? Dowd would say so. Not evidence, but strong indicators. 'These are very peculiar drawings if you don't mind me saying, Stuart. Some people might use the word *disturbing*. This one that's labelled *Edna Asleep*. Why have –'

'That's in the style of Modigliani. That's why the neck is elongated.'

'All her features seem distorted to me. And here we have another of Mr Turvey. At least that's what the caption says – *Cyril*. But unrecognisable. Broken up, one might say. Mutilated.'

'A sort of Picasso rip-off. Cubism. Breaking down an object into its visual components. I was thinking of his portrait by Juan Gris when I did it.'

'I see.'

He swallows again. Hard. Like he's got a fucking bird fluttering about in his throat. The police officer watches. There's a slick of sweat like varnish across his face, despite the room being cooler now. She watches, and waits. Dowd would be proud of her. Then: 'I have to say there is something very brutal about these sketches, Stuart, something that doesn't seem to be entirely compatible with what one would expect from a paid carer of the elderly.'

'Where did you get that?' Hibbs nods to the sketchpad. 'Did Vladimir give it to you?'

'Mr Karpin, yes he did. He also told me something that is supported by some of your other colleagues, something quite repellent really.' Her fingers dance across the Cubist portrait of Mr Turvey. 'It seems that you spend a lot of time threatening to kill the residents.'

*

It's a difficult investigation. All the residents who had been in the small lounge at the time of the attack are suffering from some form of dementia, and pretty advanced they are too. Both a doctor and the manager had been with her when she had painstakingly gone round to each, crouching beside their armchairs, trying to talk to them. Nothing. Gaga, all of them. Joan Walters, the woman Stuart Hibbs claimed hit Mr Turvey, had clapped her hands like a child, singing '*Who's sorry now?*' and blowing kisses.

And now she has a man sitting in front of her who believes he is leading an investigation into the bombing of a pub in the city centre and wants to start making arrests. 'Now. Now. Get the buggers in custody,' he barks. 'If they're Irish, arrest the bastards. Get them down to Edward Road. We'll sort them out there.' Bernadette Ryan, one of the senior carers, sits beside him, stroking his hand, but he's oblivious. He's on the case.

The police officer moves away from him and back to the window, where she takes a breath of cool air, looks out at an empty garden. A fruit tree in blossom. A bench beneath it covered in the stuff. It's ten years since she's had a cigarette, but by God she could do with one now. A long smooth Dunhill and a glass of cold Chardonnay. She turns back to the pea-green room. The man's ranting has ceased. He's looking around. Trying to work out where she's gone, probably. She hopes someone will put a bag over her head before she ever gets to that stage.

There is always a motive, she tells herself, if you know where to look. But that's in the real world. Here it is different. She looks across to the locked medication trolley standing in the corner, thinks about people like Dr Shipman, people like Beverly Allitt, Vanessa George. Cruelty. Madness. Power. Easy to see it all here. Another world. Locked away.

The man at the table has moved on from the IRA and is talking about a cruise. The Ionian sea. The blue blue sea. She won't get any sense out of him. Perhaps she should take Hibbs in for further questioning. Or maybe let things lie, go away for a day or so and think it through. Cyril Turvey has no family, so there'll be no one banging the door down for action. Perhaps she'll have a chat with Dowd, too.

She could probably pin it on Hibbs. Circumstantial, but even so. He's obviously a weirdo, the sketchbook shows that. And he's made threats. All the time, apparently. Fantasy? Possibly. But then she knows serial killers often fantasise about killing, long before their first murder. If he gets away with this one, who knows how many he might do in before they catch up with him again?

There was no wedding ring on Hibbs's finger. She wonders if he has a partner. If not, if he's a loner, that would strengthen the case. After all, why would an old lady, however dippy, suddenly attack Mr Turvey? It didn't make any sense. The manager has assured her that Joan Walters has never displayed any violence or serious aggression, other than poking people with her knitting needles, and the doctor confirmed this. *Sweet* was a word the staff used. *Funny*. Why would a sweet old lady attack Mr Turvey? No motive, nothing a coroner would see in her background as an explanation. Whereas Hibbs. He was the only one there at the time of the killing. Or, at least, he was as good as the only one. And she sees the faces – Shipman, Allitt, George – like a hand of cards before her. Yes, she'll take Hibbs in. See how he holds up to questioning at the station. Get everything on record.

The man at the table turns. 'The sea in Birmingham,' he says. 'It's much deeper than it looks. Not many people know that.' He taps the side of his nose; he is telling her a secret.

Behind Blue Eyes

JACKIE GAY

I'm outside the pub, warming up the car. Four o'clock and it's dark already. Goddamn November it hardly gets light. I only dropped in for a quick half, might have got away with that, but I'm in the doghouse now for sure.

I could just go back in. See myself doing it. The grins and nudges as I give in to a lost weekend. *See, she really is one of us.*

Or I play it safe: go home, apologise, move on from this.

There's someone in the car park. Blundering around, peering into windows. But all I can see are the patterns of ice on mine – feathers, a flock of frozen birds – then the flare of brake lights turns everything red and there's a face plastered to my window, nose squashed sideways, breath melting the ice.

His fist thuds on the roof. 'Wait!' he yells. Wild black curls, cratered face. A hole where his front teeth should be and that's how I place him. Carlo, he has gold ones – showed them to me once, drew his hand from his pocket and opened up his fist. He won't wear them in the Brook. A bad man; some say. Trouble. Terrible for fighting when he was younger. Always being lifted by the cops; picked out in identity parades. But I like the bad boys and they're golden with me. I wind down the window and his head falls in. Smells of tar, whisky. Swirls of ice-breath and exhaust.

'You've got to write it,' he hisses, grabbing my wrist. He's crouched down, squatting, his shoulders half the size of the car.

'K says you can. No one knows what it's like, see.' He moves even closer. I can see his pores; the fringes of his hair gathering frost. 'No one.'

'Sure,' I say. 'Come to one of my classes down the Adult Ed.' Trying to imagine him there – the old dears freaking out but inching closer, wanting to befriend him.

'I can't do that,' he says, and I think he means come to a class so start rattling on about all sorts coming and it's not like school and it doesn't matter about spelling or grammar and he holds up one of his great big hands and says, 'Bab, you don't get it. I *can't*. Never learned. You've got to write it down. For me mam, you see, for her.'

'I don't know . . .' I say, wavering. 'I usually just write my own stuff.'

His gaze is locked on to my face. I feel it pulling at me, look up into the craters, the gaps, the story already written right there on him.

'I can try,' I say.

Me and Kieran, K, my ex, we have a pact. I get the good bits now, the fun, the crazy energy, the magic of 'I remember that'. We meet in the pub, never alone, me pretending I'm casually passing. 'Just dropping in,' I say. 'Gotta keep the old man sweet,' and they like this, the regulars, the turning of tables, the girl who leaves her boyfriend at home, fuming in front of the rugby. We can all be rebels here, in pubworld.

And it's K that's got me into this. Him that was rabbiting on to Carlo – 'she's a writer, you know' – all puffed up with vicarious pride, but no one listens to that stuff here, and I'm grateful for that. But now Carlo's hustling me back into the bar, and I'm acting like I still need persuading while Kieran buys drinks, squeezes my arm, herds us into a quiet corner and for a second I wonder if he's planned all this, but I know it's the urgency on Carlo's face that's brought me back in. Like it's his last chance. Like if he doesn't tell his story now, this minute, then the chance is gone for ever.

I switch off my phone, hand my car keys to Wayne, the barman. Kieran's grin inches wider.

Carlo seems to have stalled now, now that I've said I'll try. We're sat down, drinks in hand. There's even a pause on the jukebox. They're waiting. Begin at the beginning, I think. 'So . . . when were you born?'

He cranks his head. 'Fifty-six,' he says, 'or maybe fifty-seven. Me mother were never too sure . . . but don't you think bad of her now,' he says, lunging suddenly. 'We were too many kids for one woman and each of us a handful. God almighty, that's the truth and he knows for sure . . .'

He crosses his chest, addresses God directly, with a glance upwards like he feels him watching, like he always has.

'I'm not thinking bad of anyone,' I say. 'It's not about that.'

I'm not sure he believes me so I move on fast. 'Where did you grow up?' I say.

'For sure it was the Ladypool Road. You know the Ladypool Road?'

I know the Ladypool Road. A bottleneck crammed with sticky Indian sweet shops and late-night Balti houses. Sari stores and more household goods than you'd think there were households in the city, but they still sell them: buckets and mops and sprays of plastic flowers. A Polish grocer's and some crumbling bedsits. Lots of Africans lately. And, of course, the washed-up druggies who hand over their scripts to the immaculate, expressionless, head-scarfed pharmacist.

'Aye, but it were different then,' he says. 'The blacks hadn't come. Not many, anyhow. Called us niggers, they did; wogs, wops, coons. Anything they frigging liked.' He sees me flinch and leans in hard. 'And don't you raise those educated eyes when I say nigger cos I've been called it all my life. Isn't that how you know me, huh? Isn't that what you've heard?'

It's true; he's Carlo, the black gypsy. 'Smoked Irish' some of the old ones say. Comes in the pub now and again and props up the bar, ticking like a clock, wound up, watching. I remember him singing once. Spring come at last and all us regulars outside, shrugging off coats and turning our pasty arms to the warmth, Carlo's voice vibrating through the flirting sunshine.

Not that I'm a regular any more but I know them all, and when I do drop by they reach out to touch me, buy me drinks; return me to the stragglers' fold. *This is where you belong*, they say. *Forget all the rest, stay here with us. Drink.* Pubworld: an irritant, a stranglehold;

a tender embrace. I was so sure I wanted out, I *am* so sure still, in the sober light of dawn.

But it's goddamn November, it hardly gets light.

'Mother pure Romany and Father straight off the boat from Jamaica and into lodgings on the Ladypool Road,' says Carlo, swigging on his pint, the rhythm coming to him now. 'Six to a room, they were, two to a bed, working shifts on the buses, in the factories. "No Blacks no Irish no Dogs." Me mother with the tinkers passing through and four kids already. When I was born she was back in Ireland – had to leave for shame. But she wouldn't leave her kids and the only other place she knew was the Ladypool Road. Four pikey kids who'd never known walls and me a big black babby no one could hide for nothin'.'

'Anyhow, she went a bit twisted you know, a bit doolally, like. Had another four after me and two were brown from old Singer from the corner, first Paki shop in the whole of Brum, I reckon. I laughed my head off when I heard that band Cornershop cos you can do that now, can't you? Take the mick outta yerself and stand proud of what you are even if it's nowt. But you couldn't back then, specially if you were a black gypo. Old Singer, he hated me, hated all of us who weren't his but me most of all, though Mam would never have bin there if it wornt for me and I told him that once. I said, you'd never have got your shrivelled old dick inside a woman like her if it wornt for me. Think you can pick a rose like me mam and get no thorns?'

He glares as if *I'm* old Singer, then his eyes slide over my notebook. It seems to settle him, the words, the writing it down.

'She were a beauty, see,' he says. 'Proper one hundred per cent beautiful, so as people would stop in the street, traffic an' everything. Feckin lunatic – soz, Ma, but it's true,' he says, crossing himself again, eyes glancing up. 'But every man's eyes follered her down that Ladypool Road, trailing nine of us scrapping and squabbling and kicking off. Have you seen those women with their hair coiling shining black and their eyes Saint Patrick's blue?'

'Yeah!' says Kieran, jumping in. 'We have. Remember, Luce? Up at Appleby Horse Fair?' Kieran's homing in, sitting closer with every drink and he knows how drink and nostalgia mix in me; that magical river of forgetting.

'The tinkers' fair?' says Carlo. 'You went there?' He's frowning now, storms gathering on his forehead. 'Aye, but you can go anywhere, can't you, what with your whiteness and your schoolin' and your ways of the world. Bet there wornt no black men up there, bet they were all feckin micks, the ones who chased me mam out, scorned her soul and twisted it.'

I open my mouth to protest but he's on it now, memories gushing like an undammed river and his eyes warn me *I hope you can take this* and I really hope I can. Write it down true. That might make it worth it; the mess I've walked back into. I can feel Kieran's heat beside me, his experimental touches, nudges, reminding my body of what he can do. His smell; his arm around my waist.

'People used to spit at us you know,' says Carlo. 'From the top of the bus. Aimin' for me but one time me mam jumped in front and this big gob hit her square on the forehead and slid down her nose. She froze solid. Turned straight to ice. She was brittle after that like you could touch her accidental and she'd break into pieces. Us boys went haring off after the bus and tried to get on but the driver shut the door in our faces. We're yelling at him, "That kid gobbed at our mam" – the gobbing kid's face in the window laughing like a loon. And the driver says, "I know who *your* mam is," and I could have killed him, I swear, murdered him savage on the spot, stamped him into the ground.'

He's cracking his knuckles, *crick, crack, crick, crack,* and I stretch out my fingers – some kind of gesture – as I watch his head sink down.

'Take it easy, skin,' says Kieran, moving round to him, placing his hand on his shoulder but Carlo shucks it off.

When he lifts his head it's slow, freeze framed as he comes up for air and turns his neck and looks straight at me with his black coal-burned eyes and says, 'How do you do this? How the feck can you?'

He means the writing and the memories, finding the words you need. The words that will tell it like it was.

I can't, sometimes, I think. That's why I come to the pub where it doesn't matter, where you can ramble on and folk'll listen and shout you a drink. You don't have to sit down and try and get it right.

'Steady, Carlo,' says Kieran. 'She doesn't have to do this. Got plenty of her own stuff to write about, haven't you, kid?' he says, pausing, looking about as if there's something we should clock.

'Never mind living with me,' he adds. And we laugh, because it's funny. Because there's so much in that recognition – that he's a nightmare to live with but a love in the pub; all these guys are and what are the women supposed to do?

'Come on, let's go for a smoke,' says K and we all scramble up and huddle outside, knocking ciggies out of their packets, cupping hands round lighters, blowing off the tension.

The outside world is frozen even harder, snow skittering across the car park, traffic slewing its icy way up the Bristol Road.

'Try a smaller story,' I say, to Carlo. 'That helps, sometimes.'

'The tramps in the shoe shop,' says Kieran. 'Or that dog on the wasteland.'

'Oh man,' says Carlo, as he penalty kicks an imaginary ball.

'Shot!' says Kieran. Carlo takes a bow.

'The look on that shop girl's face. I thought she were gonna puke right over old Robbo's skanky rotting feet when he took off his boots. But the manager, he was old school. "Yes, sir, if it's brogues you want, brogues you shall have. I can recommend the waterproofing spray."'

'What happened?' I say, though I've heard this one before; no matter – you can tell a story two or three times before its notes start to sing.

'A win,' says Carlo, 'on the dogs. And I was taking a drink down for the street guys, the ones who can't do hostels or nuttin and it was comin' on winter and I said d'you want a coat or summat? A blanket? And they all said, boots. That's what we need, so into the nearest shoe shop we go. And we sit down and I say, "Boots for the gentlemen, please." They all get into it, play acting, pretending they do this all the time. And we've took our coats off and the place is reeking, but the manager, he was cool as a morning breeze and sells us socks and insoles and even fixes steel taps on the heels himself so as the boots'd last longer.'

Me and K are laughing, but I'm hiccupping back the tears too. I mean, Carlo, he thinks he's the bad man, but who else would buy boots for the alkies on the street? Who else even *thinks* of them, their freezing feet, their stories, their mam? Carlo's shaking his head, though.

'That's not the story,' he says, and I say, 'It *is*.'

'No it's not,' he snaps, whirling around in the snow, snarling at me, filled with sudden venom. 'You know nothing.'

And here, outside, in the cold, sober air, I can see how swoony I am, making Carlo into some downtrodden Jesus and K into the loveable side of rogue. Carlo's showing the whites of his eyes and in the glare of the security light I can see his veins pulsing round his temples, like his skin's too thin or maybe the anger's too bright sometimes. And Kieran goes, 'Oi! She can just leave, you know,' and Carlo goes, 'No! Sorry, bab. Sorry, love, you've got to write it down.'

And suddenly K cuts straight through to the truth. 'She knows,' he says, looping his arm round Carlo's shoulder, 'about your mam dying. I told her.'

Under his hair, I see Carlo recoil, but he won't meet our eyes. I feel a flash of impatience: *You think you can keep that hidden? She's what this is about, is she not?* Not being kind to tramps or dogs or children, but his mam and the past and the things you can't change.

'I know it's not mine to tell, Carl,' says Kieran. 'It's hard. Jeez, I just have to *think* about our mom and me head's a cloud of bees. And mine's dead and hers is too, you know.'

'Is she?' he says and I nod.

'Have you wrote it down?'

'No.'

'God rest her,' he says, shaking his head and then his whole body, scattering snowflakes which are coming down hard now and even in the midst of this there's a bit of my brain that's concocting excuses – my car got stuck or the roads were blocked – but even as I think it I know I'm crossing a line, right now.

I draw one with the toe of my boot, in front of me, in the snow.

'Why did they think they could scorn her and shun her? Why did they think that's all right?'

None of us knows the answer to this: not Kieran nor Carlo nor me. We head inside, back to our table, peeling the labels off of bottles. I try to imagine the moment it happened, when his dad saw his mam and snagged her blue eyes and the thing that passed between them was stronger than any taboo. Into my head comes a story I've read, of lovers who hide in the Mexican night, their horses are drinking, the stars tilt and sway in the water. 'Me quieres?' she says. 'God, yes,' says he and you know disaster will follow. But it's oh so lovely, just them and the moon. The water, the horses. Sleeping cranes pull beaks from their wingpits to watch. John Grady Cole in *All the Pretty Horses* and her name was Alejandra.

'What was her name?' I say.

He lifts his head, like I've called from afar. 'Bronach,' he says. 'But she called herself Katy from Bronach Catriona. Katy Reilly of the Ladypool Road.'

'He came to fetch her, her father,' he says, 'the one that had named her for sorrow. She hid us; whipped us into silence. "He cast me out like a leper," she said. "I'll die before I go back." But my brothers went with him; my sister, too. They sent money – oh yes – but she sent it back or gave it away on the streets. "Blood money?" she'd cry. "Blood money for free." She was wild by then; her hair all knotted, her bag lady clothes. "Mam!" we'd say. "Keep it," we'd say, our bellies gnawed from the glances and whispers. Then Aimee – one twin – she died that winter, her lungs were never strong. The father took Maura, and Singer took Rav; just me and brown Mary and Mam. No one around but ourselves so empty and that's when it all comes crashing on down; when you've lost your tribe, when it's gone.'

'I tried to make it up,' he says, after a long, fidgety pause. 'Lately, like. She had everything lovely. The priest found me some nice young lasses and they had this rota and all I had to do was give them money. They dressed her proper and combed out her hair and dyed it back black; angels they were, straight from God. One day I went round and the curtains were closed and no one answered the door. But I'd seen her, those blue eyes flashing through the gap in the nets. So I went round the back and walked straight in and they were painting her face. Like a bridesmaid, a pretty young girl. I must have gone darker – God knows what my face said. "She begged us," they said: "*Make me young.*" And I ripped myself clean in half to get out of that house without wailing like a babby, like a big black babby in me mam's arms on the Ladypool Road, not knowing not caring that I wornt supposed to be.'

He's the sad man, now. In this beat-up corner of the pub, just us and the barman attending. His face carved into planes and shadow, his hand to his mouth like the *Weeping Woman*. Picasso: he painted bars like this, faces like this. And though he swears it – '*she* never cried' – her tears are here; they pour down his face.

Kieran puts his hand on Carlo's shoulder and I do, too, and he's shaking and quivering; the quivers spread through us to the drink in the glasses to the rattling windows, vibrating on, to the frozen world outside.

'Carlo,' says Kieran, low down, urgent. 'Listen to me, man. She took your money, right?'

And he nods for ages after that. Nodding and mouthing, 'At least she took my money, at least it wasn't stained.'

The last story comes from K. We're all hanging off the bar now. The evening crowd are in, dancing round the tables, and I'm dancing too, it stops my mind from jumping on. Right now it's disco lights and boogie wonderland and K's lips close to my ear and Carlo's voice in my head. *No one knows what it's like. No one.*

'Remember that day I found you in the road?' says Kieran to Carlo. 'Did I tell you that one, Luce?' he asks me.

'Anyhow, I'm driving round Highgate and the traffic's backed up solid. And when I get to the roundabout I see him, this giant in the road, his hands like plates, like trays in the air, and all the traffic roaring on past him. So I sling my van in the bus stop and go over. "Carlo!" I say. "What the fuck's goin' on?" And Carlo waves his arm at the wasteland in the middle. "She's trapped," he says. So I look over and there's this dog there, pacing and whining and there's no underpass, no bridge, no nothing. Her teats all swollen like she's had pups, but there's no pups with her now. I'm thinking, how did she get there in the first place, but all Carlo's thinking is how to set her free.'

'Been rescuing dogs all me life,' says Carlo, his neck rising from his brick-dusted collar. '"If there's a stray in the city in the whole of the Midlands my boys'll bring the feckin thing home," that's what me mam used to say.'

'It's a good thing,' I say. 'A solid thing, that.' And he kisses me, quickly; if you blinked you'd have missed it.

'I thought he'd never catch her,' says Kieran. 'Could see him chasing her around that wasteland for ever, but you know what? That dog, she crumpled into his arms at one touch. All I had to do was hold up the traffic for a moment and that was it, she was free.'

*

It's morning, and I'm sitting by the canal, still in yesterday's souring clothes. We all sloped off to some party after closing, but I was done in by then, crashed out and woke up cold as a stone in a room of slumbering bodies, clouds of wheezing breath, someone had pissed themselves. I wrapped my scarf round my gagging mouth but made myself stand there, fixed it in my memory. Riffled through my bag for a taxi number, back to the car, drove home, found the photos, quickly out again when I heard him stirring.

I sit by the cut in the frozen grass and skim stones over the layer of ice on the water. It was foggy first thing; there are tufts still snagged in the bushes, in the hollows, but mostly it's cleared and I know that I'll leave him, the man who I live with now. I knew it when I switched off my phone.

A man who doesn't drink or fight or go AWOL, who has a job and a pension; keeps regular hours.

Who I slink around like the dog in the doghouse, flinching from his disapproval.

I finger the photos in my pocket, of me and K at the Appleby Fair. I wish I could show them to Carlo, tell him the story; how we heard of the fair in a pub (where else?) and took off up there, unable to resist the draw of the oldest travellers' gathering in Europe, living like tinkers as we thought we were then, on our boat on the canal, right here where I'm sitting now. The fair was all that they'd said it would be: horses ridden bareback through the twisting turning river; caravans in circles like the wagons of the west. Girls with their jet-black shining hair crowding over trays of gold; betting on the racing on the hedged country roads.

But it's the boys I want to show him. The boys who sold gold at Appleby Fair. They're black boys, see, up north from the Smoke with their swag, their gold for the women with long, dark hair. That's what I want him to know: it can happen now, a generation later. I can picture how I want it to be when I do: we're drunk and laughing and I say, 'Hey, man, you were just ahead of your time.' Now you *can* be proud of what you are even if it's nowt.

And my mind is off, building castles like it always does; a film of Katy Reilly's life, beautiful and tragic; Carlo as the hero, the one who stayed true. Brown Mary as an impassioned campaigner. But this isn't pubworld, this is the canal and Carlo wants it told true, not my made-up, rose-tinted version.

I'm moving the words around in my head, to tell the tale, to find a way to reach out with the long arms of Black Carlo's story. 'No blacks, no Irish,' he said, last night, just before I tipped into sleep. 'So where does that leave me?' he said, and all I could see was the dog, trapped and snarling, then crumbling at the touch of love.

Write one clear shape, one vivid picture, that's how you do it, that's how you start. Katy Reilly turning heads; the dog trapped, pacing the wasteland. His face at my window, hot breath on the frost.

The black gypsies on horses in the river, their bare chests shining as the girls watch from behind blue eyes.

One of my stones chips the ice. A crack spreads outwards; filigree. The moon reflected tilts and sways. Just for a moment, if I hold myself still, I can catch a glimpse, a rare glimpse of what lies beneath.

The Cat It Is That Dies, Perhaps

ANTHONY FERNER

Professor Winegarden put his hand on the knob of the bedroom door and waited, uncertain, in the early morning light. The daily ritual, the barely resolvable daily choice: should he go back in to glimpse his wife again before he left, or not? If he did, would she wake or stay sleeping? Were she to wake, would she be irritable, saying, for example, 'For goodness' sake, Jacob, are you a child?' in that restrained murmur that made it all the more cutting. This would be painful to him. And, at the same time, like a welcome pinprick of feeling in a numb limb. But then again, she might smile sweetly and say, 'Jacob? Is that you, darling? I hope the day goes well.'

If he chose not to go in, to remain in ignorance as to whether she would wake or stay sleeping, he could speculate then on infinite possibilities, and some of these would not carry the heavy charge of loss and diminishment.

And so he waited, a burly man with thinning hair and entropic eyebrows, until some small electrical twitch of muscle led him to turn and tread down the stairs with a sigh. He would phone her later to tell her that he'd been called into the office first thing. He imagined her reproachful voice: 'On a *Saturday*? Is it that important? Are we to be ships in the night, Jacob, ships in the night?' To which he would reply, 'Miriam, darling, there's been a problem.'

A problem with the experimental cat.

Winegarden came out of the drive, glanced at the icy splendour of St Augustine's church, a fixed reference point in an unpredictable world, and turned south. He strode down the tree-lined street, past the detached red-brick houses with their self-important chimneys, dwellings fit for the professoriate. At the lights he crossed over and turned right into Norfolk Road. He could walk to his office in thirty minutes, along streets whose generous sycamores and copper beeches shaded him from the sun and kept him moderately dry on rainy days.

As he crossed the Harborne Road by the Bluecoat School, he recalled, as he often did at this spot, the four years in the nineties when he'd worked in temporary accommodation near by. While their offices were being refurbished, the research group in non-empirical experimentation had been displaced from the third floor of the Poynting Building and had settled into cramped rooms above the Harborne branch of the Cat Protection League, since closed.

Winegarden had been happy above the CPL, though he was never sure whether the location had been chosen deliberately by the hierarchs at the School of Theoretical Physics, or selected at random from a list of vacant properties by an administrator in Estates. Either way, the decision was felicitous. For the one constant in non-empirical experimentation, apart from pencil and paper, was the presence of a cat. Or at least the idea of a cat.

The manager of the Cat Protection League, perhaps as a joke, perhaps because of a problem with vermin, had lent the thought-experimenters a cat, an actual cat, a black cat so sleek it sometimes looked pearlescent grey. It served very well, prompting experimental thoughts and catching small rodents. While the scientists toyed with the former, the cat toyed with the latter and laid them out in neat ranks under Winegarden's desk. When the cat died, another was provided by the CPL. It proved unexpectedly difficult to devise a test to falsify the hypothesis that the idea of a cat (or an actual cat) aided thought experiments. In the absence of which falsification, the convention continued, even after the research group's return to the Poynting Building.

This building, square and red-brick like so much of archetypal Birmingham, was named after John Henry Poynting, an early professor of physics at the university. By some attraction of opposites Winegarden felt a hesitant warmth towards his predecessor. Poynting was an out-and-out empiricist who measured knowable unknowns (as Winegarden put it, before Rumsfeld), rather than the known unknowables of the quantum thought experiments conducted by Winegarden's research group. Poynting, the son of a nonconformist minister, was famous for weighing the earth, and something more definitive and as little open to doubt was hard to imagine. But then JHP also believed in the 'luminiferous ether', and in God – and these signs of human frailty softened Winegarden towards him.

Jacob Winegarden, despite being a non-religious Jew, an agnostic in every vibrating atom (because being agnostic was to admit to the probable impossibility of knowing), often wondered about God and the existence of God. What if God both did and did not exist, or sometimes did and sometimes did not? What if He-She-It was only forced into existence – or blocked from coming into being – by thoughts and intentions in the hearts and minds of men? Or indeed women? John Henry Poynting was, by upbringing, a Unitarian, a denier of the Holy Trinity and hence a believer in the One God. That left too little room for equivocation. At least, thought Winegarden, the Trinity allowed for the idea that God was the Father, and at the same time the Son, and at the same time the Holy Spirit, the *pneuma*, the divine breath that was immanent in this world and in human beings.

'The breath of God.' An idea – thought the professor as he made his way along the wide grass verge of Somerset Road with its lavender-scented air – an idea that was rich in arcane possibilities, even for an agnostic. He had no time for that Dawkins character and his confident atheism. How absurd, Winegarden huffed to himself, to insist that one must not believe in God. How black and white, how categorical. He smiled then and his eyebrows quivered in grim pleasure at the fleeting image of the man Dawkins standing on a street corner with an armful of newspapers, in the fashion of old Socialist Worker stalwarts, crying, '*Militant Atheist! Militant Atheist!*' Things were always more complicated, always.

Except, rarely, when they were not. When all the spins and orbits of the world's electrons aligned in such a way as to make the improbable likely, to make the incredible happen, if only for a moment.

And at such moments, things could become very simple and

you could hold in your hand the key to future states of being. Or non-being. So, in April 1936, Winegarden's grandfather, Heinz-Jozef Weingarten, a complex and cultured man, cut through all the hubbub of the times and recognised an instant of crystalline simplicity. He decided, against the wishes of his family and friends, to abandon all familial ease, pay the Reich flight tax, and leave Germany's murderous certainties for ever. He took with him his heavily lamenting wife and their teenage son Harry (who was to become Jacob's father), and they found refuge first in Belgium and then in England.

The Weingartens lived in London for a few months, changed their name to Winegarden, established contact with the *Yekkes* of Birmingham and, joining the influx of German Jewish refugees in the city, rented a modest apartment in a bulging tenement block off Sherlock Street. By the seventies, Harry was prospering as a seller of rare books and had moved his young wife, Ruth, and Jacob, their only child, out to Edgbaston.

As he hastened now beneath the shady Spanish chestnuts of Pritchatt's Road, Jacob Winegarden remembered that the family had once had a black cat called Ganef. On a Friday night it would jump on the table and rasp away at the salty surface of the smoked salmon, laid out for the Shabbes meal, until his mother chased it away, crying, 'I'm going to kill this *farshtinkener* cat one of these days.' The cat would raise its handsome triangular head and regard her for a moment before taking a final defiant lick and coolly removing itself to a place of safety.

In his teenage years, Jacob would walk with his father the two miles to the Singers Hill Shul on Shabbes and sit in the high-backed pews, marvelling at the splendour of the white and gilt ceiling. Obeying some strong force, his gaze would be drawn from his prayer book to the balcony where the women sat, where it would lock with the magnificent pale grey eyes, pulsing with their own bioluminescence, of the Rosen girl, Miriam. Or so he remembered it. Years later, having moved away, he would meet her again at a party in Moseley and, by a miraculous conjunction of subatomic particles, he would successfully woo her.

For a year or two, around the time of his bar mitzvah, Jacob became part of Rabbi Jonathan's circle of promising young men who would sit and study the Talmud on a Saturday evening in the flickering moments between Shabbes and not-Shabbes, waiting hungrily for the post-dusk meal of chopped liver and haimisha cucumbers and challa, watching the late sun stream through the windows to cast a reddish glow on the bare tables and the concentrated faces of the scholars.

The young Winegarden loved the provisionality of the Talmud, the sense of infinite exegetical shades of meaning, in which the phrases that sang out to him and entranced him were 'on the one hand . . . on the other hand', and 'but then again', and 'perhaps, perhaps'. He relished the intricately twisting logic used to examine contradictions in the scripture. *On the one hand,* some argued, there were no contradictions or redundancies in the Torah and the inability to reconcile them was a failure of logic, not a flaw in the holy book; *on the other hand,* rival scholars would argue equally persuasively, there was redundancy and contradiction because the Torah needed to reflect the redundancy and contradiction and irreconcilability of life. One day, the rabbi drew Jacob aside and asked if he, a young man of intellectual rigour and moral seriousness, would consider going to Gateshead Yeshiva and training for the rabbinate. Jacob shrugged. 'Perhaps you will think about it,' said the rabbi, and Jacob said, 'Yes, perhaps, it's a possibility,' sensing even at that age, with the pale eyes of Miriam Rosen haunting his dreams, that it was time to move on before other possible futures became foreclosed.

Professor Winegarden left the road and walked across the green expanse of the university athletics field, his shoes leaving grey-green imprints in the dewy grass. Looking back, he thought, all this Talmudic exploration had been the intellectual grounding for his life of non-empirical experimentation. But now, as he reached the careful lawns of the campus, in the sharply angled sunlight of this June morning, reveries about the past faded away to be replaced by more immediate concerns.

The dark furrows of his forehead deepened.

Whenever a problem arose with the cat, there were no easy solutions. Over the years, he and his colleagues had resigned themselves to being called the 'thought experiment people' in the popular press, and he had evolved a tight smile of forbearance whenever non-scientists – journalists, for example – asked questions about Schrödinger with that characteristically self-satisfied yet doubtful arching of their eyebrows. 'It's not really about Schrödinger,' Winegarden would say. 'Schrödinger was merely dipping in the common pool of tradition. But yes, a cat, it has to be a cat.' And Winegarden, like a rabbi with a dull student, would patiently explain.

A typical thought experiment, he would say, might be the following: a man on a motorbike (though it could be a woman as it is impossible to be sure through the smoked glass visor of the helmet) – a person on a motorbike – on the Aston expressway, is carrying a black cat in a closed fibreglass pannier. At some point an oncoming lorry bursts across the kibbled surface of the central reservation and forces the motorcyclist head-on into the concrete walls of the expressway. We may assume that the motorcyclist is killed instantly. But what of the cat, in its pannier? Does the fate of the cat depend on the intention of the lorry driver, or is it independent of it? What if the lorry driver (assuming he is a man of faith and not Richard Dawkins, for example) has prayed for the motorcyclist in the infinitesimal, never-ending moment before impact? And what hidden causal mechanisms – if one can talk of causality – at the level of medium-sized objects such as lorries, drivers and motorcycles, or at the subatomic level of muons, gluons and bosons, might influence the fate of the cat? A relaxed but intense focus on this question over days might yield unexpected insights, perhaps by closing off avenues that had seemed open, or by opening others that had seemed closed. But equally, as is the way of these things, it could prove fruitless. And the journalist from the *Birmingham Post*, or wherever, would nod with glazed incomprehension and move on.

As Winegarden swiped his card at the entrance to the Physics Department, beneath the irrefutable mass of the university clock tower, he thought of Miriam, still lying in bed, as she often did until late on Saturday mornings. Or perhaps she was now up and drinking a slow cup of coffee with a slight tremor in her hand. His wife had grown skinny. The light of her grey eyes had dimmed, and the cracked remains of her once plump lips were like beautiful ruins. He tried to focus on the cat, but he could think only of Miriam, and was tormented by not knowing whether he depended more on her than she depended on him, and whether this amounted to love – whatever love might be. He felt a longing, not for her as she now was, but for how, in his memory, she used to be. Miriam was a woman unconcerned by religious faith, or doubt, or uncertainty. She did not care. She had abandoned the orthodoxy of her Jewish upbringing without misgivings, retaining little but her fondness for its Baltic-tinged cuisine. In the early days of their marriage, the marine lubriciousness of schmaltz herring and gefilte fish and smoked salmon would send the two of them scurrying upstairs, giggling like teenagers, to mingle their salty bodily fluids. She would be uncomplicated in her pleasure. But he was more ambivalent. He was wary of orgasm because it represented an unambiguous end point, an undesired certainty, and he would lie back afterwards with profound melancholy and sigh. And Miriam would ask, with the hint of a smile, 'What's wrong, darling? Is it post-coital tristesse?' And he'd nod and say, 'Yes, PCT, perhaps, maybe,' and would wish at such moments, vaguely, that he smoked.

And then the cat clawed its way back into his consciousness. He had been woken before seven o'clock by the ringing of the telephone and, still fuddled with sleep, had lifted the receiver to hear the voice of his colleague, Dr Janet Simpson. Working into the small hours, she'd been disturbed by a terrible screeching. It was coming from his office, from the locked and windowless inner room, the 'inner sanctum' as Winegarden called it, where files were kept, all the intellectual property of twenty-three years of thought experimentation. The screeches were followed by a ferocious knocking accompanied by grunts, and then by feline squeals and yammerings of pain and anger. 'Perhaps,' Simpson had said, 'we – you – have been pushing that animal a bit hard . . .' and she'd let the note of accusation die away into silence.

As he climbed the stairs to the third floor, Winegarden was filled with dread. He entered his office and made his way to the locked door of the inner room. All was quiet. He hesitated, key in hand – he had the only key. He imagined the cat was dead. He imagined the cat was alive, and he imagined the superposition of these two states. He imagined that Janet Simpson was dreaming or mistaken. Or that the cat had slunk through a half-open window and onto the flat roof, to be joined by another. A memory slipped into his mind, unbidden and unwelcome, of the perma-tanned young woman who had lived above the baker's next to the Cat Protection League, with the tattoo at the small of her firm-skinned back, yowling her illicit passion through the partition walls on weekday afternoons when her husband was at work.

Winegarden took a deep breath to ease that beckoning tattoo from his mind. He considered again the lock and the key. Would his unlocking of the door provoke the animal's death? Or its continued existence? At what point would he, a medium-sized object, make contact with the subatomic realm and change the conjunction of particles? Really it should be very simple: this was nothing but a more recondite version of the locked-room mystery in which the murder is committed through some occult mechanism: poisoned gas, hidden passageways, false windows, now-melted icicles, stilettos through floorboards . . . The question is, always, how has whatever has happened *happened*?

The professor puffed out his cheeks and twiddled the key between his fingers. He was disconcerted, naturally, by the prospect of putting an end to uncertainty, of making a choice. Most people, when asked, hated the anxiety of not knowing, but he hated the anxiety of knowing. His heart was beating against the barrel of his chest and he wiped a film of sweat from his brow with his fingertips. This was hard. He could walk away; Janet Simpson had gone home and he was alone. But he thought of Miriam and, for her, he wished to be brave.

He put the key in the lock, turned it and pushed the door into the blackness of the room.

A dark shape snaked against his leg with an accusatory miaow and disappeared along the corridor in a pattering run, its tail lifted high. Winegarden sat down at his desk and held his head in his hands, waiting for his heartbeat to slow. One never knew, one never knew. Until one did. Every decision brought a surfeit of certainty. He rose slowly from the desk, rubbing his chest to ease the lingering tightness there, and walked from the office.

He stepped out of the shadow of the Poynting Building into the full heat of the sun. He glanced upwards at the vertiginous brick of the clock tower. Would a cat falling from the top, he wondered, have a chance of righting itself by the time it hit the ground? And, as it fell, would its whole life flash before it – its playful kittenhood, its furtive cleansing of flesh from herring bones ripped from plastic rubbish sacks, its first brutal matings on a midnight lawn? Winegarden sighed deeply. It was mid-morning now and the sun had dried the dew so that his shoes left no traces on the grass. He walked across the green and onto the athletics field and, feeling all of a sudden drained of energy, he traced a meandering line to Pritchatt's Road and headed north-north-west in the direction of home.

Jacob Winegarden climbs the stairs and stops outside the bedroom. It is eleven o'clock, but Miriam is not drinking coffee at the kitchen table, nor is she bending over the pungent roses in the south-facing flower beds. She is still in bed, asleep, or awake. Now he will be brave. He knows his bravery will change the way atoms and the particles of atoms interact and this will change the behaviour of medium-sized bodies, like wives, for example. He lays his fingers lightly on the door knob. He hesitates, contemplating the back of his hand, the finely wrinkled skin like tide-rippled sand and the pale brown spots and veins glinting in the bluish light filtering into the corridor from the high round window. It is a moment containing all possibilities, of being and not-being. He turns the knob and goes in.

Miriam lies on her back, her chest rising and falling gently. He watches her, listens for the soft, puttering out-breath. She wakes and raises her sleep-sodden head from the pillow and frowns. She mutters, 'Jacob? What sort of time do you call this?' And then immediately she smiles, gives a feline shudder of pleasure and murmurs, 'Well, hello you, hhhmm, where have you been, come back to bed.' The sleepy warmth of her voice saddens him with memories, or the ghostly trace of memories, of their younger selves. Is this love, he wonders, this constant knowing and not knowing? He sighs with a resignation that is almost contentment, and he treads softly, wearily, towards her.

One Little Kiss

ANNIE MURRAY

Two Thermos flasks; red with a white screw-on cup. One for him, tea with sugar; one for her, without.

He stood in the bright kitchen, the sky black outside. It was not yet six, but she was probably awake. She didn't sleep well. Nor, come to that, did he.

Sandwiches, already packed up. Ham with mustard, hers without butter. God knows, he thought, as if that could make any difference. She liked him to make her lunch, said it saved her from temptation. Fruit. A packet of biscuits slipped into his canvas bag.

He braced himself. 'Nora?'

Her room was dark, just the glow from the hall.

'Is it that time already?' she said.

'It is that.'

In that moment, tricked by the darkness, he thought she sounded as she always had, as if the old Nora was lying there, lithe as a pony.

'I've brought your things.' He had wrapped the portion of sandwiches in cling film: plate, Thermos, apple. 'I'll leave them here.' He didn't want the light on. 'You've got your mobile?'

'I have. Where are you today?'

'Elmdon still. I'll ring you later, okay?'

'Okay.'

'You've everything you need? And Mrs T will be in to see

you?' He was early, but there was that sense of wanting to hurry, to be out in the frosty air.

'Sure she will.' There was a moment's hesitation. 'Jim? Will you give me a kiss?'

She hadn't asked for a long time. As he bent to her, a small sound came from him, an absurd chuckle, as if they were harking back to being sixteen – *Just one little kiss, Nora Leahy . . .* His lips came upon her cheek. She smelled wrong these days, as if something in her had curdled. He thought it must be the extra weight she was carrying.

'I'll be home early as I can.'

Driving, empty crisp packets and paperwork on the passenger seat, boots and bag in the footwell, he was still looking out through a frame of ice; turning east, black tower blocks against an apricot sky. He was out, moving, the road clear. He began to whistle.

They had not been in the bungalow long – within the year. There were two bedrooms, one each these days. As the day wore on she would move herself into the living room, to have the television for company.

The house was handy for this job all right, a stone's throw from the A45 out of Birmingham, towards the airport. When he reached the site the lads were gathering, a white van emptying dark figures, Poles mostly, stamping their feet, breath rising in clouds, one or two black faces.

He parked up, keeping his distance for a few moments. In the turned-up light, he longed suddenly for a drink, something harsh and cockle-warming. Not on the job though, never. He was known for it, Jim Monaghan, sober, solid as the rock of St Peter, cheerful with it.

'Morning, lads!' Key locking his car – the central locking had long packed in – he slipped into himself, the man he needed to be for the day. Keys, hard hat, air of command.

'Morning, Mr Monaghan.'

They were respectful: they wanted work, they'd got it, even in a recession. Over a hundred homes to finish, of a size that would have suited a colony of rabbits.

Faces, some with chiselled cheeks, others bull-necked, thickset as steers. Close up now, they were differentiated; the silent one from Lithuania, a broken-nosed Russian and Gregory, the well-spoken Nigerian. Unlocking the gate, Jim remembered that Gregory had been touching the lads for money earlier in the week, had even come sloping into the office, asking if he could spare a tenner. He needed to get to the bottom of that.

'Right –' He turned as he led them in. The usual: hard hats, reflective gear, regulations. Tight ship, that was him – Christ, the injuries he'd seen in his time.

They'd reached a more relaxed stage now. The main structures were in and there were tons of bricks to lay. You still had to watch some lads or there'd be houses with no windows. The cement lorries were already roaring at the gate. 'Go and get started. I'll be out in a few minutes.'

In his cabin he sat at the desk, scattered with curl-edged papers: order sheets, specifications, timesheets. A week-old copy of the *Sun* lay with the front page hanging open over the side of the desk. Who'd left that there? He yawned, stretched both arms above his head for a moment, then poured a cup of tea and ate a couple of digestives. Sounds came to him from the site; the cement lorry disgorging, a shout here and there, Polish. Would she have gone back to sleep? A feeling, for a moment, like his lungs being squeezed.

When he was out, in the fresh and chill, he could scarcely believe in her, there in the house all day, just one room then another, lights on, never feeling the sun on her. There'd been a time they took nice walks; the canal bank wasn't far.

'Mr Monaghan?'

A dark face at the door, between white hat and yellow fluorescent jacket.

'Morning, Gregory!' Jim cursed himself for always being the top-of-the-morning Irishman. It was like a glove he couldn't seem to pull off.

Course, everything was all mixed up these days. Those Romanians who'd worked three years in Dublin and kept saying *Jaysus!* Time was, the sites were full of real Irish lads. You could have a laugh, talk about home, compare watering holes in Dublin or Waterford. Now it was all United Nations stuff, tell me about your country. At least the Poles were Catholics; there was something in common.

'You are not like the other English,' Gregory said to him once. 'You will talk with us.' He did, he spent time with them, his lads.

'I'm not English,' he said. 'I'm Irish.'

This had come as a revelation. 'Ah, Irish. Yes – Mr Monaghan! We have a priest at home . . . Ah!'

The lad waited politely on the step.

'What's up?'

Gregory stepped inside. 'I would like to ask a personal favour.'

'Not money again, is it?' He spoke too sharply, remembering. *Could you please let me have, for example, ten pounds?* He was a spruce feller, must be getting on for thirty. Too well educated for this. There was a story there all right, but Jim didn't want to know what it was. The lad brought out a tenderness in him that he tried to guard himself against.

'No, sir. I have been sending medicine home to my father in Nigeria. He has been sick. But now he has passed away. My sister texted me just moments ago.' The lad looked composed; he usually did, but there was that underlying wretchedness, always.

'Well, I'm sorry to hear that, Gregory.' Jim thought of his own father, dead years ago in Wexford. He'd never seen him again.

'I would like to go home, sir.'

'To Nigeria?' For a dizzy moment Jim thought he was asking him for the fare.

'No, sir; to Coventry.'

Jim told him to clock out, that the lads would have a whip round. Gregory slunk away, the dazzling jacket hanging from his shoulders. God now, he was like a father to them, him two years off sixty! Not that he'd been a father to anyone else, as it turned out. Something to do with her womb being tilted. These days they'd likely get it fixed. He'd never kicked up a fuss about any of it. What was the use of keeping on, upsetting Nora?

'We'll be all right, my sweet, we've got each other.' He'd never wanted to adopt, though she had raised it, more than once.

She wouldn't leave him today. That kiss; he kept thinking of it, on and off, uneasy. To distract himself he pulled the *Sun* towards him. Mother of God, page three, he'd forgotten! Had

Gregory, another good Catholic boy no doubt, seen it on his desk?

He rubbed a hand over his face and sat back. Outside the window a scaffolding pole passed horizontally. Hadn't it all started after her op? Six or seven years ago she'd found the lump. At that time, women in their fifties seemed to be forever happening upon alien presences in their chest area.

Jim sat, besieged by memory, and found himself praying his mobile wouldn't ring. It grew bright outside. He heard scraping sounds on the icy ground.

She had the breast off and recovered well. But sometime after that she'd stopped going out. No more walks. He hadn't noticed at first; he was busy. But he started doing the shopping, braving the Swan Centre on a Saturday, Mrs T helping with bits in the week.

Nora had been getting food from somewhere, though. It showed up on the phone bill; pizza places, anything you could call out for.

'It's all right,' he kept saying, as weight slid over her in layers, like sauce.

After they took the other breast, he went in to see her, but she kept her eyes closed. It felt as though she'd never looked at him again.

He never said anything to upset her, just tried to keep going and stay cheery. 'Will I put Val on for you? How about a game of Canasta?'

Nora had never been confident. What was it they said these days, *self-esteem*. He'd always tried to show he cared about her, prepared her rations now she was watching her weight, came home every night, no hanging about in pubs. Jim and Nora, close-knit, very much in love. Not that there was anything on the love front now, not physically. But that kiss . . .

He forced himself to his feet and opened the door. A smell on the cold air startled him with a loveliness that made his chest tighten again, something sharp, of winter itself. Nora wrapped in a coat and scarf, running on the pebbled strand, screaming as waves pounded her boots. Those blue eyes. County Wexford, January 1967.

'Pawel!' he shouted. 'Get on!'

By afternoon the sunshine had defrosted the day, though breath still swirled visible. An endless exhalation of traffic came from the M42. Jim went about his work, solid, grey haired, instructing, encouraging. When they knocked off for lunch he ate his sandwiches with them.

It grew dark early. Time to pack up, lads! The vans came, took them all in again. Jim closed up, steered back along the packed A45. Everything was locked into concrete in this city, he thought. You couldn't move a hand or foot for it. Just get home, shop pie out of the fridge, spuds and greens (salad for her, perhaps the odd potato). TV and a cup of tea, biscuits on the saucer, a couple of cans for him, sitting beside her on the sofa, her thigh pressing against his.

He braked outside and collected up his bag and flask, locking the car. Only walking up the path, did he notice. There was a blood rush of joy, of searing loss, both.

No lights were on in the house. The curtains hung open and there was a bereft feel to it. When he reached the front door it was ajar, just enough to let in the cold air.

It gave easily as he pushed it. The house felt strange to him, almost as if he had wandered into a neighbour's by mistake.

'Nora?'

A small, animal noise came from the front room and his blood moved faster. In the gloom he found her on the sofa, where she always was. Awake now, stretching, she raised her head.

'You're back already!' she said, seeming shamed. 'I must have dozed off.'

'The front was open. I thought –' He stood with an arm outstretched. What had he thought? That kiss, a parting?

'Was it? God now, anyone could've walked in. Mrs T must've not caught the latch.'

He looked down at her, his heart still capering. 'Oh,' he said. It was that pulse of joyful release he would recall, guiltily, for years. 'Yes, I see.'

Brothers
LUKE BROWN

I reached the Wellington first. It's a blokey, real-ale pub in the centre of Birmingham – Tony and I had stopped meeting in bars now we didn't know which ones were cool any more. I hoped that if we continued to meet in places as drab as this, we could settle into a new kind of friendship, one that wouldn't revolve around longing for women we had not yet met. I ordered a pint of Dogbotherer and took a deep breath, preparing to enjoy it. But this was the kind of place you really felt the presence of the smoking ban.

Tony arrived. Tony is a year younger than me but looks younger; he's got a boyish face, prettier than mine. He's prone to trendiness, susceptible to the ridiculous. We go for different types of girls but there's a point where they cross over.

'What the fuck have you done to your hair?' I asked as he sat down.

'Don't ask,' he said. Tony is an actor.

'You look ridiculous.'

He moved his very long fringe to one side. It fell back down the middle of his face. 'I didn't have time to do my quiff this morning.'

'Is that what it is? Well, it's good to see you anyway.'

'Looking ridiculous.' Tony scanned the bar. He looked back at me with a brief grimace. I knew what it meant but made myself not react, not say, *I know*.

'I've got a better idea than staying here,' he said. He handed me a flyer. It advertised 'an opportunity for Birmingham's creatives to network, socialise and grasp opportunities'.

'Not the fucking creative-as-a-noun brigade. I can't stand –'

'I've heard this rant from you more than fifteen times. It was funny once. Here's the important information,' he said, pointing to *drinks and canapés.*

'I suppose a free drink wouldn't hurt.'

'Free booze and creative women.'

He mentioned the women eagerly. I was surprised; he was breaking our unwritten rule.

'Creative?' I asked. 'You know you're using the word creative as an adjective there? How so? Liars?'

'Fantasists.' Tony nodded. 'In ra-ra skirts.'

'I think ra-ra skirts were a few years ago, mate.'

'You'll fit right in,' he said.

I first met Tony when we used to work in a bar together, and for a couple of years we were inseparable. We saw much less of each other these days. There'd been no fall-out and it wasn't because we both had proper jobs now. We'd found girlfriends, that's all – and it turned out our friendship had consisted entirely, quite beautifully, of nights out with each other chasing women – that and eating fried breakfasts together the next morning to discuss the unusual features of wherever we'd slept. Sometimes it had been the same bed, we were that close. I never felt awkward on those mornings and neither did he; we liked to see ourselves as different to other men, adventurers. We were both the only men in our families. No one had taught us how to play football. We didn't lose sleep over boyfriends with unfaithful girlfriends. Or, more enjoyably, we did. I had looked up to Tony then, despite him being younger than me. I watched the way he talked to women and copied his courage.

Things were different now. We were monogamous and we had nothing to say to each other. We weren't even sure if we liked each other. We were determined to be good and so we just didn't know what to do with ourselves. And it wasn't only us – whenever we met for a drink, wherever we went, when we looked around it was clear that no one else was enjoying themselves either. We'd exiled ourselves from all the fun in the world, and it was only when we were together that we noticed this. And so we moved after each drink, looking for the next place, the new bar where the young women with daring haircuts, short skirts and high heels hung out. We never admitted that that was what we were doing, that that was what we were looking for. What we said we wanted was 'atmosphere', but what we needed was to look at women and imagine the underwear beneath their dresses – underwear we might have seen on the racks while we waited by changing rooms for our girlfriends. The world was awash with underwear, with lacy bras and glossy knickers with bows on. Thousands of these items were manufactured every minute. Everywhere women were gift-wrapped. All these unseen presents couldn't help but intrigue us – and repel us. We were as scared of the possibility of pulling these women as we were of not being able to.

We had the best of intentions. We were trying hard at love. I was going out with a girl from my home town, a girl I'd been heartbreakingly obsessed with from the age of thirteen, an age when she was so far out of my league as to be playing a different sport altogether. Which, of course, she was – with the boys up to five years older than her, the boys who we'd become to the girls in the years below us. She'd tell me all about them in history lessons. Back then, I could barely say her name without feeling like I was coming up on an E (although, unlike her, I wasn't precocious enough then to describe the feeling in those terms), and even now her name could invoke the same physical response. Some men are never free of those days, I think, when what we desired was everything and unattainable. We still feel we have so much to make up for.

I'd bumped into Claire in a bar two years before, when she'd been visiting a friend in Birmingham. She was soppier than she'd been at school – she was a trainee vet now – and made such a fuss of the coincidence that I was able to be calm and droll, quietly, endearingly masculine. She was amazed it was me and I was amazed that she didn't exert the same power on me, that she wasn't her – despite the fact that I thought she was still the most beautiful woman I'd ever seen. In bed with her, feeling the warmth of her pale legs behind mine, saying her name quietly in my head – *Claire Greasdale,* her glorious, ugly name – I felt myself on the verge of tears. I'd watch her dress in the morning, each casual gesture a miracle she was unaware of. We were completely unsuited and fought constantly. Our outlooks on life couldn't have been better designed to piss each other off. But, by dint of imagination, and sentimentality, we stayed together. We loved each other. We always would.

Tony had met Lucia, a Spanish girl who was studying fine art at Margaret Street. She was talented and friendly, with a dry sense of humour – perfectly aware of how silly Tony and I were – for an art girl she was surprisingly together. Especially given her name; we'd developed a theory that all Lucys were unhinged. We suspected it was because they were the daughters of hippies who had valued 'creativity' above industry, who thought we should all live in the Sky with Diamonds. And, accordingly, it was in the 'creative sector' that you found Lucys. We'd both been out with a few, including the same three – we were the kind of guys who found it easy to meet Lucys. When I mentioned to Tony that Lucia is Spanish for Lucy, he gave me a hard look, a shocked look, and said, 'I don't speak Spanish.' He was serious about her, and I didn't blame him. We weren't so shallow that we didn't notice when we met someone exceptional.

The creative networking 'opportunity' was being held in a bar on Colmore Row where the lawyers and accountants and other realists went on Friday nights. There used to be a stock-exchange theme where drink prices went up and down depending on how frequently people bought them. We always bought the cheapest, the least popular. It was a bracing and unpredictable way to get drunk. It was years since I'd last been.

When we arrived we were given poker chips – to exchange for drinks at the bar or to use later, 'at the casino'.

'I hadn't realised it was going to be *this* much fun,' drawled Tony. 'Better than a plastic cup of warm white wine, though.'

In our heyday, we'd been regulars at Birmingham's private views, its press nights, its opening performances. They'd pretty much let anyone in. We'd turn up whether we were invited or not – we knew how to read a programme for the promise of a piss-up.

A tall blonde in hot pants walked past. We looked at her and pretended we hadn't noticed.

'Yes,' said Tony, though I hadn't asked him a question.

People began to introduce themselves. We stopped being cynical and talked to them. About making dieting programmes, cosmetic surgery programmes, programmes about extraordinary weather, home décor and bizarre pets. Sitcom/alcopop synergies. Micro-blogging, virals and flash-mobbing. Leveraging, amplifying, monetising the content. We nodded and enquired politely about all these things. We were much nicer than we'd have ourselves believe; it was only when we were on our own together that we were such iconoclasts. I was a journalist for a dying regional newspaper. He was a sporadically employed actor. We relied on each other to invent each other's personalities, and we were out of practice. We were separated for about half an hour before Tony came towards me with two full pints.

'Fuck me,' he muttered, 'let's down these.'

Ten seconds later we were two-thirds of our way down when a friendly looking girl approached us. She had on a denim skirt, leather boots and a glimmery silver top.

'Are you two brothers?' she asked.

'No, we're lovers,' I said.

'That's brilliant!' She beamed, bouncing right back.

'He beats me,' said Tony, downbeat. She looked concerned for a second. 'But only when I want him to!' he reassured her, patting her arm.

We liked to be creative with what we told women, and pretending to be gay wasn't as counter-productive to our aims as you might think: we'd met women just as kinky as we were. There were many more of them still out there, all so fascinating. I felt very sad for myself suddenly. There were so many stories I would never know or tell.

'What do you do?' she asked.

'Isn't that a bit of a forward question?' I asked, smiling.

'I didn't mean that, I meant –'

'We know what you –' But now I was turning to Tony to see if he'd noticed what I had, for she had astonishingly prominent nipples pressing through her top in a way that couldn't possibly be accidental. I had the luck to catch his expression as he saw them – he stiffened and raised himself up a couple of inches, as if he was trying to infiltrate her top by method-acting.

'We're only joking,' I said, trying to concentrate on her face and failing. 'I'm a soundtrack composer; he's a choreographer. What about you?'

She was in radio. Heart 105.7FM, an eighties commercial music station. She told me she worked as a producer. Her tight top was embossed with braless nipples. She wasn't at all self-conscious about them. I had no idea what she was saying. Tony had gone to get us another drink, shaking his head in bewilderment.

It was an act, of course, for both of us, that we'd been shattered by this young woman's protruding nipples. They were only nipples and it is very easy to see nipples if you want to see nipples, whether you have a girlfriend or not. We wanted to understand why these nipples were so nipple-like, so unrestrained, and we were not allowed to. It was for *our* restraint that we expected sympathy. And we did expect it, even though we knew no one would give it to us. Hunger for catastrophe is still hunger, and as physical. Or so we wanted to believe. And when I say we, I mean me. It explained why I still made efforts to see Tony, to hide behind the plural from what *I* wanted to do. And what I had done – or, as I liked to think, *nearly done* – two weeks ago with Lucia.

I found myself outside with Nipples, offering her a Marlboro Light. She was wearing the kind of tights with a criss-cross diamond pattern on them, a thick, spongy type, a cosy winter tight. I could imagine their crackle, their snap and their pop.

'You seem to be staring at my legs,' she said.

I looked up into both barrels and quickly looked back down at her legs. 'Oh look, sorry, it's just – I've got to say this . . . I can't help noticing . . .'

'What?'

'That you . . .'

'What?' she said, and now she began to blush and I couldn't say what I'd been planning to say.

'What?' she asked again.

'Oh, don't worry, it's nothing.'

She reached forward then and touched my hand, looking up at me. 'It's all right,' she said. 'You don't need to be so shy.'

I looked down into her hazel eyes, and beyond, everything perfectly paired.

'But – you must have a boyfriend,' I said.

'No,' she said, 'I just dumped him.'

'It's probably not the right time then to . . .'

'To what?'

'To . . . I don't know. Poor guy, is what I'm thinking. Are you sure you're doing the right thing? Why did you –'

'He was cheating on me.'

'Oh.'

'With one of my friends.'

'*Oh.*'

'It's all right. It's fine, tonight. You know, you're much shyer than you first seem. It's sweet.' She finished her cigarette and threw it on the floor. 'I'm going back in, okay? Just don't leave without saying goodbye.' At that she turned away from me and I began to breathe slightly easier. She passed Tony coming out as she went in, and I watched his eyes flash downwards, his lip make a theatrically pained O for my benefit.

'I've just met a girl who freelances for the Adult Channel,' he said, excitedly.

'In what way?' I asked.

'Oh, I didn't ask that,' he said. 'Wouldn't you rather imagine?'

Although Tony and I had always come as a pair, we'd managed to achieve very different reputations. I was the nicer of the two, the more honest, straightforward, better read; Tony was duplicitous, more depraved, the better fuck. We played up to our roles. Tony was joyfully uninhibited about his depravity. Visitors to his room would see his riding crop proudly hanging from the wall, and if they stuck around they'd likely get a tour of his collection of women's knickers, dating from as far back as a pre-Labour government, or through the contents of his hard drive. His taste there was straightforward: he liked women with big tits who wouldn't stop saying how nasty they were; in other words, he liked watching pornography, which, take it or leave it, was what most pornography seemed to be.

I hated that kind of pornography, which isn't the same as never watching that kind of pornography. But I do think I would prefer it if they'd tell me how nice they were instead. Tony was more honest about his appetites than me. And so, because of my shyness and my niche tastes, I was cast as the sensitive one, Tony as the sexual decadent. I'd always thought we both got what we wanted out of this: Tony got the notoriety and the outrageous girls, the piercings and the hot pants and the sex toys; I played the straight man and got fashion designers with luxuriant fringes and anthologies of Metaphysical Poets left ostentatiously on their bedside tables. Until my teenage fantasy and trainee vet.

But it turned out I'd been underestimating Tony.

We were quite drunk now, buying our own drinks since all the free ones had run out. Half the crowd had dispersed – though Nipples was still in the building – and I was hiding out with Tony in a far corner of the bar. He'd become maudlin, all of a sudden.

'We never really talk, you and I, do we?' he said.

'Talking,' I said, with a dismissive wave of the hand. 'Anyway, we do talk.'

'Only about girls. And now we don't know any.'

'What about Lucia?'

'That doesn't count, we can't *talk* about her.'

Two weeks ago, I'd run into Lucia in the Bull's Head. Tony wasn't there. My girlfriend wasn't there. As far as I'm concerned, I wasn't there either. It's easy to end up in a toilet together, doing coke. You can do things in a split second that aren't either of you, that shouldn't make any difference. It's stupid all the things you can't do, when in fact you can. Why not? We both agreed. And hardly anything happened, certainly nothing momentous.

'What's up, mate?' I asked.

'Oh, nothing,' he said, as though changing his mind. 'Lucia can be quite hard work, you know. She's not very happy.'

Lucia is one of those girls you see in bars on Friday nights, bright eyed and magnetic, talking about music and art, kissing hellos, knowing everyone, where three different parties are, who's got the best drugs, everything that seems to be necessary at that moment. Because you don't see them on the other days, it's easy to think they're always like that.

'Look, mate,' he was saying, confidential again. 'You really can't tell anyone what I'm saying here, okay?'

I agreed.

'The thing is,' he went on, 'it's embarrassing. You really can't tell anyone. A couple of nights ago she suddenly confesses that she got off with another guy when I was away on tour. She *had* to tell me, she said. We need to talk about what it *means*. What it fucking means! *We* need to talk about what it fucking *means*!'

'God,' I said, appalled. 'Has she gone mad? Who was it? Where did it happen?'

'Moseley. The Bull's Head. Which makes it even worse. Anyone could have seen. People I have to face every week. And she won't tell me who it is. I mean, she says she didn't even know him. As if there's anyone in Moseley she doesn't know. She didn't even want to tell me where it had happened. Did *you* see her?'

'No. No! But was it just a kiss?'

'A kiss and – I don't know what to believe.'

'Not sex?'

'Not sex. So she says.'

'Well – it could be worse. It's easy to kiss someone when you're drunk.'

'But there's an agreement not to! I never have.'

'Of course,' I said. 'But, I mean, really? You're saying you've never even . . .?'

'No.'

'Seriously? Just a little bit?'

'No!'

'You remember when you told me that the secret to lying and getting away with it is to lie to everyone, even your best friend, even your brother?'

'You don't have a brother. And I'm telling the truth. You know I'm telling the truth. You've been out with me this last year. How much fun have we had?'

I understood his righteousness. We had not been enjoying ourselves. I believed what he was saying. But this made me wonder if he was lying.

'What are you going to do?' I asked.

'I don't know,' he said. 'I know her too well. I know how depressed she is. She does this stuff to punish herself. She thinks that . . .'

I wasn't listening any more. Behind him I could see Nipples

looking over at me. She gave a little wave. What else wasn't she wearing? I forced myself to concentrate again on what Tony was saying. It wasn't him who I used to emulate; it was the character I'd made up for him. He was nothing like that man. He was sensitive and faithful, vulnerable. Everything we'd decided was feminine and throwaway. Everything we had been for each other, that we missed the most.

I loved him.

Nipples began to walk over.

'You might feel better if you get your own back a bit,' I said. 'You don't need to see it as revenge. I mean, is it natural to be monogamous? We're all trying hard, isn't that enough?'

He looked up at me, his head still down, peering over the top of imaginary spectacles. It was an inquisitive look. He knew it was bad advice but was deciding if he might choose to act on it. I didn't know if it was easier to be the one wronged, to only have to focus on your own pain and not the guilt of inflicting pain on others. All the expectations went the other way.

'Hello, lovers,' she sang as she approached our table.

I left them talking and slipped out the front for a cigarette. Now that Nipples had put her denim jacket back on, looking in her direction was no longer like staring into the sun. Tony was talking more easily to her without the razzle-dazzle. She seemed to have forgotten our conversation outside – which I wanted to be grateful for – but as Tony's hand casually, accidentally, landed on her knee, I began to think I had done him a disservice.

For a second I thought about going back in there, pulling him out and getting him in a taxi (I'd known as I was walking to the door that the cigarette was my cover to escape). I looked in at them through the window. She had her head cocked. He was speaking earnestly. I didn't belong with them. I wasn't sure if I belonged anywhere. My girlfriend was too good for me and I had an awful feeling that, if I spoke to her that night, I would manage to convince her of this. There was still time to make it to the bar in Moseley, ring a half-gram in, abandon choice for an hour or two. I might see Lucia and get chance to remind her that our coordinated whim hadn't actually happened. And, momentarily, I wondered if I'd made it all up. It was the kind of thing I probably thought I was supposed to do. I'd just been in character, the character Tony and I had made up together. I'd been doing it a long time, but it was fine, because it wasn't really me. It wasn't even half of me. I looked through the window again; Nipples had her hand on Tony's shoulder, leaning in and telling him something, insisting. He was nodding his head. I was struck by how convincing he was, how much I believed in him. And then I felt silly, standing outside, pretending to a great wealth of emotion I had no right to. Who did I think I was? A black cab approached with its light on, dark and glossy Topshop satin. I felt something clench within me and held out my hand.

Adult Beginners
GAYNOR ARNOLD

He didn't have anything of hers. Not a handkerchief, or a broken necklace, or a chewed Biro. Nothing, in fact, that she had ever touched. People had gone to the flat afterwards, he knew that. They'd laid hands on all the things that had belonged to her. They'd sifted through the rancid contents of her kitchen drawers, put their gloved hands into mangled piles of unwashed clothes, thrown out furry hairbrushes, mouldy handbags and worn-down shoes. Everything had been gone over and examined in detail. But no one had asked him if he wanted anything to keep. After all, who would want the remains of last week's dinners? Or a couple of soiled mattresses and three threadbare blankets? Or the piles of unpaid bills under sticky, tea-stained mugs? Certainly not a three-year-old child. He was to be rescued from all that, put into clean pyjamas and given three square meals a day. He was to forget his old life for ever.

He watches Lorraine as she stands at the sink scraping the burned bits off a slice of toast, then buttering it with the breadknife. 'Why don't you go back there, then?' she says, turning to him with her usual brilliant smile.

It's simple to her, he thinks: confront the past, or forget it. She's sympathetic up to a point, but she doesn't believe in too much introspection. She'll let him spend an hour or so at the kitchen table trawling back over court reports and newspaper cuttings; she'll even tolerate him going to 'research' at the library on a Saturday, when she'd rather they were in front of the telly watching *Gladiators*. But if she suspects he's getting *morbid*, she'll sneak up and kiss him, tickling him in his armpits to make him smile, draw him back into the here-and-now, where she seems to live with such contentment. He'll smile back, kiss her, try to be cheerful. But he can't let it go. He's convinced that one day he'll find some clue that will help him understand it all.

There'd been a photograph, once. Someone must have discovered it in an abandoned wallet or taken it from her mantelpiece, because it had been smudgily reproduced in a cutting from the *Evening Mail*, its 'Tragedy of Unknown Woman' headline next to an upbeat advert for Christmas bargains. He'd been about eight when he first saw it, stuck into the Miscellaneous section of his case-file with yellowing sellotape. He'd bent over it excitedly, hopes high. But it was hardly a face; just a black and white pattern on the page. And however hard he'd concentrated, squinting at it from all angles, it remained a defiant blur. Maybe the camera had moved – or maybe she had turned to say something, and in that split second had rendered herself unrecognisable for ever. Or maybe the photo had been poorly copied. There was no way of knowing; the original had gone missing. At least three social workers had said how sorry they were. They'd looked everywhere, they said (Sonia had spent hours on it), but it must have got lost in the panic of those first few days. And the police and the newspaper were admitting nothing. Not after all this time, they said, when Sonia had phoned them: *you must be joking*.

All through his childhood, he'd kept asking. Whenever they'd talked about his 'wishes' in one of those meetings packed with people he didn't know, he'd come back to the same thing, like a broken record. The photo, he'd said. He wanted the one she'd kept, the one she'd touched, the one that had belonged to her. He was convinced that, once it came into his possession, she would be real to him at last. They'd all sighed, coughed a little, turned pages, said they understood how he felt but they had really done all they could. The last time he brought it up, the man with the high-domed head and drooping moustache had closed the file impatiently and said,

'You must try not to obsess about it, Lee.' When he'd pushed back his chair and run out, saying that they were all wankers – that they didn't care; that nobody cared – there'd been an embarrassed silence.

Then Sonia had gone after him, and guided him down a long corridor. 'Look, Lee,' she'd said, opening a door. 'Just see what we mean.'

And there in front of him was shelf upon shelf of cardboard folders. Some beige, some green, and some an indeterminate buff colour, but all bulging and straining with details of children's lives. If the photo *had* ever been in the office, Sonia said, it might have got slipped into any one of these folders. It might even have got moved to another room just like this, in Moseley or Acocks Green or, well, anywhere. It might have been archived; lying in a giant shed, never to be disturbed. 'It's gone, love.' Sonia had put her arm around him. 'I'm very sorry, but you have to accept that it's gone.'

He hadn't accepted it, though. His stubbornness on the subject had defeated several child psychologists, and a couple of adult psychiatrists. In the end, they'd thrown up their hands and said it was up to him – he could let the past define him, or he could move forward, refuse to be a victim. He'd come away from the last session holding his grudge even closer against his heart. He was entitled to victimhood, he felt. Everything he'd ever had – everything he'd ever loved – had sooner or later been taken away. Like Marcia with her rolling chuckle, who'd pulled him on her lap when he was ten and said: *I too old for dis now, son. I on my way to the Lord.* He'd said she was not too old at all and had held on to the banisters when they came to take him away. Laughing Dave Hadley was his social worker then, and Lee had kicked him in the shins and bitten his fingers so hard that Dave had let him go. *Fuc–rying out loud!*

And then there was Bill 'n' Brenda who'd met him at their front door with big smiles and bigger promises, but who asked for him to go after six months (*we don't know what it is, but he won't fit in with our kids*). Dave had tried to make them understand, sat in their comfy lounge with endless cups of tea – but they kept on about being fair to their own children and *to be honest he needs more than we can give.*

So Dave had taken him to Audrey, who thought he was cute

but who was committed to a family of three at the end of the month, so couldn't keep him.

And then there was Pat - nice, gentle, grey-haired Pat - who gave him grown-up books, let him use her Amstrad and took him to the Lickeys at weekends to walk her Jack Russell. Once, when they'd glimpsed the reservoir glinting below, she'd asked him if he remembered anything about the actual event. *Only water*, he'd said, turning quickly away. But one day he'd come home from school to find her lying motionless on the kitchen floor with a strange sagging to her mouth and peeled potatoes spilled everywhere. She'd held his hand and said something that sounded like 'sorry'. When Sonia drove him to the Cedars that night, she said he was not to blame: *It's not your fault, Lee. It's just bad luck.*

But it felt like his fault. As if *he* was the Bad Luck. As if there was something about him that infected people. That he did less damage if he kept himself to himself. He became more inward, more silent. Refused to be fostered, refused to have friends. Most of the kids in the Cedars thought he was weird anyway, with his interest in software and 'programming'; his lack of interest in the latest type of trainer. He spent all his time in his room with monitors and keyboards, and got a reputation for being a loner. *Weirdo wanker!* they'd cry, kicking his door as they raced down the corridor.

When they closed the Cedars, Stella with the cornrow hair came and sat on his bed and said a new place had been found for him. *In Dudley*, she said, smiling broadly, as if it were the best place in the world. He said he didn't want to go to Dudley, and he didn't want another foster mother, thank you. But Stella held his hand and said, 'Mrs Deans won't be your mom, Lee. It's more like lodgings. Just give her a try.' And to his surprise, Mrs Deans (she never said *call me Eileen*) suited him exactly. She liked to lead her own life and didn't mind if he spent all day in his room as long as he turned up to meals and held his knife and fork in the right way. She was very particular about her carpets, though, and he learned to take off his shoes the instant he came home, balancing on one leg in the little glass-paned porch, trying not to let his rucksack touch the floor. In return she kept his clothes - even his underwear - beautifully ironed.

On his eighteenth birthday he'd kitted out his flat with Pauline from Aftercare, choosing the latest computer from Dixons and a purpose-built desk; thinking his life had taken a turn for the better. But after a year or two, he began to wish that Laughing Dave was back to have a matey chat with, to advise him on how to make friends, how to attract a girl. He'd done what he could – invested in some tight-fitting jeans and had his hair cut by a proper barber so it didn't mass about his face like dark candyfloss. After work he'd stand at the saloon bar alongside the others from Technical Support (weight on elbows, bum out), melding his Brummie accent into a Black Country one, trying desperately to fit in. But none of this seemed to make any difference. Even when the Baggies scored and everyone in the pub rose and embraced one another in delirium, he felt out of place.

In the end, he decided, it wasn't the accent, or the clothes, or the way he stood. It was him. Everyone could detect the sour smell of his unhappiness and they kept their distance accordingly. So, he'd never understood how Lorraine hadn't noticed it. Even now, when he woke in the mornings and heard the soft sound of her breathing, he couldn't believe that she was still with him – still, apparently, happy. At least, he assumed she was happy. Lorraine never seemed to have bad days, even bad moments, so it was hard to tell. He made the most of every limber movement of her body, the way she shimmied across the carpet, humming and drinking coffee, because he knew that one day she'd meet a nice cheerful man at the swimming pool and the game would be up. She'd withdraw her lovely long arms from his neck and give him a sad kiss and tell him it was over.

She said he was paranoid – *You're off your head, you are* – and that he was the only bloke she'd ever really fancied. But all the same, he couldn't help wondering about all the fit young men who powered up and down the pool every day in front of her. He'd been tempted to go back, eye up the opposition. But he couldn't face the water.

It had taken him all his will power that first time. He'd kept telling himself that he wasn't a kid any more; that it was ridiculous for a grown man to be afraid to cross a bridge or walk along the canal, let alone take a holiday by the sea. But at the first sight of the swimming bath, with its shimmering wiggly lines and hypnotic depths, he'd turned tail and run. He'd been so terrified he'd hardly noticed the attractive black woman with the clipboard and whistle, standing with the motley group of adult beginners, eyebrows raised. Back in the changing rooms he'd curled up on the narrow wooden bench in the cubicle, panting and gasping for a full twenty minutes before he could summon the strength to get dressed.

But she had been waiting for him in reception, her orange T-shirt glowing gaudily, the word 'Staff' in letters two inches high. She'd put her hand on his arm – *Okay, now?* – and he'd felt the connection straight away. And when he murmured that he had a phobia about deep water, she smiled and said she thought it was something like that, and suggested taking him to a café round the corner so he could get himself together. It was on her way home, she said. *And I got nothing else to do.*

Over coffee, he'd found himself making jokes about sitting in bathtubs and being afraid of the rubber ducks. And she'd laughed. *Laughed.* And then she'd squeezed his hands in a way even Sonia hadn't. And suddenly it had all poured out of him: his mother, the water, everything he knew or didn't know. He was conscious of going on for hours. 'Sorry,' he said. Then, 'Didn't mean to bore you.'

'You didn't,' she said. 'I knew I was right about you. I could tell straight away.' Her eyes twinkled. 'And I've got plenty of bath toys at home. If you want, you could try them out.'

He'd had visions of her putting him into the bathtub, naked except for an array of rubber ducks. And then coming in, dark and slippery beside him. Only that couldn't be what she meant. Except she'd stroked her tapered forefinger along his, sending electric pulses along his skin before saying: 'Shall we give it a go?'

His answer came out before he realised it, before he could think about it, before he could find a reason why it was out of the question. 'Okay,' he found himself saying. 'Why not?'

Everything had been dreamlike after that. She'd walked him to her battered Fiat and placed him in the front seat as carefully as if he were a sleeping child. He didn't try to speak. His whole body seemed to have collapsed into a boneless heap, and he felt unaccountably tired. As the car started, he drifted off into a world of bright lights and darkness; bright lights again, then darkness. And the sound of her radio playing Heart FM, the repeated jingle, over and over: *Hea-art FM!* The car rattled and revved, the heater blatted out too much heat, but he felt the most astonishing sense of contentment. He would have been happy to stay tucked up in that little car for ever, with all thoughts and decisions banished and Lorraine's smiling face always beside him. But then there was the ratchet of the handbrake as the sound of the engine died away.

'Come on, Sleeping Beauty,' she'd said. 'I'll run the taps.'

He looks at her now; the easy, lithe way she leans against the worktop, how her plucked eyebrows arch so perfectly as she says, 'Why not go back and take a look? I mean, you've tried almost everything else.'

'I suppose I could.' He hasn't seen the reservoir for years. Even when he'd lived in Northfield, it had been easy to avoid. It was at the very edge of the city, jutting out into the countryside – no shops, no bus routes. Just water.

'I'll come with you, shall I?' She comes close, puts her arms round his neck. Her breath smells of coffee and burned toast.

It's tempting to take her with him, but he can't trust himself not to run away and disgrace himself. 'No, bab, I'll be better on me own.'

'Sure?' She frowns. 'I could take the day off. We could make a little holiday of it.'

'Holiday?' He laughs, touched by her attempt to brighten the whole thing. 'What, in Brummagem-by-the-Sea?'

'I dunno why not, bab. I hear they've spruced it up no end. Lots of nice places down by the canals where you can have a drink.' She stops, winces. 'Except that wouldn't appeal, would it? Sorry – I'm not thinking.'

'It's okay. And thanks for the offer. But this is something I got to do for myself.'

It's late afternoon when he gets to the ruler-straight road that runs along the top of the dam, its high wall hiding the terror beyond. He recognises the little turret in the middle. Some boys once dragged him here, tried to make him scale the wall, pushing him up on their shoulders: *What can you see?* He'd kicked out wildly, knocked them to the ground. They'd turned up later with bleeding noses at Marcia's front door, but she'd sent them away: *This boy nearly drown, you know. You want I tell the policeman you nearly do it again?*

Some instinct takes him unerringly through the twists and turns of the estate and all at once he comes out on top of Ley Hill. The ground falls away down to Merritts Brook, and on the right are three massive tower blocks. And, further to the right, the Highlander – beyond which he would never go.

But this time he puts his foot on the accelerator and suddenly there's open sky above, open space beyond. He wants to shut his eyes, but he's afraid of driving full-tilt into it, like a lemming off the edge of a cliff. Because it's here. In front of him. Grey and huge and terrifying. There's a chain-link fence and an expanse of scrawny grass between him and the water, but there are still fathoms of it. Fathoms and fathoms and fathoms. It's deeper than a hundred swimming pools. And colder; much colder. Death in minutes, they'd said. Especially in winter.

He brakes and pulls the wheel round to the left, bumping along in hysterical fashion, feeling the hypnotic lure of what lies to his right. He mustn't look. But it's like the scene of a road accident; his eyes can't keep away. He over-steers crazily and embeds himself in the hedge. The car slides along scratchily for a couple of yards, then stops, petrol sloshing in the tank. He turns the ignition off and rests his forehead on the steering wheel. He's sweating. It's how it always was when they'd tried to tease the story from him, when he'd always been too scared to let himself remember. He tries to breathe slowly. *Relax and let your mind go blank. Relax . . .*

He's sitting on the floor. It's cold and gloomy as usual in the room, but there's always something to play with – coloured pills or bottle-tops. He's been pretending he isn't really there; staying as small as possible; doing nothing to annoy her. But suddenly she's yanking him off the floor by his arm. He cries out with the pain, but she ignores him, pulling him out of the room and along the passage like one of her sacks of rubbish. The floor rushes past his nose and he can't help letting out a squeal of terror. She rips open the front door and they are out onto the walkway. It's even colder outside – he can see his breath in the darkness. Now the stairwell gapes at him and he's being bumped down the concrete steps, his elbows and knees scraping the walls, the nasty smell of pee in his nose and throat. Now they're out of the building and she's pulling him over broken glass. She's going so fast he's almost horizontal, twisting and turning and stumbling so much that at times he's nearly facing backwards. He doesn't know how to keep up, but he has to; she won't let go. There's pain in his shoulder, and his fingers are crushed in her grip. His knees sting. He tries again: 'Where we going?'

She doesn't answer. Just goes faster. He can see her short skirt, and her big, white legs moving relentlessly in front of him. He shivers. He's only got a thin jumper on and the wind keeps whipping at his skinny ribs. He tries not to whimper; it makes her even madder. She keeps going. Now there's a long road with a tower thing sticking up, outlined against the moonlit sky. A car goes past, and then another. The headlights pick out the whiteness of her legs, the blackness of her long hair, but she doesn't stop. She pulls him away from the lights. Now he can't see her, but he can smell the familiar tang of her body as she bends close. Now an edge of broken wire scrapes near his eye as she forces him through a hole. And now they are running down a slope. The rough grass scratches him on his bare, cold legs.

She stops suddenly, and he cannons into her. As if by magic, there is a lake beyond them, a narrow moon shimmering on the choppy waves. He looks up. He can't see her face but her hair's being blown back like a horse's mane and she is staring at the lake. He's afraid now. 'What we doing?'

'Swimming.' Her voice sounds strange, croaky. She pulls him forward again, until they are nearly at the edge and he can hear the water lapping.

'I'm cold.' He shivers, putting his free hand under his armpit.

'It's warm in the water.'

He shakes his head. It doesn't look warm.

'Take your shoes off.'

'You got my hand.'

She lets go. He feels the blood run back into his fingers, tingling and burning. He bends and pulls at the Velcro straps, eases his feet out in their soiled grey socks, feels the prickly grass under his toes. She pushes off her own shoes. Then she grabs his hand again, jerks him forward once more.

He can see the tower thing from below now. He doesn't like it; he thinks there might be a witch there. He tries to turn, to run back up the grassy bank. But she has him tight; she pulls him closer to the water. He feels its icy slap and gasps. Now she has him in her arms, her big, white, soft, strong arms, and she plunges forward and starts swimming. The freezing water bites into his body. He has never been so cold. He can't think of anything else but how cold he is. Now there's a light, and someone is shouting, *Oi! Who's that?* She turns and the moon shines faintly on her face. She seems to smile at him, just for a second. A strange, almost triumphant kind of smile. Then, quite suddenly, she lets him go. And before he can shout, the water closes over him. It rushes into his lungs. He can't breathe. He can't see, he can't hear. He panics and flails his arms. He wants to call out for her, but he can't make a sound. The water pulls him down; he hears gurgling in his ears. He is going deeper and deeper. His thoughts begin to fade.

Then there's someone beside him, grabbing hold of him, and he's being pulled up into the air, into the stinging wind. There's a man – no, two men. They pull him up onto the muddy edge. They lean over him, dripping water. He looks around, lungs bursting. His mother is nowhere to be seen.

He's slumped over the steering wheel when Lorraine finds him. From the look on her face when he opens his eyes, he knows that for a split second she'd thought he was dead. He wonders how she's got here – Lorraine, who never drives further than West Brom; Lorraine, who has phobias about motorway gantries and roundabouts with more than three exits.

Her relief turns to belligerence. 'What you been up to? It's nearly six.'

'You knew what I was doing.'

'I knew where you was *going*. I got worried, all this time. You should have had somebody with you.'

'I'm all right, honest.'

'I should never have let you go.'

He sees now that there are tears running down her cheeks. He has never seen Lorraine cry. He's astonished. He climbs out of the car and holds her to him, feels her heartbeat, the shake of her body. *I should never have let you go.* She stays still in his arms.

'Well?' she says, after a bit.

'I don't think she ever loved me. I think I got on her nerves.'

'You'd get on anyone's nerves.' She gives a teary laugh. 'Anyone except me, that is.'

'Yes,' he says slowly. 'Anyone except you.'

She pulls back, looks at him again, suspicious. 'You really okay? You been here hours.'

'Sorry. Time just went. But I'm glad I came.' He squeezes her hand, then wipes her cheeks with his fingers. 'And I'm really glad you came after me.'

'Are you?' She softens for a minute. Then she laughs. 'Well, I nearly didn't. And if I'd had any sense I wouldn't have, neither. Them motorways – all them you-know-whats . . .' She flaps her hand in the air.

'Overhead gantries?' He can't help smiling.

'Yes, them. How should I know if I want Birmingham North, West or Central? I thought I'd end up in Kidderminster or somewhere weird. I tell you, I'll never drive round here again.'

'Don't worry. You won't have to.'

He turns to look at the reservoir. It's calm, and very clear. Just water. Just a sheet of water.

He can imagine himself swimming in it; strong, confident strokes.

Sugar Crash

RYAN DAVIS

My grandpa died a few weeks ago. I sat alone with him, surrounded by white curtains and felt his hand go slack as the morphine swamped the pain from the twisted bunch of cells that had taken over his stomach.

He left my older brother Pete his armchair. Mum got his books and records and he left me a small amount of money, which would come in handy for me and Shell, for Barney's clothes and food. I love Barney so much, but I swear his tantrums are getting worse – he spat at me the other day and told me to leave the house. Shell's become like some zombie slave for him – twenty-four / seven. The trip to give Pete the chair was a legitimate opportunity to get out and away from it all for a while.

Pete used to live down the road in a similar terrace to us in Bearwood. After writing Hot Rods in his bedroom, a fly-fishing app that went on to sell over a hundred thousand – of what he called *units* – Pete wrote a few more apps and sold the company.

'It was only for a couple of million. I could have held out for more but I'm not greedy,' he said.

'You could be out of here and in the Bahamas now, you idiot!' I said, then laughed, hoping he thought I was joking.

Instead Pete had moved to some confectionary of a cottage in the Cotswolds that seemed to be woven together by roses and whipped cream, with Annie and her Swedish-blonde hair, her long, brown body, a dog called Thompson, no kid – not yet – and an unlimited amount of time to think of what he wanted to do next with his money and life.

I have to say, it was an enviable position. My own attempt to set up Download Drinks, an online booze store, failed. After a conversation I had with him about the letters from the bank, I thought Pete would come forward and offer a helping hand, but his hands seemed to stay firmly in his pockets. I got a little lost last year and some things got out of control. He'd lent me money to get myself back together. I was still paying him, so maybe that was why. Anyway, eventually I returned to IT support, becoming a punchbag for customers' complaints and filling my time with as many late shifts as I could.

To leave the lights of the city and disappear into the black motorway that ran through the countryside was like opening the door from a steam room and feeling the cool tiles on your feet. For a while the motorway was clear, just me alone on the road, the staggered yellow lamps and the stars lighting my way as I floated through the night. But then a car crash near Gloucester meant I was stuck in traffic for three hours, so by the time I came to turn off I was sick of the drive-time DJ, thirsty and bursting for a pee.

Having driven through the warm light of the limestone village, it was a dark ride down narrow lanes to the base of a long, low hill where Pete's home sat at the end of a white shale driveway, surrounded by its own small wood. Annie opened the door, looking all city girl gone country, decked out in Hunters and a blue and white stripy shirt.

'Hello,' she said, looking the chair up and down.

'Grandad's chair?' I said.

'Oh. Okay . . .' she said, squinting at the worn yellow fabric thinning on the arms.

'Annie, is it all right if I use –'

'Well. I've got nowhere to put it. Can't you put it in the garage?'

'Yeah . . . sure.'

I dumped the chair in the musty garage and walked back over the icy ground and into the kitchen, aching to pee. I apologised again for being late, explained about the crash and being stuck in the car for hours. Annie nodded, harassed, and began looking for her handbag.

'Pete's out night fishing and I'm off to the village AGM. I'm in a bit of a rush,' she said, slipping on her coat.

'Lady of the Manor these days!' I said.

She pursed her lips, flashed a sour smile.

'I'm really, *really* late, Dan.' She pulled a pink bottle out of her bag, crossed herself with its sherbety perfume and slid it back in. The sweet smell filled the room, but it didn't suit her at all. If Shell wore it, it would smell good, I thought.

'Okay . . .' I said.

'I've really got to go,' she said, stomping out the door with me following her.

She locked up, slipped into her car and drove off beeping the horn.

Desperate now, I looked around at Pete's expansive front lawn for a place to relieve myself – and then I spotted the perfect receptacle. I walked over the ice-crusted grass and pissed in the empty bird bath by the shed. I zipped up, smiled and then began my journey home. The image of Pete chipping out the iron-hard block of yellow ice, wondering how it got there, rolled over and over in my mind, and every time I sniggered out loud I took myself by surprise as I drove back down the now cleared stretch of motorway.

At midnight, apart from the Nigerian woman with a lisp who was on the checkout, I was the only other person at Frankley services.

I got a table by a giant window. There I was, reflected in the glass, a ghost with puffy eyes and thinning hair amid the smudges made by toddlers' sticky fingers and their gluey mouths. I sipped my coffee and listened to the buzz of the overhead air con and the vending machines' mono hum. It was oddly joyful – those simple sounds; a white noise so undemanding and so far from data inputters' rants, Barney's squeals and Shell's needs. Far away from people wanting a part of me.

My peace was broken by the sound of a heavy diesel engine. A rusting, powder-blue Transit van pulled up in the car park. The side door slid open and a rucksack was thrown out, followed by a girl. In her early twenties, she had white and pink striped hair that reminded me of coconut ice. She wore faded black jeans, clunky black boots and a white vest that was tight over her small breasts. Her plump arms were covered in a rainbow of tattoos.

As the van drove off the girl spat on its back doors then ran after it, her breath visible in the cold night air, banging her fist on the side. She was just about to reach the driver's window when it gained momentum and slipped away, out on to the light-studded motorway. She yelled at the empty road, grabbed her bags and made her way into the food area.

Even though it was just me and the woman behind the counter, she placed her bags down in front of the coffee machine with a flourish and a loud huff worthy of a larger audience. She plunged her hands into her pockets, rooted around then pulled out the fabric of the pockets themselves.

Then she kneeled down and began scrabbling through her bag, throwing out its contents as she went: a multicoloured Indian scarf, a grey towel, many white vest tops, batches of black rolled up socks, a box of Tampax, small white pants and then two blocks of Dairy Milk – a big bar and a standard-sized one. The standard-sized bar left the bag with such force that it skidded across the white tiles and landed at my feet.

I didn't say anything for a moment, guessing she would notice. She didn't. She just sat on her now empty bag, head in hands, surrounded by what looked to be her whole life.

'Do you need some change for the machine?' I said.

She lifted her head. 'Huh?'

I could see her face clearly now: a small high nose, full lips that fell into an austere pout and big blue teary eyes.

'No. I've got some money somewhere. I just can't seem to find it . . .' she said and put her head back down.

I took a sip, wincing over the last dregs of the thick, syrupy coffee. My teeth were squeaking. After my fifteenth filling my dentist told me to stay clear of sugar, fizzy drinks and snacks, but I needed to stay awake. With things getting out of control last year, a coffee with three sugars was the only thing my body could tolerate to keep me functioning these days.

'I can buy you one, until you find it . . . your money I mean.'

She didn't move for a moment, then she sat bolt upright. 'Okay. Great. Why not? Yeah, I will have one. It's cold out there.'

She began gathering her things and pushing them back in her bag. I picked up the chocolate bar, placed it on the table, then went and bought the coffees.

When I got back she was in the chair adjacent to mine with the bigger bar of Dairy Milk torn open and a triangle of chunks broken off.

'Thank you so much,' she said.

I smiled and handed her the cup.

She poured in two UHT cartons and began sipping.

'Lost your lift?'

She picked up a square of chocolate from her palm and began munching on it. After a while she said, 'Lost my lift . . . lost my boyfriend.'

'And now you've been left here.'

She looked at me with an inquisitive frown. 'You're not one of those men who hang around places like this, waiting for girls like me, are you?'

I sat back in my chair. 'No,' I said, shaking my head, smiling gently, so I didn't look like I was one of those men. Then I gave her a 'Like, duh' look. I tore open three sachets of sugar at once and tipped them into my cup. For some reason I couldn't tell her that I was going home to my wife and baby boy.

'I've just got back from a conference. A new app I'm developing. I'm here to freshen up.'

I put the spoon in and stirred.

'Freshen up. Okay . . .' The girl raised her eyes at the stack of empty sugar sachets. 'That's freshening up, eh?' She held her hand to her mouth and laughed.

Her hair was greasy. She had a shiny red spot on her forehead, but other than that her skin was without a blemish, almost liquid. She was good looking, but I didn't find her attractive until that moment when she began to speak. I could smell the chocolate on her breath, see the tackiness of it sticking her tongue to the roof of her mouth and then something inside me flipped.

'Fair enough,' she said.

'More to the point, do I have to worry about you?'

'That's up to you,' she said, raising a thick, mousy eyebrow.

'You've been dumped?'

'I pissed in his beer tonight.' She sniggered, looking around the room.

'Really? I pissed in my brother's bird bath tonight.' I smiled.

'Nice . . .' she said coolly. 'He was bringing girls on stage and singing to them. Can you believe that? He thought buying me this chocolate would make things better.'

She quickly snapped off another chunk and popped it in her mouth. Her left arm was mostly taken up by a large red heart tattoo in an elaborate green frame. In the middle was written 'Bobby 4 Jocelyn 4 ever'. At the top of her arm, above a TB jab scar, was the name of a local band I recognised – it looked like it had been composed with a compass and an ink cartridge.

'Don't say you're a fan of the Creators.'

She looked at her shoulder. 'Bobby, the lead singer is my – was my – boyfriend. He did that for me.' She ran her thumb over it.

'Aren't they, like, a skinhead band?'

'Yeah. Well . . .' She shrugged and took another chuck of chocolate.

The Creators had been going since the eighties and their gigs were known to be hateful affairs. BNP supporters pushing each other around to racist chants. Gay-bashing lyrics and songs of pointless hate. Bobby must have been at least twenty years older than her.

'Okay,' I said, loading the word with as much disapproval as I could muster.

'No, it's just good music, you know. I don't really listen to the lyrics. If you want to know, we argue a lot. It's part of our relationship. We're what you call fiery.'

She was getting a little defensive now.

'No, no . . .' I said with a grin. 'I just wondered about the tattoo, that's all.'

'I don't agree with what he sings. He says he doesn't really mean it these days anyway. Most of it's for the crowd. Bob says he wouldn't have an audience if he sang about peace and harmony. He'd be out of a job.'

Back when we were teenagers, my brother had gone night fishing and a load of pissed up skinheads had thrown him in the canal. He said he remembered that their T-shirts all read *The*

Creators, their heads shining yellow in the street lamp as he looked up at them from the water.

Talking about Bobby was getting her upset. I wanted to say, well, if he has changed, why can't he leave it behind him? Why doesn't he just join another band?

But what I said was, 'How could you love someone so angry and attention seeking?'

She stared at me like I'd told a bad joke.

'Look, I'm not a racist,' she said, glancing over her shoulder at the car park. 'We've been together five years. It's got nothing to do with that. Anyway. This is the last time he does this. The. Last. Time. I've had enough.'

She took another chunk of chocolate.

She told me Bobby was her first and only boyfriend. He'd never been violent with her, she'd never seen him be violent with anyone. Looked after his mom, too. They wanted to start a family next year. She knew what he was really like. She went silent for a while as she chewed on the last block of chocolate, nodding, as if willing what she'd just said into life. Then she looked blankly at her coffee and told me her friend lived on the other side of town. She would have to call her if she wanted to get back tonight. I said town was on the way and I would drop her back if she wanted. She smiled then leaned over and gave me a kiss on the cheek. Her lips were warm and soft. The chocolate on her breath and the smoke and patchouli smell of her hair was like the perfume from a bouquet of wild flowers. I felt my face flush with heat. It was a feeling that I thought I'd left behind, a long time ago.

I knocked back my coffee and looked at the time.

I told the girl – Jocelyn – I just needed to use the toilet and then we could go.

As I stood at the urinal I had this shiver in my chest, like something amazing would happen. That something I never knew existed would be in the taste of her tongue. A sweet danger, laden with something that I never thought I'd want or need again. Something that would lift me up beyond this world, that would make things better for a while. I washed my hands, tidied my hair and tried not to look at the white glow of my scalp in the low lights over the sink.

When I came out, her seat was empty. I walked over to the table and through the window I saw the blue van grind away, puffing balls of black smoke in its wake.

I looked out at my battered silver Honda Civic in the empty car park and back to the space where she'd been thrown out of the tour van. I stood there for a while, the gaunt sound of the air con and vending machines churning around me again. Well, I think I was there for a while. It might have been a second, or even ten minutes, I couldn't tell you. Eventually I looked down at the table. She'd left the smaller bar of chocolate next to her empty mug. I picked it up, put it in my pocket, cleared the cups and made my way to the car.

Sad country ballads played from the radio and the sugar and caffeine comedown had hit. A sugar crash. I was feeling tired and my vision started to blur a little. My mind drifted back to the service station, to the girl with the coconut ice hair and I felt an ache in my stomach. I looked down at the chocolate bar lying across the passenger seat then up at the blue illuminated sign - only five miles until my exit.

I flicked on the air con. Turned the dial up as far as it would go in the blue section and let it blast my eyes. It was nowhere near cold enough, so I wound down all the windows. A frozen wind mobbed the car, howling out the sound of the radio, clawing at my face and my hair. I looked back down at the chocolate bar and picked it up. The wrapper glowed under the motorway lights. I thought about its inconsiderable weight in my hand, its smallness, the instant, but short shot of energy that it contained. Then, quickly, I leaned over to the passenger seat, opened the glove compartment and threw the chocolate bar in. I sat up and turned back to the road that rolled out forever before me, to places I'd never been, places I might never go, that buzzed and sang under all those stars, and I pushed my foot down on the accelerator and watched the speedo rise. If I stayed like this, with the windows wide open, and I didn't stop again, I wouldn't need the chocolate. I knew if I all I thought about was getting to the next exit, then I could just about make it back home.

Biographical Notes

Gaynor Arnold was born in Wales but has lived and worked in Birmingham for forty years. Her first novel, *Girl in a Blue Dress* (Tindal Street Press), was longlisted for the Man Booker Prize 2008 and the Orange Prize 2009, and has been sold and translated all over the world. In 2011 she published a collection of short stories, *Lying Together*, and in 2012 a second novel, *After Such Kindness*, inspired by Lewis Carroll's relationship with Alice Liddell. She has been a member of Tindal Street Fiction Group since 1988.

Alan Beard has had two collections of stories published: *Taking Doreen Out of the Sky* (Picador, 1999) and *You Don't Have to Say* (Tindal Street Press, 2010). He also edited *Going the Distance* (Tindal Street Press, 2003), an anthology of stories celebrating twenty years of Tindal Street Fiction Group. Alan won the Tom Gallon Award 1989, and was longlisted for the Edge Hill Prize 2011. He has had stories published in many magazines in the UK and USA, and anthologies including *Best Short Stories 1991* and *Best British Short Stories 2011*.

Julia Bell is a writer and academic. She works at Birkbeck in central London, teaching on the MA in Creative Writing. She is the author of two novels for young adults – *Massive* and *Dirty Work* – both published in the UK by Macmillan, and is the editor of the bestselling *Creative Writing Coursebook*, which she wrote while teaching at UEA. She is the founder and director of the Writers' Hub website and is currently working on several projects, including *Hymnal*, a memoir in verse, and a new young adult novel. She has been a member of Tindal Street Fiction Group since 1992.

Kavita Bhanot grew up in London and lived for many years in Birmingham before moving to Delhi to direct an Indian-British literary festival and then work as an editor for India's first literary agency. Kavita is currently a PhD student at Manchester University, and has Master's degrees in creative writing and in colonial and post-colonial literature, from Warwick University. She has had stories published in anthologies and magazines, two of her stories have been broadcast on BBC Radio 4, and she edited the short story collection, *Too Asian, Not Asian Enough* (Tindal Street Press, 2011). She is a reader with the Literary Consultancy.

Luke Brown grew up in Fleetwood, Lancashire, spent fifteen years in Birmingham and now lives in London. His debut novel, *My Biggest Lie*, is published by Canongate in early 2014.

Georgina Bruce's short fiction has been published in various magazines and anthologies. She is currently studying creative writing at Edinburgh's Napier University. Her blog can be found at www.georginabruce.com.

Ryan Davis's debut novel, 27, is published by Sidewinder Books. He has a background in the music industry, setting up IKS Records in 2003, and with his own band, Adventure Club, releasing an album, *Wilderness Music*, on Re-Action Records in 2007. He has an MA from the National Academy of Writing, where he was awarded the 2011 screenwriting prize for *The Box of Secrets*. Ryan's short story, 'The Conversation', appears in the anthology, *Finding a Voice*. He writes frequently about books, film and music on his blog, *Lost in Language City*.

Kit de Waal was born in Moseley, Birmingham, one of five children of an Irish mother and Caribbean father. She has an MA in creative writing, is a trustee of Prisoners Abroad and of the Inheritance

Project, and writes training manuals on children in care and judicial studies. She has had stories published in the *Fish Anthology* and by Black & Blue Writing. She is an associate member of Tindal Street Fiction Group and of Moseley WRB Writers.

Anthony Ferner is a professor of international business at De Montfort University, Leicester, and has published widely on his academic research. The story in this anthology is his first published work of fiction. He also has two novels nearing completion. He is grateful for the encouragement of Tindal Street Fiction Group, without which it's unlikely he'd have written a short story in the first place.

Jackie Gay is a writer and professional sailor and she never thought she'd be able to say that! She was born in Birmingham and has published two novels with Tindal Street Press, as well as co-editing three anthologies of short fiction. She taught creative writing at Birmingham City University and the National Academy of Writing before moving to the west coast of Canada to get married. She still teaches online and is currently writing a historical biography, a memoir and proudly wearing a maple leaf as a member of the Canadian Sailing Team.

Roz Goddard co-ordinates the West Midlands Readers' Network and works extensively as a writer in educational settings. She has recently written a series of poems for the Herbert Gallery in Coventry linked to the art of painter George Shaw, and her poetry is on permanent display in Birmingham Museum and Art Gallery. Her poetry has also featured on BBC Radio 3 and 4. She was recently awarded an Arts Council writer's bursary to work on her next poetry collection. Roz is a board member of Writing West Midlands. Her collection, *The Sopranos Sonnets and Other Poems,* was published by Nine Arches Press in 2010.

James B. Goodwin was raised in Coventry. He left school at fifteen and went to work in local factories. After twenty-two years on the shop floor and having taken A-levels at evening classes, he took an English degree at Warwick University. He moved to Birmingham in 1978 and joined Tindal Street Fiction Group in 2006. His first novel, *Bad Seed*, was published in 2013, and his second, *Power Cut*, will be published later in the same year.

Fiona Joseph is a writer of short stories, graded readers and narrative non-fiction. Her latest book, *BEATRICE – The Cadbury Heiress Who Gave Away Her Fortune*, was published through her own imprint, Foxwell Press, and was longlisted for the 2012 International Rubery Book Award. Fiona lives in Birmingham and is an associate member of Tindal Street Fiction Group.

Joel Lane lives in Birmingham and works as a journalist. His fiction touches on the genres of supernatural horror and crime, with published work including two novels, *From Blue to Black* and *The Blue Mask*; four collections of short stories, *The Earth Wire, The Lost District, The Terrible Changes* and *Where Furnaces Burn*; a booklet of crime stories, *Do Not Pass Go*; and three book-length collections, plus a pamphlet of poems. He and fellow TSFG member Steve Bishop jointly edited the crime and suspense anthology, *Birmingham Noir.*

Annie Murray has had stories published in *London Magazine, SHE, Pretext* (UEA), and in Tindal Street Press anthologies, *Her Majesty* and *Going the Distance*. She has had eighteen historical novels published by Pan Macmillan, including *Chocolate Girls* and *My Daughter, My Mother*. She is an associate member of Tindal Street Fiction Group and is currently completing an MA in creative writing at Oxford Brookes University. She lives in Reading.

Mez Packer has been a member of Tindal Street Fiction Group since 2010. Her stories and articles have been published in *Under the Radar* and *Mslexia* and on the Writers' Hub. She has written two novels, both published by Tindal Street Press. *Among Thieves* (2009) was nominated for the Commonwealth Writers' Prize and the Authors' Club First Novel Award. *The Game is Altered* was published in 2012. Mez is an associate senior lecturer at Coventry University and lives in Leamington Spa with her husband and daughter.

Sibyl Ruth is a poet who has increasingly been lured into writing prose. Her poetry collections are *Nothing Personal* (Iron Press, 1995) and *I Could Become That Woman* (Five Leaves, 2003). In 2008 she won the *Mslexia* Poetry Competition. The last short story she had published was in the long-defunct magazine, *Spare Rib*. Sibyl has worked in advice centres and arts organisations, but now earns a precarious living juggling writing with part-time work. She lives in south Birmingham.

Mick Scully lives and works in Birmingham and has been a member of Tindal Street Fiction Group for eight years. He has had stories published in a number of magazines and anthologies. His subject is usually – but not always – crime. And very often – but not always – he writes from the criminal perspective. *Little Moscow*, a collection of linked crime stories, was published by Tindal Street Press in 2005, and his first novel, *The Norway Room*, is scheduled for publication in March 2014.

Amanda Smyth is Irish-Trinidadian and was educated in England. Her first novel, *Black Rock* (Serpent's Tail), won the Prix du Premier Roman Etranger 2010, and was selected for Waterstones New Voices in 2009. It was also chosen for Oprah's Summer Reads 2009. *A Kind of Eden*, Amanda's second novel, was published in July 2013. Amanda has been a member of Tindal Street Fiction Group for seven years.

Natalie White was born in Birmingham, and now works as an English teacher. She has been a member of Tindal Street Fiction Group for three years, writes short stories and is writing her second novel. She lives in Shropshire where she leads a writing group and enjoys running, cycling and swimming. This is her second published short story.

Charles Wilkinson was born in Birmingham in 1950. His publications include *The Snowman and Other Poems* (Iron Press, 1978) and *The Pain Tree and Other Stories* (London Magazine Editions, 2000). His work has appeared in *Best Short Stories 1990* (Heinemann), *Best English Short Stories 2* (Norton), *Midwinter Mysteries* (Little, Brown), *The Unthology* (Unthank Books), *London Magazine*, *Supernatural Tales* and *Theaker's Quarterly Fiction*. A pamphlet of his poems is forthcoming from Flarestack.

Polly Wright is a writer, lecturer, and occasional performer. Five of her plays have been staged professionally and four of her short stories have been published, including two in a showcase anthology, *Are You She?* She is the artistic director of the Hearth Centre, which harnesses the transformative strength of the arts to raise awareness about health issues and is currently in partnership with the Birmingham Rep and the Birmingham and Solihull Mental Health NHS Trusts. 'Seagulls in Sparkhill' was developed from ideas which emerged from creative writing work in a mental health setting.